GOOD
YOUNG
MEN

Also by Gary Lonesborough

The Boy from the Mish
We Didn't Think It Through
I'm Not Really Here

GOOD YOUNG MEN

GARY LONESBOROUGH

ALLEN&UNWIN
SYDNEY•MELBOURNE•AUCKLAND•LONDON

First published by Allen & Unwin in 2026

Allen & Unwin
Cammeraygal Country
83 Alexander Street
Crows Nest NSW 2065
Australia
Phone: (61 2) 8425 0100
Email: info@allenandunwin.com
Web: www.allenandunwin.com

*Allen & Unwin acknowledges the Traditional Owners of the Country on which we
live and work. We pay our respects to all Aboriginal and Torres Strait Islander
Elders, past and present.*

EU Authorised Representative: Easy Access System Europe, Mustamäe tee 50,
10621 Tallinn, Estonia, gpsr.requests@easproject.com

A catalogue record for this
book is available from the
National Library of Australia

ISBN 978 1 76118 217 4

For teaching resources, explore allenandunwin.com/learn

Cover & text design by Hana Kinoshita Thomson
Cover illustration by Dylan Finney / Solid Lines
Set in 12/15.5 pt Adobe Garamond Pro by Midland Typesetters, Australia
Printed and bound in Australia by the Opus Group

10 9 8 7 6 5 4 3 2 1

The paper in this book is FSC® certified.
FSC® promotes environmentally responsible,
socially beneficial and economically viable
management of the world's forests.

garylonesborough.com

For Matthew

DYLAN

As we step into the shopping centre car park, white spray-paint on the orange brick wall catches my eye. Two council workers in high-vis shirts are on ladders, scrubbing away the words: *WHITE POWER*.

KALLUM

ONE

It's not my fault I got expelled from St Augustine's – not really.

The sun's setting when I get off my train and walk along Redfern Street. The place is abuzz with adults heading home from work, older people dawdling, a man on a mat on the corner with writing on a piece of cardboard that says *HELP PLEASE $*.

I'm on my way to Aunty Lisa's house. Aunty Lisa's not actually my aunty – she's an Aboriginal woman from Carraway's Point who moved to Sydney years ago, and her house is the go-to spot for Kooris visiting from home.

The weight of my duffel bag is killing me; all the books, clothes and shoes I could fit – my whole life as I knew it – burning into my shoulder.

In my stomach, along with the threatening vomit, there's a feeling of grief. I've lost my scholarship. The sporting college was my ticket out of Carraway's Point and I fucked it up. Mum and Dad probably want to disown me. They always said it was such a great opportunity, a chance that kids like me could only dream of. I was the potential-filled rural Aboriginal scholarship student, the world at my feet. Now, I'm an expelled disappointment who's getting a bus back to Carraway's Point in the morning.

My mates back home thought I was chasing my dreams. I was going to play for the Rabbitohs one day. The truth was I just wanted to get out. The window opened but I've managed to slam it shut again. Because of the rage.

I don't remember all I did when I was in that rage. I remember what happened before it, though – things I can't tell my parents. They'd be more ashamed than they already are. As it is, they'll think I'm violent, that I'm one of those aggro boys – but maybe it's better that way.

My feet are starting to kill me as I walk through Redfern Park. There's a big fountain in the middle. A couple sit on one of the benches nearby, and there's a young family, a mum and dad walking with their two little sons and a baby in a pram. The mum's wearing a Rabbitohs hat.

Everyone loves the Rabbitohs in Redfern.

When I was a kid, I dreamed of running out on the footy field at Olympic Park wearing the green and red jersey with the rabbit emblem on the chest.

I guess those dreams are dust now.

Out of Redfern Park, I walk onto busy Elizabeth Street. I pass the football field and the basketball courts, then cross the street into the quieter neighbourhoods. The giant orange public-housing buildings tower over the suburb like beacons lighting the way home, away from the prestigious all-boys college where I was studying and living, rubbing shoulders with boys who'd received Audis and jetskis for their sixteenth birthdays. The map on my phone is leading me to Aunty Lisa's house, near the towers.

The backstreets are quieter in Redfern. I pass a person with a backpack and a tucked-in shirt, a woman walking a small dog, and two teenagers powerwalking in hoodies and parachute pants. The townhouses and streets remind me more of where I'm from – this is more *me*.

I come to a two-storey townhouse with faded green and white paint. All the townhouses share walls, with variations in the little gates out front. Aunty Lisa's is a small white gate, which rattles when I open it and walk the few steps along the pathway, passing shrubbery and a red-lidded wheelie bin.

I knock on the door and when it opens, Aunty Lisa is standing there in a black top and jeans. Her hair is tied in a ponytail, and the greys are coming through the black. She's tall and has bags under her eyes, like an owl. She smiles then rushes to hug me.

'Took ya time gettin' 'ere,' she says.

'Yeah, sorry,' I reply. 'I need to put this bag down.'

I follow her inside and along a skinny hallway. The carpeted stairs ahead are steep. In the lounge room, Uncle Dane greets me. My cousin Hilary, who is nineteen and heavily pregnant, has her feet up on one of the couches watching *Love Island*. She offers me a 'Hey' as I drop my bag behind the couch. The smells of the house cover me like a mist – frying chicken, curry and marijuana smoke.

'You right, Kal?' Aunty Lisa asks me. 'What happened at that school?'

'Oh,' I say, still catching my breath from the walk. 'It was just a fight. They got zero tolerance for fighting.'

'Jeez. Bullshit, hey. As if teenage boys don't fight. Make yourself at home, Kal. Dinner's almost ready.'

I sit on the other couch, facing the TV.

'I hope you got 'im good,' Uncle Dane says. 'It'd wanna be worth expellin' ya for, hey? They wouldn't've kicked ya out if you weren't black. They always racist in them institutions.'

'Yeah, I dunno,' I say.

'Tellin' ya, if you was white, they'd give ya a few detentions and you'd be good as gold. Instead, they kickin' you out.'

I get his point. Maybe I wouldn't've been straight-up expelled if I was white. For sure Aaron Davies ain't getting kicked out. I guess he was just defending himself.

Aunty Lisa dishes out curried chicken with basmati rice in little bowls. She places them on the bench in the kitchen and I follow Hilary to collect mine. Hilary pours herself a glass of off-brand cola, and I do the same.

Aunty Lisa switches over to the news when we all gather on the couches with our bowls. The curry is a lot hotter than I'm used to.

'Did you hear they set a date for that trial down home?' Aunty Lisa asks me, downing a forkful of curried chicken and rice.

'Trial?' I ask, taking a sip of cola.

'The trial for that copper who shot that young fulla, Brandon Long, last year.'

'Oh,' I say, remembering when I heard the news. Some police commissioner guy called it 'an unfortunate incident'. I remember what my mates Mitch and Eric said about it: that Brandon probably tried to attack the officer or something, that it was probably his fault.

It was March last year when it happened. I was already living in Sydney then, and I found out about it because a couple of people posted 'R.I.P' messages with pics of him on their Instagram stories. Brandon was a Koori fulla that lived at the end of our street – Chopin Drive. He was the same age as me, and we used to be mates, but we drifted apart in high school. I started hanging out with the white footy boys and he hung out with the crew of Kooris, including Dylan Keenan – another lad I used to be friends with who also lives on the same street. It used to be me, Brandon, Dylan, and Jordy Danvers – another Koori fulla. We were the boys of Chopin Drive. Somewhere along the way in Year Seven, me and Jordy kind of moved on. But Dylan and Brandon were still mates.

I heard Dylan was there that night, and saw everything.

I don't know the full story, but Dad said the police were trying to arrest Brandon and he reached for a weapon. They shot him. Mum wouldn't talk to me about it when I asked, I guess because she's a police officer. She and Dad were sad about it, though.

'When's the trial?' I ask.

'November, they reckon,' Aunty Lisa replies. 'I saw a video on Facebook. They got this Murri activist from

Brisbane involved. Shirley something. She's organisin' rallies and protests for Brandon.'

After dinner, Aunty Lisa and Uncle Dane sit at the far end of the kitchen, drinking a beer each, while Hilary reclaims the TV to watch more pointless reality shows. She's got *Below Deck* on now, and it's the whitest thing I've ever seen. I'm checking the time on my phone. As the night gets later, and the stream of pointless shows keeps on rolling, I'm begging her with my inner voice to fuck off to bed so I can go to sleep on the couch.

My phone buzzes in my lap. It's a text from my mate Liam from St. Augustine's.

What's with this video of you and Aaron Davies fighting? When did that happen? I came to your room but ur not there. Where you at?

I reply: *Expelled. Not coming back. Sorry.*

What the fuck? Bruh Aaron was talkin some shit about you.

By ten o'clock, reality show number three thousand finishes and Hilary decides to go to bed. She turns off the TV and brings me a blanket from the cupboard. I use one of the cushions as a pillow and lie on the couch. My legs are too long for it; I have to stretch them over the armrest and dangle them off the edge. As I get comfortable, Aunty Lisa and Uncle Dane turn off the lights in the kitchen then head up the stairs.

'See you in the mornin', Kal,' Aunty Lisa says. 'Uncle will drive you to the bus stop.'

'Thanks,' I say. 'Goodnight.'

'Goodnight.'

The steps creak as they climb to the top. Their footsteps move into their bedroom and they close the door. I'm in darkness in the living room, alone on the couch. I pull out my phone, staring at the last text from Liam. I run through all the possible replies in my head.

Nah, not true.

Don't believe what you hear.

It was nice knowing ya.

Yeah, it's true. Sorry.

I would've told you, but I was scared.

Nah. I can't reply. In my head, I'm replaying this afternoon over and over. But I don't want to talk about this. Ever.

A messenger came to get me from class. They left me at the brown door to the deputy's office, and I knew exactly why I was there.

Inside, Mr Walker was behind his desk and Tracy, the wellbeing officer, was sitting in one of the chairs.

My palms were sweating and I could feel my heart beating like a drum in my throat as I sat down.

'Is something wrong?' I asked.

'We've recently become aware of a video that's been shared around here at the college,' Mr Walker said. 'Are you aware of this video, Kallum?'

I shook my head, but I was. A heaviness filled my stomach like cement. It was sour, poisonous. My toes curled tight in my shoes and I held my sweaty hands in my lap.

Mr Walker turned his laptop around on his desk to show me the screen. He pressed the space bar, and shouting and swearing echoed from the speakers as I watched myself on screen, banging my fist into Aaron Davies's face. The recording was shaky but I could see he was trying to fight back.

'*What the fuck…you psycho…you're killing him…*'

He was on the ground and I was on top of him, my arms swinging away. Two of the other boys tackled me and wrestled me off.

'*You fucking idiot,*' someone shouted at me as the camera came closer. The video ended on a frame of my face, someone's arm across my chest, holding me on the concrete.

'That was you, wasn't it, Smith?' Mr Walker asked me. I swallowed all the words I wanted to say and nodded. 'That was you who was seriously physically assaulting a fellow student, right?'

I nodded again.

'Can you tell me why you were assaulting Aaron Davies?' Mr Walker asked. 'Can you tell me who else is in the video besides you and Aaron?'

I couldn't tell the truth, so I kept my mouth shut.

Mr Walker sighed. 'You know St Augustine's has a zero-tolerance policy when it comes to violence, Kallum. Do you have *nothing* to say for yourself?'

'Am I expelled?' I asked.

Mr Walker reached for his phone. 'I'm going to have to call your parents.'

I swallowed hard. Even now, lying on this couch that smells like old farts, I can still taste the sour, stinging vomit threatening my throat, just as I did when I sat in Mr Walker's office. My chest feels tight and I'm hot again.

I set my alarm to seven-thirty. My shoulder is sore but luckily, I'm fuckin' exhausted. I close my eyes.

When I was a kid, camping in the bush was the only time when Mum and Dad didn't fight. I could close my eyes and listen to the bush and everything was okay.

In my head, I create the sounds of the bush – leaves and branches brushing against each other in the breeze, birds singing. I imagine the smell of the trees, hear the quiet, and it calms me.

TWO

Uncle Dane's old Kia Carnival rattles. The sound's been coming from right beneath my passenger seat all the way from Redfern into the city.

'Do you hear that?' I ask.

'It's right,' he says. 'Just another expense trying to ruin my life.'

The buildings are so tall in Sydney. They tower over people on the street like monuments of success and prestige, judging those below, including me, who will never see what the view is like from the highest windows. It's eight-thirty a.m. so traffic is crawling. I'm running a bit late because of it, but missing a bus to Carraway's Point wouldn't be the worst thing to ever happen to me.

'What's your plan for footy?' Uncle Dane asks.

'I dunno,' I say. 'Haven't really thought about it.'

'No? Well, you can't give up, Unk,' he says. 'You're

obviously talented. You got that black magic. Don't let 'em wreck it for ya.'

'Yeah, I dunno.'

Finally, we arrive at the bus stop on Pitt Street, in the heart of the raging traffic, towering judgemental buildings and people racing off to work in suits and fancy shoes, near Central Station. Uncle Dane pulls in behind a bus and taps on his hazard lights.

'Out ya get, mate,' he says. 'Give our love to your family, yeah?'

'Yeah, okay,' I say, unbuckling my seatbelt.

'Have a good trip,' Uncle Dane says. 'Nine hours goes pretty fast.'

I climb out and retrieve my duffel bag from the back seat. I lug it along the footpath as Uncle Dane drives away, and step inside the ticket office to check in and get a luggage tag.

My bus is at the front of the line of coaches. There's a woman in a business suit standing near its closed door, puffing away at a cigarette. She's thin and stands with a straight back, looking like she's somewhere else in her mind.

There's a man with a beard and hair cut short, leaning down to talk to two little boys, probably both under ten years old. They've got two big bags with wheels on the bottom.

There are heaps of old women and men standing around, chatting like they know each other, and a teenage girl with green hair and earbuds in her ears, tapping her thumb on her phone's screen. Then there's me – the expelled Aboriginal boy travelling home to his disappointed family.

At nine-thirty on the dot, a tall, round man with a blue shirt bearing the same emblem as the one on the side of the bus arrives from the building behind all the waiting travellers. He opens the door, and within seconds a line begins to form in front of him. One by one, we climb into the bus after getting our names checked off on the driver's clipboard and handing him our luggage.

Most of the seats in the front half of the bus are taken by the time I get inside. I find a seat right at the back, beside the toilet.

On my last bus trip, my phone died with ages left to go, so I slept a rocky sleep from which I woke constantly, and arrived in Carraway's Point feeling thirty times more tired than I did when I left.

We get moving through the city and I take my AirPods out of my pocket. I forgot to put them on the charger last night before I crashed, so I'm hoping they've got some life left in them.

As we leave Sydney, my mind drifts to Brandon and the officer who shot him. Something about Carraway's Point changed when Brandon died. Before, on my trips back, coming out of the bush at the top of the hill and seeing the town below always felt like coming home. I appreciated the place more. The bush was beautiful, green and brown and full of life, and the sand of the beach soothed me when I stepped on it and dug in my bare toes. But after what happened to Brandon, it feels like there's a darkness in the bush – like the brown and green colours have dimmed to a darker, colder shade. The birds and insects seem quieter, more subdued. And even the beach doesn't feel as warm or beautiful. After I moved to Sydney, I started thinking of Carraway's Point as a kind of paradise. Now, there's a weird sadness in the air.

I guess that's what happens to small towns when there's a *tragedy*.

I don't know the full story of what happened that night, but it feels strange when someone you used to know really well dies. It makes me wonder if things would have been different if we didn't stop being mates. Even though we used to be pretty close, I can't remember the last time we hung out as friends. We were probably talking shit in one of our houses – me, Jordy, Dylan and Brandon.

I wake from a nap when my head bangs on the window. Outside the sky is a dark orange; it looks like the clouds are bleeding. My AirPods are still in my ears but the music isn't playing anymore. They died hours ago.

It's Saturday evening and the bus is passing dairy farms – hills and paddocks as far as the eye can see. We're almost there – I almost live in Carraway's Point again.

As the bus travels over the final hill and begins its dip into the valley, the lights of Carraway's Point look like a Christmas tree. The town is waiting for me below, and so are all the people who want to say *I knew you'd never make it*. They'll be so pleased to see me back. I proved them right and fucked it up, just like they secretly thought I would.

We pass the Carraway's Point lookout. There are a few cars parked up there – probably couples who've done the Maccas run and headed there to eat, then dig their tongues into each other's mouths.

The bus rolls past more farms and big construction bobcats parked by the side of the road. The roadworks signs have been covered and the headlights catch the reflectors on the middle of the road.

We drive through the roundabout at the north of town and past the service station. Trucks are lined up on the road to get their fill. The servo itself looks like a lantern in the dark.

We cross the river. A mist has grown from below and the fog is mild across the bridge.

The bus rolls into the main street and the streetlights are ablaze. The town's more alive than I remember it being at night. The one Thai place in town looks full. The Maccas is packed with cars waiting their turn in the drive-thru.

The bus turns up the hill towards the church and comes to a stop outside the town hall. I pull my hoodie over my head. The cold from outside has already rushed in before the bus's door can even open all the way.

The moment my shoes touch the pavement, I feel a sour grumble in the pit of my stomach. It's there beneath my bellybutton – the feeling of loss. I've failed.

The bus driver hands my duffel bag to me. It's got my name stitched on the side: Kallum Smith.

Dad's Ford Territory is parked just down the hill. He and Mum are in the front and they both get out when they see me approach. Mum's got her hair dyed brown. She wears a puffer jacket and jeans. She opens her arms for me as I approach, so I hug her with one arm.

'Oh, Kal,' she says as she wraps her arms around me. 'We've missed you.'

'Missed you too, Mum.'

Dad's wearing a t-shirt that shows off his muscles even though it's freezing. He takes my bag and loads it into the back of the car. 'Come on,' he says. 'Keira's cooking dinner for us.'

Nice to see you too, Dad.

We get in the car and drive the five minutes to Chopin Drive. I could've walked it, I guess, but it's freezing.

We pull into the driveway of our little white three-bedroom house with a garden out front. The rosebushes are Mum's pride and joy and I can smell them as I follow my parents inside.

Through the front door, the smell of curry engulfs me. Keira's in the kitchen, dishing out the rice into bowls when she sees us walk in. It's almost the exact same dish Aunty Lisa and Uncle Dane cooked last night, except it's sausages instead of chicken.

'I told you to get out of your school clothes before we got home,' Mum says to Keira.

Dad hands my duffel bag to me. 'Take your stuff to your room before we eat.'

He's cold. I can feel his disappointment, his frustration, like each word is a tiny knife leaving his mouth, stabbing me.

In my bedroom, I flick on the light and my poster of Greg Inglis is the first thing to greet me. My single bed is made and the blankets tucked in. My pillow is waiting, calling for me to get my head on top of it. My bookshelf is perfectly stacked but there's a coat of dust on the edges. I flick on the bedside lamp and plug my phone in.

I'm home and I may never leave again. All the things I did, everything I was beginning to experience in Sydney, it's all over now. I'm back to who I was before I left last year. I didn't like that person. In fact, I hated that person. I can already feel that sad boy slipping back into my skin. I'm home and so is he.

Back in the kitchen, I take my seat at the table beside Mum. Keira places a bowl of curried sausages and rice in front of me.

'Welcome home, bro,' she says. Keira's a year younger than me. She's got long browny blonde hair that hangs straight down her back. She sits down beside Dad, opposite me. 'So,' she says, 'heard you got in a blue.'

Dad sighs.

'Let's just eat,' Mum says, taking a forkful of curry. I deliver some into my own mouth. Not as hot as I would've liked, but it's good.

'Did he press charges, or what?' Keira asks. 'What happened? Was it worth getting expelled over?'

'Nah,' I reply. If I could tell anyone the full story, it would be Keira. She used to be my best friend. We aren't as close since I moved off to St Augustine's, though.

'Kallum made a dumb mistake,' Dad interjects. 'There's no point in dwelling on it. It happened and it's done now.' Dad looks up from his bowl and his eyes on me feel like lasers. 'Did you forget who you are? Did you forget everything I taught you?' he asks me, like he didn't just say there was no point dwelling on this. 'You knew they'd look for any excuse to knock you down because you're a blackfulla. You knew that, and you gave them the perfect excuse anyway. You had a pathway right into professional footy. It was right there, Kallum.'

'I know, Dad,' I say.

'Do you still want it? Or are you gonna give up everything because of this? You can let this break you, or you can let it *make* you. If you still want it, you're gonna have to work a lot harder. And it can't wait. The getting-back-up starts now. You understand?'

I dig my fork into some more sausage.

'Do you understand, son? Are you going to let this ruin your life?'

'No,' I say.

'Good. You're back at school next week. It's all organised. The work starts tomorrow.'

Dad digs back into his bowl then he takes it to the sink. Within five minutes, he's gone up the hallway, changed into his gym clothes and left the house.

I finish dinner and Mum and Keira hog the couch to watch TV.

I go to my room, close the door behind me and fall onto my bed. I kick my shoes to the floor and let out the biggest sigh I've ever sighed.

There are a bunch of messages on my phone. A few from the kids at St Augustine's.

Bye bye abo
You're dead if we ever see your face again.
What happened to you bro? Did they really expel ya?

I'm so tired. Nine hours on a bus will tire you right out. I drop my phone back on my bedside table and surrender my head to the pillow. When I close my eyes, my mind drifts to being in Mr Walker's office, watching the video.

THREE

A knock wakes me from a dreamless sleep. It's still dark outside.

'Jump up, son. It's beach time,' Dad's voice says. My eyes are blurry, but I can see him standing at my door.

'What?'

'The work starts now, just like I said. If you want to get back to where you were, get up.'

I rub my eyes. 'Now?'

'Yes. Now.'

I yawn as I swing my legs off the bed. I go to my wardrobe and pull out my sweatpants, then a singlet.

Dad's waiting by the front door with two towels over his shoulder and a sports drink in his hand. He gives it to me and I follow him outside. He's got his gym shirt on, which smells of old sweat. I put on my runners in the driveway, then we get in his car and drive to the beach.

The beach is freezing. The blue in the sky is growing lighter and the sun hasn't come up yet.

'Why are we going so early?' I ask as we step onto the sand.

'Because this is what it takes,' Dad replies. 'Fitness needs to be part of your routine. The best way to begin your day is early and with exercise. You can make it, son. You're good enough but you're gonna have to work harder than you ever did before.'

I take off my shoes and feel the sand beneath my feet. It's so cold, I feel like my ankles are icing up. I take a sip of the sports drink as we walk closer to the water. The waves are big and crashing. There is a surfer way out. Up the beach, there are a few people fishing.

'After you, son,' Dad says as we arrive at the harder, wet sand. I begin jogging. My legs are tight, but I move them anyway. Ten minutes in and I'm puffed, but Dad is still running with me. I gulp the air, let it be my fuel.

The sun begins to rise beyond the waves. After an hour, we return to where we started. I'm all sweaty and I could collapse to the sand.

'Keep your back straight,' Dad says as I hunch over, catching my breath. 'Hands behind your head, like me. It keeps your lungs open and you can get the oxygen in better.'

I stand straight and grip the hair on the back of my head. I breathe in the sea breeze. Dad takes off his shirt and races into the waves. I do the same and the icy water shocks my bones. I dunk my head under the salt and foam.

I stand in the waves, watching Dad freestyling further out, and I don't know what to do. There's nothing I can do. This town is my life again.

When Dad comes back in, we go to our towels and wrap ourselves, then we're in the car and on our way home.

'Perfect way to start a Sunday,' Dad says as we turn onto the highway. He switches on the heater and blasts warm air into the car. My legs are sore from the beach run – sorest at the back of my ankles. My feet still feel like blocks of frozen steak, slowly defrosting. 'This is how you get back there,' Dad says. 'You keep at it. You lost your scholarship but it's not over. We're going to the footy later – we'll go talk to Mack. He's coaching the eighteens again. The regional trials are in September. We're doing beach runs every third morning. We're going to the gym four times a week. You keep up your fitness, keep your head in the game. There's no way those scouts will look past ya at the trials.'

Dad's already got it all planned out for me: impress the scouts and get a contract, get back to Sydney on another scholarship. *He* got the contract when he was a kid. He used to always ramble on about getting signed to the Cronulla Sharks feeder club when he was sixteen, but how he liked the grog too much and so it never happened for him. I guess I'm his second chance. It's not like there is any part of me that can say no. He's the boss and it's always been that way. He wrote me up a fucking exercise program when I was eleven – exercises I could do on the days I didn't have footy training. And he would do them with me, correct me when I was doing things wrong, push me to work harder. I should have known he'd be even more *Dad* if I got to this point – the point where I might actually have some chance, even if the window of opportunity has shrunk.

It's two o'clock in the afternoon when we arrive at the sportsground. Cars fill the streets surrounding it. Inside, they park along the side of the footy field, behind rows of wooden stands where people sit, opposite the sheds and the big concrete grandstand on the other side.

Dad's wearing his blue jeans shorts and Carraway's Point Roosters jersey, which is the same emblem as the Sydney Roosters but with *Carraway's Point* instead of *Sydney*, which is obviously a fresh and original take on the source material.

The under eighteens are playing now. Carraway's Point is in the blue, white and red jerseys. They're playing Belrose – I recognise their white and black uniforms. Carraway's Point just scored and a woman is changing the scoreboard at the far end of the field, behind the in-goal. Carraway's Point is winning 28–20.

I'm straggling a little behind Dad. He walks so fast and determined and I never walk like that unless I'm rushing. He stops beside an old white man – Chief Kelly. He's tall, balding and grey, with a big beer belly. Chief's not his real name, but I don't think I've ever heard anyone call him anything else. He's a coach from the old days, now club president or something. He coached Dad when he was a teenager and now they're like besties.

'Greg, how's it going?' Chief asks Dad.

'Good, mate. You remember my boy, Kallum?' Dad steps aside to reveal me – *his boy, Kallum.*

'Ah, mate, how are ya? How's the big smoke?' Chief asks. His grip is strong when I shake it, like a real man.

'I'm all right,' I say.

'Kal's back in town. He's gonna finish Year Twelve here. Thought I'd sign him up for the Roosters,' Dad says.

'No worries, mate. The eighteens won the comp last year. I'm sure if we chuck Kallum in there, we'll go back-to-back,' Chief says.

'He'd be up for first grade, too,' Dad says. 'Just chuck him in there. He's been up in Sydney playin' with those big Islander boys. He wouldn't be out of place.'

'Let's try him in the eighteens first. Go see Candy in the clubhouse,' Chief says. 'She's just sittin' on her phone up there. Go get her to sign him up.'

Dad shakes Chief's hand again then tells me to come with him. We walk through the crowd, past the filled car park. People are standing along the sideline, sitting on picnic blankets or on camping chairs. A group of kids are playing a game of touch footy over the other side, behind the stands and the parked cars on the grass. I watch one little fulla chip the ball over his opponent's head, run through and collect the ball after one bounce, then he dives for the invisible tryline they've made with two shoes. They're having fun, and I miss that: when footy was for fun. That was when I loved playing, when I was just out there to run around and tackle and score tries – when there were no stakes or consequences.

As we walk to the clubhouse, I see two boys in hoodies – Dylan and his friend Jarrod. I haven't spoken to Dylan in years. Even though we haven't spoken in years, I kind of want to detour from the clubhouse and make for him, ask him about what happened the night Brandon died, if he's going to the trial at the end of the year.

He looks up, shoving a chip drowned in tomato sauce into his mouth, and sees me. He sees me seeing him, and I turn back to Dad and follow him to the left, towards the entrance of the clubhouse.

I can't remember the last time me, Dylan, Jordy and Brandon were all in the same place at the same time outside of school or Koori Klub. It would've been in Year Seven, I think, probably early on.

A memory flickers in my mind. We were probably ten or eleven. It was a hot day, and as we walked home from school together we made plans to go to the pool. It was my responsibility to get twenty dollars for the entry fees from my parents; the other boys always thought of me as the rich kid cause my mum was a police officer. I got the money and we all met at Brandon's place. We rode our bikes through town towards the pool, all of us brown boys in tank tops and boardies, no helmets, towels over our shoulders. We turned down the big hill and as we rode into the shade of the trees that lined the perimeter of the park, the wind howled in our faces and we hit full speed. There wasn't much thought for brakes, except when Jordy hit his about halfway to the bottom. Riding down that hill felt like freedom. There was nothing to worry about, nothing to be sad about. I thought we were the coolest kids in town in that moment, and nothing would come between us.

Dad's knocks on the open clubhouse door take me out of my memory and I follow him inside. There are people watching the field from the window, young and old men, a woman in her twenties, and Candy, sitting on a couch and tapping away on her phone just like Chief said she would be.

Dad does all the talking. Candy pulls out a binder folder, hands him rego forms and he fills them out for me. I sign where it says *Player* and Dad signs where it says *Parent/guardian*. He hands Candy a hundred and fifty dollars and thanks her for her help.

'Training's on Tuesdays and Thursdays, and games are usually on Sundays,' Candy says to me. I nod.

'Thanks, Candy,' Dad says.

Back outside, the sun's coming out. Dad's saying hello to every second person that passes by and they ask him how he's going; he replies over his shoulder as we keep walking.

The eighteens teams walk into the sheds as we arrive at the grandstand. Dad sits us in the first row beside a guy around his age. He shakes his hand and introduces me as *his boy, Kallum* who has moved back to town, just signed up for the eighteens.

'He'll be in the first-grade team for sure,' Dad says. 'He's been playin' against those big Islander boys up in Sydney.'

I roll my eyes. The sun brings warmth with it. The hundreds of people at the footy grounds are talking, sharing stories and laughing. But me? I kind of want to cry.

'What the fuck?' I hear. I look up and see my friends Eric and Mitch have just come out of the sheds after their game. They're wearing their Roosters club shirts and Eric's still in his footy shorts, barefoot, while Mitch has wet hair, and has changed into blue and white shorts, white Asics on his feet. They rush to me with smiles on their faces and I force one myself. I thought I'd be happy to see them again, but I'm not really. I think I just want to go home, get back in bed.

'What are you doin' 'ere?' Eric asks.

'Moved back,' I say. I realise now that I probably should've texted them to let them know.

'For good?' Mitch asks.

'Yeah,' I say.

'You gonna come back and play for the mighty Roosters?' Mitch asks, pointing to the emblem on his club shirt.

'Yeah, Dad just signed me up,' I say. 'Sorry I didn't tell youse I was back. It all happened pretty fast.'

'All good,' Eric says. 'Had to look twice to make sure I was really seein' you sittin' 'ere.'

'Good to see ya,' Mitch says. 'We've missed ya. We'll make finals with you in the team for sure.'

In my head, I can hear Dad's voice talking about how I should be playing first grade because I played with the big Islander boys in Sydney, but thankfully, he's still talking to his friend.

'Why'd you move back?' Eric asks. 'Get too homesick?'

'Nah, kind of,' I say. I don't want to say I got expelled, that I was in a fight that was recorded. And I definitely don't want to say why I was in that fight in the first place. 'Wasn't for me anymore,' I say, instead of the truth.

'Fair,' Mitch says. 'Ebony will be glad you're back. She's volunteering in the canteen today. You should go say hello.'

'Oh,' I say. 'Nah. I'll see her at school, anyway.'

Ebony was my first girlfriend. Well, she was my *only* girlfriend. We dated in Year Eight for a few months, then broke up because she didn't feel the same way anymore. We met again at Mitch's sixteenth birthday party when I was back from Sydney for a visit. It was the first time I ever got drunk, and I kissed her while she was in the middle of telling me something. Regret set in immediately, but instead of pushing me away and slapping me, she kissed me back. We slept on Mitch's couch together that night. I cuddled her against my chest and she was warm and comfy; she fit perfectly in my arms. In the morning, we awkwardly had bacon and eggs with everyone else, avoiding eye contact.

After I went back to Sydney, we started messaging each other all the time. But the daily texts turned to once in a while, and now I haven't texted her in months, since before another party in the summer holidays, this time at Eric's house. I didn't kiss her then. I avoided her altogether, and I think that pissed her off. I was scared that if we kissed again, it would lead to more, and she might want me to have sex with her. I wasn't sure I could actually do that. I was scared I'd be bad, that I'd ruin sex for her and myself. She wasn't a virgin, but I was, and still am, so I was worried I wouldn't live up to what she was expecting.

As the reserve-grade teams run onto the field for the next game of footy, Eric and Mitch fill me in on what's been happening in town, apart from the officer's trial date being set: Stacey McQueen had an abortion, Jamie Collins got caught with a bag of weed at school and was expelled, Elijah Winters from Belrose had a car crash and got banged up, but is hoping to play footy again next year.

They continue with updates about people fighting at school, a teacher who got fired and no one knows why, and the damage done by the summer bushfires, but I switch off when I see Jordy, another face I haven't seen in a long time. He's walking along the sideline with Amber and Hamish – his new, weird friends.

Jordy came out as gay last year. Mitch said he was worried Jordy fantasised about him, that he didn't under-stand how a guy with a penis wouldn't want to put it inside a vagina. I felt proud of Jordy, though. We used to be close, and if we still were, I'm sure I would've been one of the first people he told. I thought he was brave, and I was kind of jealous that he could just do that – come out of the closet, stay out and be himself.

I'm jealous of Jordy, because for the past few years, sometimes, I've been thinking that I might be gay too.

FOUR

Carraway's Point High is surrounded by tall black fences. I'm walking through the open gates in casual clothes for my first day back because my old uniform is too small for me now. All the memories of why I was so glad to be out of this place are flooding in: the classrooms that are like ovens on warm days, the teachers who seem like this is their back-up profession, the people who are all related to this person or that person and everyone knows everyone.

The first thing I do is get bigger clothes at the uniform shop with the cash Dad gave me. Then the next few hours of the school day I'm with Ivy, the Aboriginal liaison officer, and the deputy, Mr Keating, selecting my electives and building my timetable. Mr Keating asks a lot of questions about Sydney, about the sporting college. He's already received my last school report, so he knows about my grades and how shit I am in just about everything.

When the bell sounds for recess, Mr Keating rushes to print off my timetable for me.

'I'll let your teachers know over recess that you're joining their classes,' he says. 'Welcome back.'

'Thanks,' I reply.

'I'll walk you out,' Ivy says. Ivy is a short Aboriginal woman. She's young, probably only in her twenties, and used to have long brown hair, but she's wearing it short now. She wears glasses with black frames, and has a lanyard around her neck, just like always.

I study my timetable as we leave the office. I've got English and Geography after recess, then lunch and a free period, then Wood Tech in period six. I can't think of a worse way to end a school day.

We exit onto the wide concrete pathway where students are rushing out of classrooms.

'I know this has all been a bit of a whirlwind for you,' Ivy says. 'I want you to know I'm aware of what happened in Sydney. I'm here if you ever need to yarn about anything. You remember where my office is, yeah?'

'Yeah, I remember.'

'Good. Well, welcome back. I'll see you round.'

'See ya.'

I walk through the square and under an arch between two of the conjoined buildings. Stairs lead up the hill towards the oval and canteen and gym, but I turn to the left. I've never actually set foot in the seniors' area before.

I pass a long rectangular building where they do Drama and Photography classes, and follow the footpath around to the other side. Trees stand tall and in the spaces between are picnic tables, some with shelters over them, some without. Senior students in white shirts sit at the tables and on the grass, all the way up to the black fence at the back.

'Howdy, stranger,' I hear behind me. I turn to see Ebony approaching, next to her friend Cassie. Cassie continues walking while Ebony stops with me. 'I thought I saw you at the footy yesterday – wasn't sure though.'

'Hey,' I say, and I can feel the blush rushing to my cheeks. Ebony's got blonde hair, tied in a ponytail, and she's gotten taller – we're the same height now. Her cheeks are red and she's tanned.

'Why are you back in this dump? Seems kinda weird to be moving back to Carraway's Point a few months into Year Twelve.'

'Yeah, I dunno,' I say. 'Got sick of it.'

'Really?' she asks, tilting her head to the side in a way that tells me she doesn't believe me.

'Yeah. How you been?'

'Fine,' she says. 'You?'

'Yeah, fine,' I say, and my throat is suddenly very dry because I don't know what else to say. 'Good. Fine. All right.'

Another two people pass by on the footpath, talking about something I can't register because I'm too busy thinking about how awkward this is.

'Well, I'll see ya round,' she says, smiling. She walks past me and continues to the seniors' area. I follow, spotting Eric and Mitch sitting with our other mates. I see Jordy with Amber and Hamish, and a blonde girl who I think is called Krystal. They're on the grass, in a spot near the back fence where a ray of sunshine is getting through the trees.

I start towards Eric and Mitch, ready to be social again.

———

After school, I follow Eric, Mitch and our mate Tom to Mitch's car for an after-school Maccas run. We drive over the hill and past the church where a hundred old white-fullas are gathering outside, down past the bus stop and onto the main street. Mitch just got his licence, and it's nerve-racking being in the car with him. He howls and sings and steers with one hand – he leaves his left hand on the gearstick the whole time he drives. But it feels normal, kind of. It feels like I'm back with my mates, and they're not judging me or disappointed in me, like I thought they would be. We're just hanging out.

Our car crawls through the Macca's drive-thru and I order a double McChicken meal with a Coke. We get our food and head back along the main street to the wharf.

We pull into one of the parking spots facing the water.

The boats are lined up near the piers. Two women jog past and make their way around the harbour where seagulls are circling above.

I buzz my window down halfway. A cold breeze rushes inside and skims through my hair.

'So, did you have a girl in Sydney?' Mitch asks.

'Nah,' I reply. 'Hooked up with this girl April, but that was a while ago.'

'Aw yeah? What, did she break your heart or some-thing?' Mitch asks.

'Nah, it was just a one-time thing.'

I remember Mitch once describing the appearance of a vagina. He said it was like a *delicate rose,* a *flower with silky petals.* The first time I saw one in real life was in my first semester at St Augustine's in Sydney. There was an all-girls school across the suburb and the guys I became friends with would hang out with them sometimes. One of the girls was having a birthday party and I went along with my mates. I'd had a few drinks and eventually, I started kissing April. We were around the side of the house, on the grass, making out, and I slid my fingers into her jeans. She was the first girl I'd ever gone that far with. It felt okay at first, and she moaned and kissed me harder. I was feeling really turned on, and I started thinking maybe I was straight after all. Then I kissed her and made my way from her lips to her waist.

'What about you, Mitch?' I ask as I dig into my Maccas.

'Tunin' a couple of tens at the moment,' Mitch says. 'Becka Costigan and Leah Hill. Leah's harder to crack but I'm gettin' there.' Mitch tosses one of his chips into Tom's face. 'Meanwhile, Tom here's been stuck with the same hole since Year Seven.'

'Oh, you're still with Ashley?' I ask Tom.

'Yeah, still with Ash.'

'Goin' strong,' I say.

'What about you, Eric?' Mitch smiles, looking in the rear-view mirror at us in the back seat. 'Why don't you tell Kal about Rita?'

'You're dating Rita?' I ask.

Eric finishes swallowing his McNugget and clears his throat.

'We're not dating, exactly,' Eric says.

'You comin' on the weekend?' Mitch asks me. 'Eric's eighteenth.'

'Oh? I forgot it was your birthday,' I say to Eric.

'Yeah, you're invited, obviously,' he says. 'I didn't send ya the invite cause I didn't know you'd be back. We've got the bye this week, so no footy. Party starts at seven.'

'Sweet. Yeah, I'll have to check with Mum and Dad. They've been hard arses since I got back.'

We finish our food and Mitch drives me home to Chopin Drive.

I don't think I really like Mitch anymore, or Eric, or Tom. I've changed somehow, and they've stayed pretty much the same. If they saw that video, if they ever knew why I was fighting Aaron Davies, they'd never hang out with me again.

Before I step inside my house, I pull my phone from my pocket. There's a text waiting on the screen, from my mate Liam.

Are you gonna reply? Let me know ur good?

A twisting feeling grows in my stomach as I remember the friends I had in Sydney. I could tell Liam what happened. I could tell him the real truth, but when I think about doing that, it's terrifying.

———

Mum's at work, and Dad makes beef rissoles and mashed potato with gravy for dinner, though I don't finish my plate because I'm still full from my McChicken earlier. Dad reminds me I've got footy training after school tomorrow, tells me he'll pick me up at six-thirty.

After dinner, Keira lazes on the couch and watches *The White Lotus* while Dad goes to the garage to lift weights and listen to music. I pack my footy boots and a spare shirt for training tomorrow and have a shower. Dad's standing at the door when I exit the bathroom, sweat all over his face and a towel on his shoulder. He passes me on my way out with no hello or anything.

In my room, I change into a singlet and my red pyjama pants. I get in bed at nine-thirty and I'm stuffed. My muscles feel like they're relaxing for the first time today. Everything that's happened in the last few days has been chaos. It was just five nights ago when I got into a fight with Aaron Davies, three days ago when I was expelled, two days when I got on a bus back to Carraway's Point. Things can change so quickly. The middle knuckle on my right hand is still a little sore.

Even though my body is tired and I need to be asleep right now, my brain doesn't want to turn off. I'm thinking about the fight, how stupid I was.

I get up and go to the kitchen. It's just past ten-thirty; Keira's gone to bed, and I can hear the radio on in Mum and Dad's room.

I pour myself a glass of water and as I sip, I hear the front door open. Mum walks in with a sweaty face, hair tied back, her blue police uniform on, and a navy-blue jacket folded in her arms.

'Kal,' she says, surprised to see me. 'Thought you'd be asleep.'

'Trying,' I say. 'Brain won't shut up.'

'I hear ya.'

She drops her keys in the bowl beside the front door and steps into the kitchen. Her heavy boots thud on the wooden floor. She takes her dinner from the fridge, unwraps the cling wrap and puts the plate in the microwave.

'How was your first day at school?' she asks, undoing her hair and letting it fall over her shoulders.

'It was okay,' I say. 'Bit weird.'

'Yeah? Your friends glad to have you back?'

'I s'pose.'

'I wanted to give you a few more days, but your father insisted you get back to school as soon as possible,' she says. 'You *are* in Year Twelve, so I guess he's probably right.'

'Yeah.'

The microwave buzzes. Mum opens the door and touches the centre of one of the rissoles. She closes the door and starts the microwave again for another minute.

'How was work?' I ask. 'Anything interesting happen?'

'Interesting? No. But I guess that's a good thing,' she says. 'Just Old Toby stumblin' around drunk, so I gave him a lift home. That was about as eventful as Carraway's Point got tonight. Then again, the interesting stuff usually happens after midnight.'

She pulls the plate out of the microwave as I finish my glass of water. I want to ask her about Brandon, about what happened to him. I wonder if she was working that night, if she went to the scene. I want to ask if she thinks that officer deserves to go to jail. She knew Brandon too. Surely she has an opinion on the colleague who killed him.

'You wanna talk about what happened? In Sydney?' Mum asks, her voice softer now. She's staring at me.

'Nah,' I say. A part of me wants to tell her everything, but I don't know how.

'Get some sleep,' she says. She places her hand on my cheek and kisses me. 'It's good to have you home.'

I go back to my room and climb into bed again. I pick up my phone, and read the latest message from Liam: *Are you gonna reply to me? I thought we were mates.*

I type some words, let them sit there beneath my thumb for a moment: *Sorry I didn't get to say goodbye.*

I'm a bad friend, holding things back from him. He always seemed like a great mate, someone I could talk to. But we talked about girls – girls he was interested in, girls I said I was interested in, how he made out with a girl from the other school, how I did too.

The part I left out when I told Mitch, Eric and Tom about April was that we tried to have sex that night at the party, and I couldn't get it up. I thought maybe I was just tired, but I remembered the fantasies I used to have when I was twelve and thirteen, where I would imagine kissing my friends – kissing Mitch, kissing Eric, kissing Jordy, kissing other boys at school. They were bad thoughts, scary thoughts. I didn't want to have them anymore, because the only person I knew who was gay, who wasn't a character in a TV show or a movie that Dad would call *fruity* or *faggy*, was my cousin Aisha. She was my mum's cousin's daughter. She moved to Sydney when she was eighteen, came out as lesbian and I never saw her again. Mum and Dad always referred to her as *the dyke*, saying, *there's always one in the family*.

I knew I liked boys, but I was so scared of it until earlier this year, when I heard about Maneatr – this app where men can meet other men for anonymous hookups. I turned eighteen in February, and the first thing I did when I woke on my birthday was download the Maneatr app. It was so exciting. I could explore this part of myself that I'd tried to make my brain kill for years, and I could do it all in secret. No one would have to know my name. No one would have to know anything about me. Then I realised there was another boy at my school who was on the app, another Year Twelve. We talked for days, weeks, late at night, real cute shit. He was scared of sending a face pic, and I was okay with that. But I wanted to meet him, because I was sure he was closeted like me.

Turned out the boy was Aaron Davies and his mates, playing a massive prank on the parts of myself I was slowly becoming less ashamed of. The flashlights came on when I met the mystery boy behind the canteen block at midnight.

They were filming me, filming my outing. Something took me over when I saw them: rage, embarrassment, dread. I don't remember launching myself at Aaron – all I remember is the blood on his face and the burning in my hand as I pounded my fist so hard it was like I was trying to kill a mountain.

It's behind me now. I need to get a girlfriend and find a way to make that work. It'll be like learning to love strawberry milk. I'm sure if I try it enough, I'll talk myself into it. It's the only path to having a happy life. I'm sure of it.

No good can come from that part of myself. Thinking of those parts of me makes me hot, makes my muscles tighten. To free myself, I close my eyes and picture trees. I imagine I'm standing on dirt, feeling the roughness beneath the soles of my feet. Looking up, I see the blue sky breaking through the treetops. The branches brush together and I listen to them, take a deep breath and suck the bush air into my lungs. The birds are singing, and even if just for this moment, it feels like I'll be okay.

FIVE

It's Tuesday morning and I'm walking to the bus stop at the end of Chopin Drive. It's not far, but it feels like a long walk in the chilly air.

Jordy and his brother, Lewis, come out of their house. Lewis powers off but Jordy offers me a half-smile as we meet on the road.

'Saw you back at school yesterday,' he says.

'Yeah? It's been a while.'

'When did you move back?'

'On the weekend,' I say. 'Congrats, by the way.'

'For what?'

'For coming out,' I say, and as soon as the words leave my lips, I know I've made this awkward before we've even begun talking properly.

'Oh.' Jordy chuckles. 'Thanks, I guess?'

We pass Brandon's house at the end of the street, and I think about the police officer's trial. I'm about to ask

Jordy about it when we arrive at the bus stop and I see Lewis is talking to Dylan and Jarrod.

I don't think Dylan likes me very much anymore. I think he avoids me because I hang out with the footy boys.

The bus arrives and I find a seat at the back, beside Tom. Tom's playing Pokémon Go on his phone. Mitch is sitting behind us with Eric.

'People still play that?' I ask Tom. He looks up from his phone with a raised eyebrow.

'Yeah, mate,' he says. 'This'll never get old.'

'Didn't know you were a Pokémon nerd.'

'I'm not a nerd. It's just fun. I got into it over summer.'

Tom goes back to his phone and I look down the aisle of the bus. Jordy is sitting with Amber.

It's a ten-minute journey from Chopin Drive to school. I take out my phone and start scrolling Insta. Liam has posted a photo of the sunset from the window of his train with the caption *TIRED*. He hasn't replied to my text from last night. Maybe he's decided to forget about me.

I have Photo/Vid first period. None of my mates are doing this class, except Ebony and Jordy.

Ms Kennedy tells us to divide into pairs for a photography assignment. We have to go with our partner and scatter around the school, taking photographs that represent *hope*.

Ebony zeroes in on me as everyone else finds a partner. 'How about it, Kallum?' she asks.

'Sure.'

We stroll off along the path like the rest of our class-mates. Ebony is carrying our Canon 700D because for some reason, she is its keeper.

We walk to the oval and find a picnic table under the shade of a big gum tree by the old demountables. There were none of those at St Augustine's – just state-of-the-art tall buildings.

'You're going to be the model,' Ebony says.

'What? Why me?'

'Because I'm holding the camera.'

'Sure, but you could pass it to me, then I'd be holding it.'

'Models keep their mouths closed and do what they're told.'

'Wow,' I say. 'You're meaner than I remember.'

We sit at the table and it's colder under the shade of the tree.

'Do you still hang out with Nerdy Pete and Dawson?' I ask.

'Yes,' she says. 'And don't call Pete that.'

'For real? Even *I'm* more interesting than them.'

I'd always found it weird that Ebony was this sporty girl but she hung out with people who play Dungeons and Dragons and watch professional wrestling religiously. She doesn't seem like the type, she doesn't fit with them. But maybe those labels they tell you about in high school don't really exist.

'Sit up on the tabletop,' she says. 'Feet on the seat. And look towards the demountable. Pretend you're thinking deeply, if you can.'

I climb on the table and look towards the demountable.

The paint is a faded yellow and there's a class inside.

'Okay, now, rest your elbow on your knee and lean forward,' she says. 'Cup your chin and look to the clouds.'

'Okay.' I do what she says. I can't help but laugh my arse off at how stupid this is.

'Hey!' she barks. 'Be serious. You're contemplating something.'

'Contemplating?' I chuckle.

'Just...think about something that worries you, and search for the solution in the clouds. It might not be clear, but search for it.'

Okay, she's making me feel weird. I look to the clouds and try not to laugh again. I think on it for a moment. The dread, the fear comes back. Ebony snaps shot after shot. I don't like thinking about this while she is watching, so I turn my thoughts to my dad. I won't ever be good enough to impress him. He'll never be happy with what I'm doing. I don't know if there's any solution to that. Maybe there *is* an answer in the clouds somewhere.

'That enough?' I ask.

'Yeah, that'll do.'

'Can I see?'

'No, not until I've put it through Photoshop. She scrolls through the photos, glances up to me. 'Why'd you get expelled, anyway?'

'What?'

'Was it drugs? Alcohol?'

'Wow, is *Ebony Green* being racist right now?'

'No,' she replies sharply.

'How'd you know I got expelled anyway?'

'Everyone does. It's a small town, Kal. And besides, it kind of goes with the whole *tall, dark and mysterious* thing you got going on.'

'Tall, dark and mysterious?' I chuckle.

'Yeah,' she says. 'You're, I dunno, kind of guarded. You hide things. I'm just not sure exactly what you're hiding yet.'

'I'm not *guarded*,' I say, and a cold shiver comes over me. She knows I've got a secret. 'How am I guarded?'

'You keep things to yourself. Like, you never talk about your family or home or anything.'

'It's really not that interesting.' I chuckle again.

'Not interesting? Your mum's a cop and your dad's like the boss of the Aboriginal land council. Probably got some stories there.'

I sit back and sigh. I guess I don't talk about my family to anyone. I don't really like to.

'So,' Ebony says. 'Why'd you get expelled?'

I sit forward again and rub my eyes. 'I got into a fight with someone and it was videoed and reported to the principal,' I say. 'That's it.'

'Yeah, that'd do it. And no,' she says.

'No what?'

'You're *not* more interesting than Dawson or Pete. Dawson's a brilliant piano player. She's also going to be a world-class vet one day. She could tell you all about a cat's anatomy without even thinking about it. And Pete, he's the only person who knows Star Wars better than me. And it's not just Star Wars – he loves all film, and he writes stories. He could damn well write a better story for the school play than the bullshit they stitched together for our Year Eleven Drama class last year.'

'Language,' I say. Ebony laughs. 'Ready to head back to class?'

'Yeah. I need to swing by the bathroom.'

We cross the oval to the bathrooms. Ebony walks in and I lean against the wall outside. I don't know why I'm waiting for her. She didn't ask me to. Ebony's very attractive. She's tall and walks with a straight back. Plus, she's really fun to talk to. Maybe if she liked me, and I liked her back, I could convince myself I don't need to worry about what happened in Sydney. We've made out before, and there's definitely *something* between us. Maybe I can ask her out, now that I'm back for good. Maybe she's waiting for me to do that. Maybe I really am straight, and she can help me be sure of that.

SIX

Mack wears sunglasses when he trains us. He has a big mole on his left cheek and his voice sounds exactly like Woody from *Toy Story* when he shouts. We did sprints with burpees for thirty minutes, now we're doing ball work. The team runs pretty much the same plays as we were running in Sydney – block plays, overs and unders, arrow ruck attacks – so it's not like learning a whole new sport. I pick it all up pretty easy. Maybe I am as good as Dad says I am.

'Yes, shift,' Mack yells. 'Shift it to the wing!'

The ball passes through hands and finds me on the wing. I catch and run into the in-goal.

'Good work, back to the fifty,' Mack calls. 'Now, two forward hit-ups and we'll run the superman play.'

'What's superman?' I ask Eric, who's my centre.

'It's a kick downtown,' Eric says. 'We do it on the second or third tackle to catch 'em off guard. You or Tom will be runnin' after it.'

One of our forwards plays the ball, then another runs. Mack calls out to signal the tackle, then our forward plays the ball. Mitch takes the next run, sprinting straight at our assistant coach. As Mitch gets to him, Mack calls another tackle.

'Superman!' our halfback calls. When he receives the ball, he kicks it down the field and it veers to my side. I sprint after it and pick it up after two bounces, just before the ten-metre line, and race it into the in-goal again.

'Good work, boys,' Mack calls.

I'm out of breath, panting like a dog. I place my hands on the back of my head, straighten my back and open my lungs, just like Dad told me. Sweat is dripping into my eyes. The smell of the night dew on the grass is something I've missed from Carraway's Point – it didn't really smell the same in Sydney.

'Good effort,' Mack says. 'Let's wrap it up. See you all on Thursday.'

Dad's waiting for me beside the grandstand, wearing a dark-green jumper and folding his arms, leaning against the post.

'Already feels like a better team, now you're here,' Eric says to me as we walk off the ground. 'I smell a premiership coming.'

He gets to his bag and pulls out a Gatorade, takes a big gulp.

'Season's only just started,' I say. I take out my deodorant and spray my underarms.

'Me and Mitch are gonna start hitting the gym Mondays and Fridays,' Eric says. 'You should come.'

'I'm sure my father would love that,' I say. Eric chuckles. Dad's shaking Mack's hand, smiling and talking. 'I'll see ya tomorrow.'

Eric gives me a nod and I start over to Dad and Mack.

'How'd he settle in?' Dad asks Mack. 'You should put him forward for first grade once he's got a few games under his belt.'

'Well, I'm sure if he plays well enough, I won't have to put him forward,' Mack says.

Dad turns to me. 'Ready to go?'

'Yep,' I say.

We head to the car park, where some of the reserves and first-grade players are climbing into their cars and speeding out of here.

'How'd you go?' Dad asks.

'All right,' I say.

'We'll hit the beach in the morning. Gotta keep consistent on that cardio.'

'Yep,' I say. I just want to sleep, to be honest. I feel like I've hardly slept since Friday. And every time I hear Dad's voice, a little bit of fire grows in my fists and I begin to feel hot again. Sometimes, I wish he would just shut the fuck up.

Back home, there are three slices of pizza saved for me. Mum and Keira are on the couch watching a movie – it's got Denzel Washington in it and he's killing some mobsters. I eat in the kitchen and Mum's telling Keira about a driver she pulled over for a random breath test this afternoon – Brandon's mum, Kathy. She was over the limit and Mum felt terrible about having to place her under arrest. Keira's reassuring her that it was better Mum picked her up than one of the white police officers. Mum is saying she still feels like the bad guy. I feel sorry for Kathy, but not for the breath test – for the dead son. We used to say hello to each other, me and Kathy, whenever I'd see her in the street, or out the front of her house. If I was hanging out with Brandon at his place, Kathy would always put on some chicken nuggets or party pies and feed us. She'd always be smiling or I'd hear her laughing in the other room at the TV or on the phone. A part of me feels like I should stop by and visit her, tell her I'm sorry about what happened to Brandon, but she probably hates my family these days – we're the family with the Aboriginal police officer. It's been too long now, anyway. Too much time has passed for it not to be awkward.

I finish my pizza as Dad is heading out to the garage in his training singlet.

'Remember to set your alarm for six o'clock,' he tells me as we pass in the hallway. How could I forget?

After a quick shower, I'm in bed and my body is so sore. There's a text on my phone from Liam: *U right bro? Wanna talk about what happnd?*

Right now, all I want to do is close my eyes and get through this week. I wish there was some way to set my body to autopilot, so I could breeze through days and nights without feeling anything, without feeling exhausted all the time, or angry and disappointed in myself. I feel like no matter what I do, or how hard I train, Dad'll never be satisfied unless I'm playing in the NRL and representing

New South Wales in State of Origin, pulling in hundreds of thousands of dollars a year.

———

At six-twenty a.m. on Wednesday, there is a cold wind howling along the beach. Thunder groans in the grey clouds. I feel like my bones have turned to ice as I stumble from the waves in to shore. I trudge the wet sand, wrap myself in my towel and shiver as Dad emerges from the water. He shakes his wet hair and sprays like a dog, picks up his towel and buries his face in it.

'I'm gonna start going to the gym with Eric and Mitch,' I say, hoping that will satisfy him.

'Tonight?' Dad asks.

'They wanna go Fridays and Mondays,' I say.

'Good. Make sure you do some cardio. Your fitness needs improving. I'm fifty-two years old, and I can outrun and outswim you. Should be the other way around.'

Dad steps into my space. I try to hide my shivering. The sound of the waves crashing drains away and there is only Dad's voice now.

'Do you still want this?' he asks. 'Do you want to play in the NRL?'

I nod. 'Yes.'

'Then show me. Show yourself.'

He grabs his shoes and starts up the beach. He's daring me to push myself harder, to prove to him that I still want this dream I've had since I was a kid watching Greg Inglis carve it up on TV. He's always been hard on me. Even when I was little, he would stalk the sideline of my games, shout instructions, tell me to tackle harder, tell me to run faster, tell me to use my palm, use my shoulders. After a while, I found a way to tune it out. I stopped hearing the words, even if I could still hear his voice.

Back in the car, Dad blasts the heater. Sand litters the floor and water is still dripping from my hair. We aren't talking, and the silence feels comfortable to me – more comfortable than trying to make conversation.

———

It's period four and I don't have to go to class because there's a Koori Klub meeting in the school hall with Ivy.

Ivy enters the hall with Glen Wright, who works with Dad at the land council. His neat black beard has some grey sprinkled through it now. The sight of him reminds me that for the past few years, he's been organising celebrations for graduating Koori students who finish Year Twelve. He wears a black shirt with Aboriginal art splashed across one sleeve and the body. His glasses look like they've come straight out of the two-dollar bin at The Reject Shop.

Gathering at the front of the hall are the five other Kooris finishing Year Twelve with me – there's Jasmine Turner, who is one of Ebony's friends, Billy White, who's one of the footy boys, but he and his family mostly keep to themselves outside of school, and Kaz Granger, who hangs out with the popular girls. Then there's Dylan and Jordy, the wannabe-gangster and the gay kid who defi-nitely seems to be treated differently by all of our old mates because of his sexuality.

Ivy has gathered chairs from the front of the hall and set them out in a semicircle. The only empty seat is beside Jordy, so I take it.

Ivy and Glen are moving slowly towards their seats at the centre of the semicircle.

'So, the time has come for us to start planning our Future Leaders celebration,' Glen says, sitting down. 'I just came in to get some ideas from youse, see what you'd like to do to celebrate. You're all finishing Year Twelve and it deserves a celebration. And if any of youse have any questions, I'm here to answer. Speak now or forever hold your peace.'

Glen's always making these left-field comments, like he thinks he's hilarious.

Jasmine asks for a barbecue, which Glen says is possible.

'Will it just be us, or graduates from the other schools?' Jordy asks.

'We'll be joined by four students from Carraway Catholic,' Ivy says, 'and two students from Belrose High.'

We all know the Kooris that go to Carraway Catholic – Elijah, Doreen, Maddie and Corey. Elijah plays footy for the eighteens with us, so I know him pretty well. I used to, anyway. I only know the others by name and face.

I don't know who's at Belrose High. Belrose is thirty-minutes down the highway. It's more inland and there are a couple of smaller localities surrounding it, so most kids from that area go to Belrose High, but some go to our school.

'Why don't we do a camp, like you guys did last year?' Kaz asks.

'Yeah?' Glen says. 'Would everyone be happy with a camp? We'll go to Camp Kamble, so we got a bit of privacy. Week after you graduate, before the HSC exams.'

'What do *you* reckon, Dylan?' Ivy asks. Dylan's been sitting there with his hands in his pockets, hood over his head.

'Yeah, I don't care.'

After the twenty-minute meeting, it's decided we're doing the camp. I leave with Jordy towards the seniors' area. As we walk along the path, I spot Ebony sitting at one of the tables under the shelter, opening her laptop. Nerdy Pete is at the table too.

'I didn't think Dylan would make it this far,' I say to Jordy. 'Finish Year Twelve, I mean.'

'Yeah, I'm as surprised as you are,' Jordy says. 'Especially with what happened last year.'

'Yeah.'

'He was there that night with Brandon,' Jordy says. 'He saw the whole thing. That would fuck you up.'

'Definitely.'

Eric joins from one of the walkways, arriving for lunch. Jordy glances at him, looks away, then increases his speed a little to get ahead as Eric says hey to me. Weird.

Jordy leaves to join Amber and his friends by the back fence. Ahead are the popular girls, Rita and Stacey. Rita gives Eric a wave.

'I'll catch ya later,' Eric says to me.

'Okay,' is all I can say, before he jets ahead. Ebony spots me, glancing up from her laptop. I offer her a smile, which she returns.

Okay. I can do this. I can flirt with girls. It's what boys do. I can do it.

I walk over. 'Hey,' I say.

'Hi,' Ebony says. 'Can I help you?'

I look at her screen. She's reading an article on the flat-earth theory.

'I didn't take you for a flat-earther,' I say.

'Oh, god no,' she says. 'I'm not at all. The earth is round. Duh. I just find it interesting that people actually believe in this. Like, a thousand years ago, I could understand, but in this day and age, I don't get it.'

'And you're interested in why people think that nowadays?' I ask.

'Yep. I've been researching the whole thing, hoping one piece of writing might convince me to think about it differently.'

'No luck yet?'

'Not yet. Lots of wild conspiracy theories.'

'My favourite conspiracy theory is the JFK one,' I say, hoping this might make me seem more interesting. 'We watched that JFK movie in History up in Sydney. It was really interesting. I reckon the mafia did it.'

'The mafia? Really?'

'Yeah, it's possible,' I argue back. 'And you know about the magic bullet thing, right? There was obviously multiple shooters.'

'There *were* obviously multiple shooters,' she says,

correcting my white man's English for me. 'Okay, that one I do kind of agree with.'

Me and Ebony chat for ages under the shelter. Nerdy Pete puts on his headphones – big black bulky things – to block us out. I think Ebony is warming back up to me. She's nice, she's pretty, she's smart, and most importantly, she's a girl.

My phone vibrates in my pocket. I take it out and there's a text from Liam: *Is it true? Aaron said you're gay and that he catfished you.*

I'm quick to put my phone away. The bell sounds to end lunch. Ebony closes her laptop and makes me get up to let her out of the shelter.

'See you,' she says.

'See ya.' I should have said something funny, witty, flirty, but Liam's message has hit me. I'm still standing beside the shelter. The seniors' area empties, as students head for period five. I need to get to my class too, but I'm frozen where I stand. My legs are like trees growing into the ground beneath me. The words I need to reply blast in my head like fireworks. He was my friend – my best friend. I owe him the truth.

I type a text and hit send: *I don't know if I'm gay, but it's true. Sorry if this changes anything.*

I stuff my phone back in my pocket. My heart is beating like a jackhammer.

I walk along the path, through the square, up the stairwell and arrive at my English classroom.

I pull my phone out to see if Liam has replied yet. He has. His text waits on my screen.

What a fucking cock he is. I'm sorry that happened to you, man. Doesn't change anything obviously. Hope you're okay!

Liam hopes I'm okay. Liam says it doesn't change anything. For a moment, my heart smiles and the jackhammer in my chest stops. I feel my muscles relax.

Liam has said it's okay – it's okay to be gay. Liam's in Sydney, though. Liam isn't in Carraway's Point. Liam has the most laidback, loving parents I've ever met. Liam doesn't know what it's like to be me.

A new text pops up at the top of my phone screen – a message from Ebony. She's sent a photo. I open the message and it's the photo she took of me sitting on the picnic table, staring off into the distance, edited in a dark black and white.

Ebony: *Mysterious boy…*

Me: *I actually don't look too bad lol*

Ebony: *Nah you're pretty cute* 😊

Me: *Wow at least buy me dinner first lol*

Ebony: *Nah, the guy buys the dinner*

Me: *In this day and age? Lol what about breaking those gender stereotypes?*

Ebony: *Fine, we'll split the bill. 50/50.*

I think we are organising a date. I feel a kind of energy in my stomach, a stirring of heat and a tingle. It's not butterflies – it's worry. What if I let her down? What if I try this and I can't convince myself not to be gay? It would just hurt her, and hurting her would hurt me too.

SEVEN

It's Thursday evening and tonight's session was all fitness – running, burpees, push-ups, step climbing. We're the last grade to finish training.

Ebony is sitting in the grandstand waiting for me. I'm all sweaty down my back, under my arms, my groin, my feet, everywhere – not exactly how I wanted to be for our date tonight. But she's been at Oztag training so she's probably sweaty too.

I change back into my school shirt and spray myself with deodorant before I start over to Ebony. She's wearing a white hoodie and her training shorts, and her legs look shiny under the lights of the footy field.

'Pizza? Really?' she asks.

'Not just *any* pizza,' I say. 'The best pizza in Carraway's Point. One of the few things I've missed from here.'

I'd thought pizza was a great idea.

We walk to Ebony's Suzuki Swift and climb inside. There's a rainbow-coloured penguin on the air-freshener dangling from her mirror, which I didn't expect to see. I want to ask her about it, but that would arouse suspicion – or she might even think I'm homophobic.

We drive through town then onto the coastal road towards the wharf. There are boats docked, and moonlight blazing over the water, which seems steady tonight.

'Have you got your Ps yet?' Ebony asks.

'Nah, I got my Ls. Didn't feel the need to get my Ps in Sydney. I should though.'

'Then you can get a car and drive next time,' she says.

'Do you not like driving?' I ask, brushing over the fact that she said there'd be a next time.

'No, it's just usually the guy who picks up the girl.'

'Again with the gender stereotypes.' I chuckle.

'Just saying,' she says. 'It'd be kind of nice, like in the olden days. In my head, a guy would pick me up, I would introduce him to my parents, he would walk me to his car and open the door for me.'

'Well, I can do that, but I'd be walking you to the driver's seat of your own car after trekking it to your place,' I say.

'I guess that would do.' She giggles.

We arrive at the pizza place opposite the docks. It's between a fishing shop and a takeaway shop. Nothing's really changed since I moved away, but as I look at the boats and the bay and the moon, I think this might be the first time I've thought of this place as pretty.

Inside, the smell of cooking pizza and garlic bread instantly makes my mouth fill with saliva. I follow Ebony to the counter with the pizza slices on display for six bucks a slice, which feels like a bit of a rip-off.

'Could I get two slices of margarita?' Ebony asks the server.

'And I'll take two slices of pepperoni, please,' I add. The server is a short bald man with a goatee and thick-rimmed glasses. His forehead is all sweaty, glistening under the light above him. He uses a spatula to scoop out our slices, places them into separate paper bags. We pay for our own food and sit at one of the little round tables outside.

'So, Ebony,' I begin, 'what are you planning on doing after we graduate?'

Ebony sits back, sucking a long string of mozzarella into her mouth.

'I was thinking of doing veterinary science, like Dawson,' she says. 'I don't think I'll get the ATAR for that, though.'

'Really? But you're heaps smart.'

'Not as smart as you think,' Ebony says. 'For some reason, everyone thinks I'm this academic whiz. I'm smart with some things. It just doesn't translate into good grades. Exams fuck me up. If I can work on something for a while, I'm good, but if I have to sit at a desk and get through fifty pages in two hours, I'm doomed. I need time, and exams don't give you that.'

'True,' I say.

'What about you? What are your plans?'

'Well,' I begin, 'I guess I'll do those footy trials in September, see how I go. If it goes well, I'll move back to Sydney and play footy.'

'What's your back-up plan?' Ebony asks, and it catches me off guard.

'Umm, back-up plan?' I ask. 'I . . . I don't know. Haven't really thought about it. There's only one plan.'

'Maybe get yourself a back-up, in case the trials don't work out.'

'You don't think they'll work out?'

'I didn't say that.' Ebony smiles. 'I'm sure you'll do well. I know you're a great footy player. But, I mean, thousands of people try to make it to the NRL, you know? A lot of good players never make it that far.'

'Still, even if I don't make NRL, I can play professionally somewhere.'

'Sure. Yes,' she says.

I'm making this awkward and all about me. I honestly hadn't even considered not doing well at trials. I assumed Dad's pushing would be enough to get me there. But what if it's not enough? What if I don't enjoy it? I hardly enjoy playing anymore as it is. What if it's worse playing professionally? What if that takes the last ounces of fun out of the game for me?

'I haven't thought about what else I would do,' I say.

'What else are you into?' Ebony asks.

'I don't know.'

'Surely you have other things you're interested in.'

'Umm, well, yeah,' I say, trying to think of something. It was always footy. Dad always envisioned me playing footy. Mum always envisioned me playing footy. But in my head, I find myself beneath trees. I can almost hear the birds clicking and whistling around me. 'I like the bush,' I say.

'The bush?' Ebony giggles. 'What do you mean, the bush?'

'I don't know. I like being in the bush.'

'I'm pretty sure *being in the bush* isn't a job someone can get paid for,' Ebony says. 'Maybe you could be a park ranger or something.'

'Oh, I like that,' I say. '*Kallum, the park ranger.*'

'Your dad works for the Aboriginal land council, doesn't he?' Ebony asks. 'Maybe they have jobs doing things in the bush.'

'I don't know,' I say. I don't think Dad would be too thrilled if I came to him and said I wanted to work in the bush for the land council, back-burning and looking after vegetation and whatnot. But now that I think about it, I could enjoy that. I could check in on wombats and make sure their homes are free from rubbish, teach people about the flowers and bush food and medicine.

'Isn't Jordy's dad a park ranger? Why don't you ask him to take you out for a bit one day, show you what it's like?' Ebony asks.

'Yeah, that could be fun,' I say. I don't think I've talked to Jordy's dad in years. And there's something about asking Jordy to ask him for me that makes me feel anxious. Jordy's gay and he's open about it. What if he has a sixth sense for seeing that in someone else? I'd be found out before I've even figured it out myself.

We finish our pizza and get back into Ebony's car at about eight-thirty. We drive back through the quiet town. Everything is closed. I spot Dylan and Jarrod on the main street.

Rory is walking a few metres ahead of them. Rory's this weird Aboriginal guy who lives a few blocks from Chopin Drive. He's tall, skinny and has a terrible goatee that's longer every time I see him. I don't think he works, but he's known as the local drug dealer. Mum reckons he'll be dead before he's thirty.

Ebony turns onto Chopin Drive and pulls up in front of my house. Mum's highway patrol car is in the driveway; she must've finished work already.

As I unbuckle my seatbelt, Ebony clears her throat.

'So,' she says. 'Are you gonna kiss me, or not?'

'You want me to kiss you?'

'Well, only if you want to,' she says.

I smile, lean over and plant a kiss on her lips. The worry stirs in my stomach again, telling me I'm only going to hurt her.

'Did you have a good time?' I ask.

'Yes, I did,' she says. 'But you need to get in the shower, asap.'

I chuckle and give my armpit a quick sniff. She is absolutely right. 'See you tomorrow,' I say.

'Bye.'

I climb out and Ebony drives away. As she reaches the end of the street, I hear shouting from inside my house: Mum and Dad, and Keira yelling for them to shut the fuck up. I haven't heard them fight for years – I guess

I haven't been around that much. Suddenly, it feels like not a day has gone by since their voices shook the walls of our house, and all I want to do is hide under my blanket and close my eyes.

Instead of starting for the front door, I go back to the street and walk along the road. It's so quiet out here that my shoes are clapping on the bitumen. I turn into Jordy's yard. It could be a bit late to visit, but this is less exhausting than being at home.

As I arrive at the door, the tingling returns to my stomach. It's telling me to turn away, that Jordy will be annoyed that I showed up at his house like we're still good friends. It was on me to reach out to him, to keep in contact, and I didn't. He'll be annoyed that I expected to knock on the door at nearly nine o'clock at night and be greeted with a smile, like our friendship didn't dissolve when I moved away in Year Nine.

When the four us used to hang out, Brandon was always the brave one, and I was jealous of that. One time, there was a big black dog loose in the street when the four of us were walking home from school. It was massive, almost the size of me, and lived in one of the houses halfway along the street. It would always be barking at us from behind the steel fence, and we used to joke that one day it would break the fence, chase us down and kill us.

Dylan and Brandon lived in the first two houses in our cul-de-sac, but my house is right up the end, and Jordy's is in the middle, across the road from where the dog lived. Me and Jordy were going to have to get past it to get home. Jordy was terrified and wanted to stay at the end of the street.

Once the dog spotted the four of us standing near the street sign, she started barking aggressively and rushing towards us. Dylan bolted to his yard and jumped his side fence. Brandon could've done the same, and left me and Jordy there. Instead, he took a few steps towards the dog and crouched down on the road, held out his hand and began calling her name: *Zelda*. I didn't even know that was her name until he said it. She stopped her charge a few metres from Brandon, but kept barking like she wanted to tear us to shreds.

'Zelda, Zelda,' Brandon said calmly, encouraging her to approach. Eventually, she stopped barking and walked to him, and Brandon patted her head. I remember the feeling that I was about to shit my pants turning quickly into jealousy. I wanted to be brave like him.

I decide to be brave now. I raise my fist to knock on Jordy's door, but before I can, the door opens and the light from inside hits my eyes. Jordy goes to walk outside but stops with a gasp at the sight of me. He's holding a plastic box with beer bottles and paper bags from McDonald's, still in his school shirt but with his pyjama pants on.

'Jesus, you scared the shit outta me,' Jordy says with a giggle.

'Sorry,' I say.

Jordy catches his breath. 'You right?' he asks.

'Yeah, yeah,' I say. 'Sorry. I just wanted to see if I could ask your dad something.'

'Oh. He's asleep already, big day at work,' Jordy says. 'Everything all right?'

'Yeah, nah, all good,' I say. 'I...I was thinking about maybe working in the national park. I wanted to see if he'd take me out to his work sometime, show me the ropes.'

'Oh, okay,' Jordy says. 'Umm, yeah, I can ask him in the morning if you want.'

'Yeah, that'd be good. Thanks.'

'No worries.'

I smile and nod, and maybe thirty seconds have passed before I realise we're both just standing at the front door smiling in silence. Jordy's still holding his container of recycling.

'Well, text me after you talk to him?' I ask.

'Yeah, will do,' Jordy says.

'Okay. Goodnight.'

'Goodnight.' Jordy giggles. I turn away and Jordy heads for his bins at the side of the house. I start back up the road for home.

There. That wasn't so hard. Jordy's nice, he wasn't annoyed, and he's gonna ask his dad for me, even though it was awkward as fuck. I think Jordy was always my favourite of the Chopin Drive crew growing up. I kind of wish we never stopped being mates.

EIGHT

It's an overcast Friday morning and the cold has invaded the house. There's a little fan heater on in the lounge room but it's not doing any good. I pack my lunch box and pull on my shoes by the front door.

'You're going to the gym tonight, right?' Dad asks.

'Yesss,' I reply. He knows I'm going to the gym, and it annoys me that he's asking in a way that sounds like he wasn't completely sure. I wouldn't be surprised if he's written my whole schedule out in a calendar or something. And I hate how he and Mum can fight all night, yelling and swearing at each other, banging things and calling each other the worst names, and then just wake up the next day and act like nothing happened.

'I'll pick you up about seven o'clock,' he says. 'We're going to dinner with a few of your mum's colleagues, remember.'

'Okay,' I say. I check my phone and there's a text from Jordy: *Hey, dad said today's the best day to take you out as big boss is away and he usually bludges. He said he can pick us up from school if ur still keen.*

I text back: *Yes plz!*

I'm going to go out with Jordy and his dad to the national park to see what it's like being a park ranger today. I won't tell Dad or Mum about it. They would think I'm wasting my time – time that could be better spent working out or something.

———

Jordy is waiting at the gates at the end of the school day. He's leaning against the fence watching the crowd of students leaving. Eric's walking with me, talking about how his birthday party tomorrow night is gonna go off, that he's hired a DJ and even a security guard. Eric's got a hectic house. It's up on the cliffs over the bay, where the houses are big and most of the driveways have boats parked in them. He had a party for his sixteenth; I wasn't there, but I saw the photos he posted on Instagram. It looked pretty spectacular.

'I'll meet youse at the gym around five-thirty,' I say to Eric as I cross towards Jordy.

'No worries,' he says.

I didn't tell Eric I was going out to the national park, either. For some reason, I don't want anyone else to know about it. What if I go out there and I realise that I hate everything involved in being a park ranger? What if Eric thinks it's a stupid back-up plan to have, or stupid to have a back-up plan at all? I realise these thoughts are silly. Eric knowing I am interested in being a park ranger won't hurt me, but a part of me wants to keep it between me and Jordy.

'Hey,' Jordy says.

'Hey.'

'How was your day?' he asks.

'Umm, it was fine,' I say. 'Shit, actually. I hate this school.'

Jordy giggles. 'Yeah, me too.'

Before long, Jordy's dad, Lee, rolls up and pulls into the bus lane in his little Ford Laser.

'Let's go,' Jordy says. He climbs into the front seat and I get in the back, where his little sister, Josie, is sitting.

'Hey, boys,' Lee says. 'How was your day?'

'Fine,' Jordy says.

'How you going, Kal? Didn't know you were keen on parks work.'

'Yeah, maybe,' I say. 'Just exploring my options, I guess.'

'Well, if you love the outdoors, it's the job for you. It's not all that flash but it's great,' he says.

We drive past the school, back through the main street and onto the highway. The trees line the sides of the road like a guard of honour as we join the queue of cars slowly leaving town. Lee then turns onto a dirt road with a sign that says *Carraway's National Park*.

'So, why national parks work?' Jordy asks.

'Umm, I don't know,' I say. 'I always loved being outside, I s'pose. Love being out bush.'

'Yeah, less people to deal with.' Jordy smiles.

'Be a lot different than Sydney,' Lee says. 'I used to run around there myself, when I was younger. City's too loud for me now – everyone's always in a rush. Out in the bush, it's quiet.'

'Yeah, it's like my happy place,' I say.

'Your happy place?' Jordy asks.

'Yeah, you know...that place in your head you go to when you need to chill out.'

'Right,' Jordy says. 'I guess that's Kylie for me.'

'You still listen to Kylie?' I ask.

'Yeah, always,' Jordy says. 'Can't believe I was listening to Kylie Minogue my whole life and no one knew I was gay.'

'You used to do that "Can't get you out of my head" dance with the music video on the telly,' Lee says to Jordy. 'In hindsight, there were definitely signs.'

Jordy and Lee both laugh, and I'm a little jealous, to be honest. I don't think I could laugh with my dad about the childhood signs of my gayness. Jordy's luckier than me, though – he was born to more relaxed parents.

The Laser rattles and shakes as we drive along, and I begin to worry it might fall to pieces. Jordy's dad slows as the road narrows, and we turn onto another one where the dirt is smoother. There's a long green building at the end, standing before the heavy surrounding bush. Nearby, a big shelter covers barbecues and picnic tables. We pull into the car park beside a dirty Toyota HiLux.

'Here we are,' Lee announces. 'We'll grab the jeep.'

We climb out of the car. There's a breeze rolling through the trees and the branches sway against each other, like an earthly wind chime. The sound makes my heart rate slow, steadies my breathing and relaxes my shoulders. The smell of rain lingers in the air and the grey clouds in the sky are threatening another downpour.

'This way,' Lee says. 'I've got some interesting stuff to show ya.' I walk behind him with Jordy and Josie.

We climb into a jeep that looks about forty years old, parked by the green building. Josie's with me in the back seat, and buckles her seatbelt before any of us. She peers out the window as Lee drives us onto the dirt road, pointing out birds she's spotted. The jeep feels much more comfortable than the Laser.

'So,' Lee begins. 'Being a ranger is all about protecting the environment. A big part of that is maintaining the camping grounds near the beach.'

The jeep travels along narrow dirt roads, where potholes make us bounce in our seats. We pass a small wooden block of toilets and showers, and drive through a series of clearings. There is one big tent set up next to a ute.

'Every day we inspect the camping areas and make sure there's no rubbish anywhere,' Lee says. 'We also charge campers eighteen dollars for each night they camp, except for the Kooris here for cultural camping.'

There are two more tents in a clearing that looks down to the beach. The sand stretches on for hundreds of metres to the water.

Lee slams on the brakes and the seatbelt pulls against my chest, holding me in my seat.

'Dad, what the hell?' Jordy shouts. Josie is laughing her head off like she's on a rollercoaster.

'Look,' Lee says, rolling down his window and pointing towards the bush. We all peer out the windows on the right side of the car, but all I see is bush and trees and fallen leaves and branches. 'Do you see it?'

'See what?' Jordy asks with a sigh. 'That big tree? Yeah, that's pretty cool.'

'Getting warmer,' Lee says, shutting off the engine. He climbs out and tells us to follow.

The sprinkling rain is beginning to fall as I walk behind Lee and Jordy off the dirt road and into the bush. Josie's legs are rushing as she tries to keep up with us. We walk towards the big tree Jordy was talking about. The leaves and twigs break beneath my shoes and the smell of eucalyptus finds its way to my nose.

'Probably our most important job is protecting wildlife,' Lee says. Finally, he stops at the big gum tree. When he crouches down, I finally see what he's seeing. There's a small, furry possum at the base of the tree. Its paw is extended and holding the trunk. It is staying still, watching us with its little black eyes.

'What is that?' Josie asks.

'It's a ringtail possum,' Lee replies. 'He would've run off when we got closer, but he must be injured. They usually sleep during the day, so he shouldn't be down here.'

Lee brushes away some leaves around the possum, slowly brings his hands to it and gently picks it up. The possum makes a chirping sound, very high-pitched. It is so small, it fits perfectly in the palm of his hand.

'He's hurt his leg,' Lee says. 'He must've fallen out of his nest. He couldn't climb back up.'

'He doesn't look real,' I say. 'What do you do with the injured animals?'

'We take them in and nurse them back to health, then return them to where we found them,' he replies. 'It's a very important job, because these little fellas are so important to this bush. Once he's fit and healthy, we'll bring him right back.'

We return to the jeep, where Lee instructs Jordy to get a small blanket out of the car.

'Maybe you can hold him till we get back to the office,' Lee says to me.

'Oh, okay,' I say. I buckle my seatbelt and let Lee pass the possum and its blanket into my hands. It hardly weighs anything, like I'm just holding a piece of cloth. As we begin the drive back, I think I'm in trouble, because holding this little injured ringtail possum in my hands, knowing that this is an actual job someone can get – to look after the bush and the animals in it – makes me feel like footy doesn't matter at all.

It's nearing six o'clock when Jordy and his family drop me off at the gym.

'Thanks for today,' I say.

'That's okay. I hope it helps a little,' Lee says.

'It did. See you at Eric's party tomorrow, Jordy?' I ask.

'Yeah, maybe,' he says. 'See ya.'

They drive off and I think of Jordy's *see ya*. We used to be such good friends. I want us to be friends again.

Eric and Mitch are waiting for me, leaning against the back of Eric's car. I don't know how I replaced Jordy with them, or why. It seems like it was a stupid thing to do now.

Eric's wearing a tank top and short shorts, white runners on his feet. He used to be this rough-looking chubby guy, but now he's fit and muscled. Bodies became important, how we looked became important. Muscles. Abs. Calves. Chests. I got caught up in it with them, and in the process, I left Jordy behind. Feels like wasted time now.

'Pumped?' Eric asks as I arrive.

'As pumped as I'll ever be.'

'Noticed things with you and Ebony pickin' up where you left 'em,' Mitch says with a sinister grin that's begging me for details. I shake my head.

'This place looks exactly the same,' I say as we walk inside, hoping that changes the subject. The gym is busy tonight.

'Nothing changes round here,' Eric says. 'Those footy trials in September could be our tickets out.'

We hit the dumbbells first, where Tom is already lifting. We all stand in a line and lift tens and twelves, except for Mitch, who's lifting fifteens.

Eric and Tom go to the bench press while me and Mitch do some boxing. I hold the bag while Mitch throws his punches. He hits slow at first, then increases his speed, landing left, right, left, right, over and over.

Sweat is pooling in the hollows of his collarbones. My eyes stray to his neck and his skin is covered in it. I don't know why sweaty, muscly Mitch is turning me on so much right now, but I need to look elsewhere. I stare at my feet. I'm wearing cheap runners from Kmart. Mitch is wearing Asics. I love the ASICS logo. I study his shoes as he hits the bag, now grunting with each punch. The logo is turning me on, knowing that it's on Mitch's shoe, which contains Mitch's foot, which connects to his manly legs and his fit body.

Maybe the smell of sweaty men is fucking up the signals in my brain. A brand logo can't be sexy, yet I'm getting hard in my shorts.

'Your turn,' Mitch says. He moves in to hold the bag and I pick up a new pair of boxing gloves. They feel damp inside, and any normal person would think using them was unhygienic or yucky, but I'm imagining a hot guy like Mitch wearing these gloves before me. I imagine him throwing hooks at the punching bag, exhausting himself, and leaving his sweat in these gloves for me.

I throw my fists into the bag, trying to replace the men in my head with Ebony, memories of kissing her, thoughts of running my fingers along her back, holding her.

'Settle down.' Mitch chuckles, jolting back as I hit harder and harder.

With each punch I land on the bag, I tell myself I'm wrong, I'm disgusting, I can't be attracted to men.

I can't.

NINE

Mum and Dad are waiting for me when I leave the gym with Eric, Mitch and Tom. 'See you tomorrow night,' Eric says as they go to Mitch's car. 'BYO.'

'Gotcha,' I say.

Mum and Dad wave to me from the front of their car, and I'm already dreading this dinner. Mum used to make us go to dinners and lunches and afternoon barbecues with her police friends all the time when we were younger, and it was always awkward because they'd make me hang out with the white kids, and white kids who have police officers for parents are somehow different. They're more sure of themselves, more confident, they like to stand over you. Maybe I'm stereotyping.

I walk across the car park and when I get into the back seat I immediately smell my sweat.

'Do us a favour and spray yourself,' Dad says. I take my deodorant out of my backpack and spray under my arms.

'We brought clean clothes for you to change into when we get there.'

I spot the buttoned shirt and black jeans, folded neatly on the seat beside me.

'How come Keira doesn't have to come?' I ask.

'She got an assignment,' Mum says.

'Lucky,' I say under my breath. I take my towel out of my backpack and wipe my forehead.

It's a short drive out of town on the highway, into the hills that look down over Carraway's Point. In the daylight I'd be able to see the farmland that stretches for miles, but in the dark, all I can see is the dirt road ahead and the wire fences alongside us.

'Now, Miles Higgins is gonna be there tonight,' Mum says. 'Just... don't talk to him, if you can help it. And if you do talk, don't mention anything about Brandon or the trial.'

'Umm, okay,' I say. 'I'll make sure not to mention the black kid he murdered.'

'Kallum,' Mum says.

'What?' I ask, feeling the heat rising in my chest, blazing along my arms to my fists. 'Are you defending him now?'

'It's going to trial,' Mum replies. 'He hasn't been convicted of anything yet.'

'I don't get how you can continue to work with these people after that.'

'Because I have to,' Mum says. 'It's important we have Aboriginal people in the police force. We can make sure that doesn't happen again.'

I want to ask where she was when Miles Higgins shot Brandon, but I know that'll just make all of us angry, and then there'd be shouting and swearing and I might just as well open the door and roll out of this moving car if that happens – the dirt would be less painful.

I wish I could remember the last time I hung out with Brandon as friends. When I try to think of it, all I can recall are times when we were younger – playing Xbox in one of our bedrooms, kicking the footy in the street and calling each other by the names of Aboriginal NRL stars (I was always Latrell Mitchell), barbecues at Jordy's house where we'd pretend tomato sauce was blood and act out a war against each other.

I hate that I can't remember the last time we were together as friends, before we all changed.

'I know how you're feeling, Kal,' Mum says.

'What?'

'I feel similar. We just gotta get through an hour or two, then we'll go home. Deal?'

'Fine.'

We drive through an open gate and I see a horse standing on the other side of the fence, looking at us. We continue up a small hill to a long house with all its lights on.

Dad parks beside a paddy wagon. Outside, the night air is close to freezing, with a howling wind. The air is a mixture of meat on a barbecue and cow shit.

Beside the car, I change into my nice, ironed shirt and my black jeans. I slide my shoes back on as Dad takes a deep breath. He's being especially quiet tonight. I know he doesn't like hanging around Mum's police friends any more than I do.

We walk past a neat garden and to the steps leading up to a deck, where bodies linger beneath an outdoor light and a haze of smoke. Mum's carrying a bottle of wine, and Dad's tucking in his shirt as we climb the steps.

I think back to the ringtail possum I held in my hands today. It was so fragile, wrapped in its blanket. I wonder if it's okay, how they're going to nurse it back to health. It must be terrified – fallen from its home with an injured leg, trying to climb back but unable to, then a human comes and wraps it in a blanket and takes it away. I wish I was with the possum, looking after it, instead of here.

'Marge,' Sergeant Gray says to Mum as she reaches the landing. He's a tall man with a beer belly and grey hair; I remember him from the barbecues back in the day. Mum greets him with the bottle of wine, congratulating him on his retirement. After Dad, Sergeant Gray shakes my hand tight, like he's trying to squeeze the life out of me. 'Make yourselves comfortable.'

There's an officer in uniform at the barbecue, transferring sausages and steaks onto a foil tray. He's still got his gun at his waist – he must still be on duty and making a pit stop here.

'Hello, Kallum,' a woman says, approaching me with her hand out. She's drinking a Canadian Club, has blonde hair and is smiling from ear to ear. 'Remember me?'

'Uhh,' I say.

'Kal,' Mum interrupts. 'This is Constable Shelley. You've met her.'

'It has been a while, though, Marge,' she says. 'You were probably about eleven, last time I saw you. Now, you're a big footy star.'

'Well, nice to meet you again,' I say, shaking her hand.

'Over there at the table are Jorgia and Keith Peters,' Mum says, pointing to the woman with short brown hair and the man beside her with the neatly trimmed beard. 'Against the railing is Ivan Harlen and Marlon Dwyer,' Mum continues. 'At the barbecue is Constable Ryan, and behind the barbecue smoking the ciggie is Miles Higgins.'

Miles Higgins has white skin and neatly combed hair that covers his ears. He's wearing a plaid shirt tucked into his blue jeans. He smiles as he exchanges words with Ryan at the barbecue.

'Why don't you go sit over with the young'uns?' Mum asks me, pointing to the picnic table at the end of the balcony, beneath the window to the kitchen. Three teenagers are sitting there and I only know one of them – Trent Harlen. He's Ivan's son, and he was a year above me at school. I've heard things about his older brother, Terry: that he's a racist, that if you're a blackfulla walking around Carraway's Point at night, you need to watch out for Terry Harlen's ute. He and his friends live in a few granny flats on the Harlen property somewhere out here in the hills.

I remember Keira told me a story she'd heard about Ivan a few years ago. The story was that back in the nineties, him and his racist partner would pick up Aboriginal teens, drive them to the middle of nowhere and leave them there without their shoes. They'd have to walk back into town barefoot in the black of night.

I chalked those stories up to elders trying to scare us out of doing anything illegal.

I take a seat next to Trent and face the younger boy across from me. I realise the girl is Stacey from school. One of these officers must be her parent.

'Kallum Smith,' Trent says. 'I heard you moved back to town.'

'Jeez,' I say. 'Word travels fast.'

'You playing footy with the Roosters this year?' Trent asks.

'Yeah. We've got the bye this week.'

'Probably be a walk in the park for ya, after Sydney.'

'I guess we'll see,' I say. I take the bottle of Coke on the table and pour it into one of the paper cups in a stack.

'I heard you and Ebony have been hanging out,' Stacey says to me, sipping her Coke from a straw.

'We're mates,' I say.

'I wish we didn't have to be here,' Trent says. 'Why do they always make their kids come to these things? Why do I care Sergeant Gray is retiring? Like, honestly.'

'I hear ya,' I say.

'You used to be mates with that Jordy lad, didn't ya?' Trent asks me. 'The gay one?'

'Yeah,' I say. My shoulders tense and my back muscles tighten when I hear the word *gay*.

'My cousin was in this play last year, that Shakespeare shit... *Midsummer Night's Dream*,' Trent continues. 'Jordy was in it, playing some fairy in tights. I remember he used to play footy, now he's on stage, flamin' around like a sissy.'

'Don't be homophobic,' Stacey says.

'I'm not,' Trent says. 'I'm just sayin', you really don't know people. I didn't think there were any gays in this town.'

'*Seriously* homophobic, what you're saying,' Stacey says again. I should say something too, but my lips have sealed shut.

'Whatever, snowflakes,' Trent says. 'I'm getting food.'

He gets up and walks away. I take another sip of Coke as a plate of sausages and steaks is placed on the table in front of the younger boy, who barely looks up from his phone. It's Miles Higgins's arm delivering the food. He smells like cheap cologne.

'That enough for you, Tobes?' Miles asks the boy.

'Yep,' Tobes replies. My eyes follow Miles back to the barbecue where he stands in a huddle with other people, including Mum and Dad.

I don't get how he can be here, mingling, delivering barbecued meats to his son, when he ended the life of an Aboriginal boy who was my age. Now he's laughing at something someone has said, throwing his head back, beer in his hand. He's a life-ender, a destroyer, and he's walking around free. I hope he gets jailed for shooting Brandon. Brandon wasn't exactly a good kid, but I don't think he deserved to die. And he doesn't deserve for his killer to be having a great time, like nothing ever happened.

TEN

Keira rolls her eyes at me when she gets home at five o'clock on Saturday. She could probably hear me yelling from outside.

'Just let me go, please?' I beg Dad.

'Son, I told you,' Dad says, 'partying is not what you want to be doing right now. You told me on that beach that you still wanted to make it to the NRL. Parties are not going to get you there. Only hard work and fitness will get you there.'

'I'm not gonna drink,' I shout, as Keira escapes to her room. 'I told you I'd be sober. For fuck's sake, it's not hurting anyone.'

'No,' Dad says. 'Your mum agrees that you need to be at home. You need to be dedicated if you want to make it. I'm not seeing the dedication yet.'

'Fuck dedication. I want to see my friends. You can't lock me up here.'

'Son, it's for your own good,' Dad says. 'I know how parties work. You ain't goin'.'

I stomp to my room and slam the door shut. I'm so close to telling him that I don't want to play footy anymore, that I'd rather be a park ranger, that I want to move out of this fucking house and never see his face again.

I drop onto my bed, bash my head on the pillow. I feel like a ball of fire that's about to explode and burn this whole house down. Keira doesn't have to deal with this shit. She doesn't have to ask permission for anything. She just does what she wants, walks into the house, walks out.

I watch the hours drift by: six, seven o'clock. Then Mum's car pulls up in the driveway. When I hear her come inside, I rush out of my room to ambush her.

'Mum,' I say. 'Dad won't let me go to Eric's party. It's his eighteenth and I'm one of his mates. I should be there. I even told Dad I won't drink and he still won't let me go.'

'Kallum.' Mum sighs, kicking off her boots by the front door. 'We don't want you going to parties. I know you hate us for it now, but you'll thank us once you've done all your training and you're running onto the field in a Rabbitohs guernsey.'

'Oh, come on,' I say. 'I'm not gonna drink. I swear! Just let me go.'

Mum sighs again, rubbing her eyes. 'Let me talk to your dad.'

She pours herself a glass of water and leaves through the back door to the garage, where Dad's probably just starting his nightly workout. I powerwalk to my room.

I know whenever Dad won't let me do something, Mum can convince him.

In my room, I change into a nice purple shirt and the black jeans I wore last night. I slide on my good Converses and then I hear the yelling begin in the garage. I can't make out the words, but Mum's voice is dominating. The yelling finishes after a few minutes.

Dad arrives in my doorway with sweat on his forehead.

'Come on,' he says. 'You always get your way.'

'Good,' I say. I follow Dad to the car and then I'm off to Eric's.

Eric's house is two storeys, with golden lighting inside. It looks like a castle to someone from Chopin Drive. As Dad pulls up to drop me off, he turns to me in his seat.

'Now, no drinking tonight,' Dad says. 'Alcohol is your worst enemy. If you do drink, you'll be ruining the progress you've made this week with the beach runs and the gym and footy training.'

'It's fine, Dad,' I say. 'I said I wasn't gonna drink.'

'I know what you said,' Dad says, his voice deeper than usual. 'But I was a teenager once. I know at a party, if your mates are drinking, they'll try to get you to drink. And drinking is fun. I get it. But you lost that scholarship. There's no easy path now. If you really want this, you need to make sacrifices. Sometimes, those sacrifices include friends who influence you into making bad decisions.'

'Dad, I'm not drinking,' I say. 'And shut up about the fucking scholarship.'

'Kallum.'

'I know I lost the fucking scholarship. You don't have to keep reminding me that I'm a failure, that you're disappointed in me. I know all that.'

I can't control the words coming out of my mouth. It's like water has been building up at a dam wall inside me all day and the dam is starting to crack.

'Kallum, don't yell at me,' Dad says. His eyes are wide, like he's so shocked that I might be angry.

'I'm sick of you treating me like I'm a fucking project,' I say. 'Just let me go have some fun for once. Jesus.'

'Okay, okay,' Dad says, his voice trembling. The anger is still red hot in my chest and my fists, but now there's a sour feeling in my stomach because Dad looks upset. 'You can go,' he says.

In a second I'm out the door and slamming it shut behind me. There's a lump in my throat and tears beginning to burn my eyes. I take a deep breath as Dad does a U-turn and disappears back down the hill.

My hands are shaking when I straighten my fingers. I didn't plan to say all that stuff to Dad, but it happened. I've surprised myself. I didn't think I could stand up to him. I feel like I should be proud, but instead, I'm worrying that I was too harsh, that I scared him when he was just trying to make sure I didn't do anything bad tonight.

I take another breath and think of trees, think of the sound of them brushing each other in the breeze. I listen to the soundscape in my head for a moment, then it's overpowered by the music playing in Eric's house.

I start up the driveway and let myself inside. I immediately see Eric, Mitch, Rita and Stacey in the kitchen, making a bowl of punch. Eric's pouring a bottle of gin into the red-coloured mixture.

'Kallum, finally,' Eric says, seeing me. 'Party started an hour ago. Help us, will ya?'

I carry paper cups and plates while the others take the punchbowl and cutlery and bottles of alcohol. The sliding back door is open and there are fairy lights strung along the fences and across the backyard above our heads. I can see the beach, way down below our spot on the cliff. It looks like something from a Hollywood movie.

There are so many people in Eric's backyard; most of the kids from our year are probably here. I spot Jordy and Amber, standing with two other guys and a girl, each with a Vodka Cruiser in their hand. I see Dylan with Jarrod, both in hoodies and drinking longnecks in paper bags near one of the barrel fires. Everyone is here and everyone is drinking, except for me.

'Didn't you get the memo?' I hear. I turn to see Ebony, dressed in a nice black blouse and blue jeans, sandals on her feet. 'It's BYO.'

'Oh, nah, yeah, I knew that,' I say. 'I told my parents I wouldn't drink tonight.'

'Brave man,' she says. 'Are you sad?'

'Sad?'

'It's our last year of high school. This is one of the last times we'll be together as a group outside of school.'

'If we're lucky,' I say. Ebony giggles. I walk with her to the barrel where Jordy and Amber are standing. 'What are you drinking?' I ask Ebony.

'Ciders,' she says. 'They're five per cent alcohol. Do you want a try? Or are you strict on the non-drinking?'

Saying *no* is what Dad wants me to do. He wants me to be sober so I can continue chasing this footy dream he has for me. But I don't want to do what he wants anymore. I take the can from Ebony's hand and sip. It's fruity, sweet, delicious. My tongue tingles all the way to the back of my throat.

'Damn,' I say. 'That's pretty good.'

'Do you want one?'

'If you're offering.'

'I'll be back.'

She walks towards the group of eskies by the back door – there are five of them.

'I wanna hook up with someone,' I hear Amber say to Jordy. She takes another sip of her Cruiser.

'What? Who?' Jordy asks her.

'I don't know. Maybe one of the footy boys.'

'They're all dickheads,' Jordy says, and he's kinda right.

'Ouch,' I say, interrupting their private chat.

'Not you, Kallum,' Jordy says. 'You're all right.'

'Hmm. What about Tom?' Amber asks. She nods across the backyard and there's Tom standing by the fire with a can of Great Northern. 'I always thought he was pretty cute.'

'He's pretty chill,' I say.

'He also doesn't stop his buddies from making their homophobic comments,' Jordy adds.

'He's not as bad as them, though,' Amber says. She turns to Jordy. 'Will you come over with me? To Tom?'

'What? Why?' Jordy asks.

'I can't go over by myself,' Amber says. 'Come on. I'll give you one of my Cruisers as a thank you.'

Jordy sighs, then starts across the backyard with Amber to where Tom is.

Ebony's making her way back to me with another cider in her hand. Beside the barrel fire, it's warm and smoky. It reminds me of camping with my family. We'd all drive out to Dennard's Beach, thirty minutes up the coast, deep inside the national park. The campsite usually fills with tourists in the summer, so we'd go in March or April. Me, Mum, Dad and Keira. Mum always called it a reset, to go out bush. She said it was like plugging in a phone and recharging the battery.

'There you go, mister,' Ebony says, handing me the can of cider. It's pear flavoured. I take a sip and let it wash down my throat, knowing Dad wouldn't be happy with me.

I walk with Ebony past the beer pong table where Mitch and some of the footy boys are having a game. Mitch's partner downs a cup, then rushes away from the table and vomits it all out on the grass near the fence. Laughter rings out. Mitch tries to get him to come back but he refuses, so Mitch stumbles over to Tom.

'I need a new partner, Tommy,' Mitch says.

'I'm busy, bro,' Tom replies, gesturing to Amber.

'Fine,' Mitch says, flinging his arms around Jordy's shoulders. 'Jordy-boy, I need a partner. Fletch and Aido are killin' me.' Mitch directs Jordy towards the table, and Jordy tries to shrug his arm off his shoulder.

'No thanks,' Jordy says.

'C'mon, it'll be like old times,' Mitch replies, slurring his words. He grips tighter and I can see Jordy trying to shuffle out of his hands.

'Jordy,' Amber says, 'everything all right?'

'We're all good,' Mitch says to Amber. 'Jordy's partnerin' wif me.'

'No, I'm not,' Jordy says more sternly as he shoves Mitch's arm off his shoulder.

'Weak as piss,' Mitch says, then turns back to Amber. 'What about you?'

'No thanks,' Amber says.

'Why do you always wear that jumper? You look pretty decent without a jumper on. You got nice arms.'

'Excuse me?' Amber says, eyes wide and her jaw about to drop to the damp grass beneath our feet. I feel everyone's heart rate quicken. Something's about to happen.

'C'mon, partner with me. I bet you're good with little balls,' Mitch says, then he steps towards her. He reaches out and she shoves him back.

'Hey!' Amber shouts. Mitch is laughing.

'Fucking virgin,' Mitch says. I see the colour of Jordy's face turn from brown to red and he launches his fist at Mitch's head, gets him on the cheek.

Mitch's head flicks away and he drops his beer. It fizzes and foams on the ground, but Mitch's eyes are on Jordy. He launches at him.

Jordy hits the wooden fence with a bang, right where the boy is still sitting beside his spew, and it feels like the whole earth just shook. His glasses fall from his face, bounce off his stomach and onto the grass.

I rush to stop Mitch as he throws himself onto Jordy. Others join the pile; someone else shouts to let them fight. Eric's arm swings around Mitch's throat and I help him pull Mitch away.

Someone screams as the three of us fall and Mitch's body lands on top of me. Mitch bounces up like I'm a trampoline and then he's on Jordy again. Jordy tries to shove him off but Mitch's forearm is on his throat, pinning him against the fence, which is now beginning to bend.

I'm back on my feet with Eric, and wet blades of grass are sticking to my neck and cheeks. Now Mitch has got Jordy in a tight headlock.

Amber and Hamish grab Jordy from his side and it feels like a tug of war as me and Eric try to pull Mitch away.

'Fucking poofter,' Mitch shouts. Amber's laying punches into him. It looks like an all-in brawl. Now people are pulling Amber away and Eric is ripping at Mitch's collar. I swear everyone in the backyard has joined this cluster-fuck now.

'Fuck you,' Amber shouts. 'Homophobic prick!'

'Let me go!' Mitch yells. 'Let me fuck 'em all up! I'll take anyone!'

We fall to the ground again, and I have the weight of bodies on top of me. Everyone scrambles, tangled and pulling and shoving, and I try to get to my feet but wet shoes land on my legs and people climb over me. Feet push me into the ground and it's like being punched in the lungs over and over.

'Get off!' I shout, but no one hears me. 'Get off!'

A man's voice begins to yell – Eric's father.

'That's it!' Eric's dad shouts. 'It's over! Everyone out! Get out of my backyard! All of you! Out, before I call the cops!'

The bodies above me begin to separate. Eric's father passes me and grabs Jordy's arm, lifts him to his feet.

'Shit,' he says. 'You right, Jordan?'

'Good as,' he says, wiping blood from his lip. His eyes are teary as he slips his glasses back on, though one wire arm is bent out of shape. I kind of want to hug him.

Jordy's the first to leave with Amber and his friends, then everyone else begins exiting through the side gate.

And just like that, I remember the last time I hung out with Brandon. It was the April school holidays in Year Seven. Me, Dylan and Brandon were at his house – Jordy couldn't come for some reason. It was a warm day, and we were playing Xbox in Brandon's stinking hot room. I had sweat all over me. I said we should go to the park and kick the footy. Brandon and Dylan didn't want to, they were too busy playing *Call of Duty*, they said they had a *duty* to continue playing, which they laughed about, thinking it was a hilarious thing to say. I was annoyed. It had been the same thing on repeat for a few weekends. I remember feeling over it. I sighed and said I was bored and it was too fucking hot in that room, and I was going home.

'Bruh, there's a third controller, ya know?' Brandon had said, but I didn't care. I walked out of the house, thinking that was it for our friendship. I'd made some new friends who I played footy with, but Dylan and Brandon weren't into it.

I remember feeling like I wasn't going to miss them at all. And maybe I'd still feel okay about that if Brandon hadn't died.

'Coming?' Ebony asks.

'Oh. Yeah.'

I walk with Ebony through the side gate and out to the front of the house. Everyone is littered down the driveway and onto the road. Mitch is on the street with Tom and some other footy boys.

'Don't fuck with me!' he shouts. His voice echoes into the night. 'I'll fight any of you dogs!'

'Jesus,' Ebony says. 'What's with guys and the whole, *I'll fight anyone, anytime* thing?'

'I don't know,' I say. 'Toxic masculinity?'

Ebony chuckles. 'That was wild.'

I turn back to Eric, who is standing there with his dad and Rita. The music is still playing in the backyard but finally stops as the five of us are standing out front.

'Scram, kids,' Eric's dad says. 'Party's done.'

'You good, Eric?' I ask. He notices like I do that his hands are shaking. He's catching his breath and his face is covered in sweat.

'Oh,' he says. 'Yeah. You guys should go. Sorry about that.'

'Do you want me to go too?' Rita asks Eric. 'I can get my mum to pick me up.'

'Nah, you're good,' Eric says to her. 'Let's just go inside.'

Me and Ebony watch Eric and Rita disappear through the back gate, which clangs shut.

'You reckon they're gonna fuck?' Ebony asks me,

nodding to Eric's house. I laugh hard and it bursts out of me like I've been holding it in all night.

'I mean, that's what it looks like,' I say. 'I'm gonna get going. You could walk into town with me, if you want. Get your mum to pick you up in there?'

'Okay,' Ebony says. We start walking down the hill. Somewhere in the distance, Mitch is still shouting. I hope he hasn't gone after Jordy.

The clouds have cleared completely and a starry blanket covers the sky. Below, the waves roll in, glistening under the moonlight. And suddenly, Ebony is feeling like my only real friend. Our hands brush as we walk, then she slips her fingers between mine.

She likes me. She thinks I like her back, which I do, but not in the same way. She thinks we're gonna become something – that sometime soon, I'm gonna ask her to be my girlfriend. And I could, but I would only hurt her. This whole week, I've been trying to convince myself that I *am* straight, that I *do* like girls, that I could get a girlfriend and be a good boyfriend and not think of guys as attractive, but tonight, I thought Jordy was cute, and at the gym yesterday, I couldn't stop looking at the muscly men. I just don't look at girls that way, and I think I can accept that because I don't want to hurt Ebony.

We arrive at the bottom of the hill and there are some teens on the street ahead, on the way to the beach. They're probably strays from Eric's party, wondering what they're gonna do next.

We turn left towards town. Soon, the lights of the main street paint our bodies, and we're not protected by the dark anymore. Ebony pulls out her phone and calls her mum, releasing my hand. After filling her mum in on what happened, she tells her that we are outside the supermarket, which is closed now.

Ebony hangs up and then her eyes rest on me. She smiles, like she's waiting for me to walk up and kiss her. I could do that, and then ask her to be my girlfriend, and force myself to be straight forever. I'd treat her kindly, celebrate her achievements and do whatever I could to make her feel special, but I know I'd be lying to her the whole time.

Ebony reaches for my hand again but I pull it away. The smile fades from her face and she narrows her eyes.

'Ebony, I need to tell you something,' I say. My heart is beating fast in my chest, my legs feel like they're trembling beneath my weight, and I can't believe that a week ago I was arriving back in Carraway's Point, feeling like the smallest person in the world, and now, I'm about to tell Ebony my deepest secret. My stomach feels like it's about to explode and my hands are shaking. Instead of standing here on the main street of Carraway's Point, I imagine for a moment that we're in the bush, that trees are brushing against one another, that birds are singing and talking to each other.

'Well, spit it out,' Ebony says, chuckling a little, probably because of the suspense. It's been nearly a minute since I last spoke and it's becoming awkward now.

'Well,' I begin, 'the thing is...I'm...I think I'm... I think I'm gay.'

Ebony's face doesn't change. She doesn't blink. She stands there, still, half her face lit by the shopping centre lights, the other half draped in dark.

'You're gay?' Ebony asks.

'I think so,' I say. 'No...I *am*. I'm sorry.'

'Oh. Okay.' Ebony clears her throat. Now she looks sad. Her eyes go to her feet, and she steps back from me.

'Do you hate me? I'm sorry.'

'I...Don't be sorry. I don't hate you. No way. I just... I thought you liked me.'

She shakes her head, smiles again.

'I *do* like you,' I say. 'I think you might be the only person in this shithole who makes me feel like I can be myself.'

A tear slips from Ebony's eye, rolls down her cheek. She's quick to wipe it away and shakes her head again. 'I'm sorry. I'm not mad at you,' she says. 'I'm...I'm happy for you.'

She looks up at me again and smiles, then she hugs me. It's a warm hug – a hug that steadies my knees, slows the thumping of my heart, makes me feel like everything isn't going to fall to shit.

'Have you told anyone else?' she asks.

'No,' I say. 'I guess I'm still figuring it out. I just... I wanted to be honest. Is it good I told you?'

Ebony releases the hug, sniffles back her tears. 'Yes, it's a good thing you told me. I'm *glad* you told me. I'm *honoured* you told me first.'

I smile and she smiles, and now my eyes are burning and there's a lump in my throat. Tears leak from my eyes and Ebony's hands rest on my cheeks. She wipes away my tears with her thumbs.

'It's gonna be okay,' she says.

Headlights turn onto the main street and Ebony removes her hands from my face. The car pulls up on the other side of the road and Ebony's mum gives us a wave.

'At least now you can talk to someone about it,' Ebony says. 'If you ever want to. Do you want a lift home? I'll get Mum to drop you off.'

'Yeah, sure.'

As we move towards the car, I brush Ebony's hand with mine.

'Hey, Ebs,' I say before we cross. 'Are we still friends?'

Ebony smiles. Her eyes are glossy as she looks at me. 'So long as you never call me *Ebs* again. Fucking hate that.'

We climb into Ebony's mum's car. The heater is on and it feels toasty, like I'm already in bed. I suddenly feel like being expelled from St Augustine's was an age ago, and it might have been the best thing that's ever happened to me.

JORDY

ELEVEN

A rustling in the bushes outside my window wakes me, followed by Sophie, our little Australian Terrier, barking like mad. It's Monday morning and the light is bleeding in through my blinds. Sophie settles and whimpers, and I check my phone – it's just after six-thirty.

I know what that rustling is. I'm going to catch my little brother, Lewis, red-handed.

I put on my glasses and stagger out of my room – my glasses arm is still kind of crooked from that fight I had with Mitch four months ago. I go down the hallway and open Lewis's door slowly. As I enter, his window slides up and his long brown hairy leg reaches in, hitting his blinds which in turn bang on the walls and make a racket that sounds ten times louder this early in the morning. The rest of him follows.

'Well, well, well,' I say. His whole body jolts; I've just scared the crap out of him. I close the door and lock us in.

'Jesus,' he says.

'You can call me Jordan,' I say. 'I do accept *Jordy* from close friends and family, though.'

'I just went for a walk,' Lewis says. As he removes his hoodie, the drifting stench of cigarette smoke finds my nose.

'Oh yeah? A morning stroll to get some ciggies?'

'I don't smoke,' Lewis scoffs, trying to keep his voice just above a whisper.

'Oh please, I can smell it from here. You're fourteen, dickhead.'

'I know how old I am.'

'Do you? You're a child. Why are you coming back so late? It's six-thirty in the morning. When I used to sneak out, I'd always make sure I was back before sunrise, at least.'

'Don't tell Dad,' Lewis says. His eyes are big and glassy, like he's begging me.

'Dad already knows you're being a dumb-shit.'

He sighs, kicking off his shoes.

'I was just playin' Xbox at Riley's,' Lewis says, heading to his wardrobe. He takes out a clean towel and starts for the bedroom door, but I'm in his way.

'Playing Xbox and smokin' ciggies?'

'I only had one,' he says. 'Maybe two.' He tries to get past me, but I step in front of him again.

'I know all about Riley, his brother and his parents. I know what kinda shit they're into,' I say.

'So?'

'So, you can hang out with Riley and play Xbox or whatever, but I don't want you gettin' involved in any of their shit. Got it? And I want you to stay away from Dylan up the street.'

'Whatever. Calm down.'

'I'm calm,' I say, imitating a Buddhist monk. I step aside and follow Lewis and his cigarette stench out of his room. He locks himself in the bathroom and I go to the living room.

There are empty stubbies on the little table by the couches, and more empty bottles on the coffee table. I count them as I scoop them up in the mist of alcohol smell. I've counted ten by the time I've placed the last one quietly into the recycling carton.

Last night, me and my little sister, Josie, watched *Barbie as the Princess and the Pauper* in my room. I even microwaved us some popcorn and carried Josie to her own bed after she fell asleep. Dad was drinking in the living room, watching Channel Nine half the night, and on the phone with my aunty for the other half.

When Lewis is out of the bathroom, I get in the shower to get ready for school. As I stand under the warm flow, I listen to the sound of water powering through the pipes in the roof.

Here I go, about to do some deep thinking again.

Mum died last year. Brain aneurysm. Before she died, if you had looked at us from the outside, we were a happy family. Now, Lewis is acting out and Dad's drinking. But the slowly arriving collapse of my family doesn't feel so important, because I'm about to finish Year Twelve, and next year, I'm going to acting school in Sydney.

Back in my bedroom, I check my reflection in the mirror as I dry myself. I've put on some weight this year. It's all around the lower part of my stomach and my hips. I haven't really felt fat before, but I do now as I gaze over my naked body in my full-length wardrobe-door-mirror.

I pull on my Calvin Klein underwear and my black pants. My school shirt is a little tighter than it was at the start of the year. I sit on the end of my bed and stretch the bottom of the shirt over my knees. I hold it stretched for a moment. Maybe I should exercise more, like Eric. Eric goes to the gym. Maybe I could go with him sometime.

I put on my glasses again and in the hallway, I hear Dad's alarm going and him snoozing it. Josie's in the kitchen opening the fridge. It's becoming a pattern now: Dad being too hungover from drinking the night before, so it's me who has to make Josie breakfast.

I take the eggs from the fridge while humming 'Come into my world' by Kylie Minogue. On the fridge, pinned by a magnet, is a letter with info about the Aboriginal graduation camp happening the week after I finish Year Twelve. I am so not looking forward to camping – it's not my thing – but Ivy, the Aboriginal support officer at school, was very insistent.

I cook scrambled eggs and toast, pile all the food on a plate and sit it at the centre of the table. I dish some up for Josie, and Lewis joins us. We're eating when Dad emerges from his bedroom with a sock on one foot and his other sock and shoes in his hands.

Dad's rubbing his eyes as he makes his way to the kitchen and flicks on the kettle. I want to yell at him, tell him he needs to stop fucking getting up hungover because I'm sick of being the extra parent in this house, making breakfast for *his* kids. It's supposed to be the other way around.

As Dad makes himself a coffee, I feel the yelling and the swearing threatening to burst out, but I funnel my angry words into the bottle I keep inside. It's growing quite full in there, but at this point, I've made bottling-up into an artform. One day, people will study the way I've bottled things up.

Dad sits down at the table with his cup of coffee and takes a slice of toast. His eyes are bloodshot and his face is looking very haggard. He hasn't shaved in a few days, and his stubble is looking dirty.

'I'll drive youse today,' Dad says.

'You sure you're right to drive?' I ask.

Lewis finishes his food and turns on the TV. The morning show is on.

'I'm right,' Dad says. I open my phone and find the email I received on Friday – the acceptance email from the acting school – and slide my phone across the table to him. I've taken a few days to process it, and now I'm ready for him to know.

Dad looks down at the screen, narrowing his eyes, then they burst open like he's seen a ghost.

'Jordy,' Dad says. 'You got in?'

'I did.'

'Son, I knew you'd get in!' Dad smiles wide and it looks like it's hurting his face. He scrolls the email. 'I'll talk to Aunty Lisa, see if she can put you up for a while when you move to Sydney. I think her daughter's moving out soon to live with her boyfriend. They just had a baby.'

'Yeah, that'd be good,' I say.

'Once you've made some mates at the acting school, you can move out with them. Those were the best years of my twenties, when I was living in share houses with my mates.' Dad looks to Josie. 'Jordy's moving to the big city,' he says.

'I don't want him to go,' she says, stopping eating and looking at me.

'It's okay,' I say. 'I'll come back and visit.'

Dad drives me, Lewis and Josie to school, and it's always better than getting the bus. Josie's the first drop-off, as her school is closer. After that, it's a surprisingly quiet car ride – quiet enough to think about the future.

I always imagined I'd live with Eric after we finished Year Twelve. I can't wait to see his face when I tell him I made it into acting school. He's going to be so happy for me.

Me: *Hey! I have some news and was hoping we could meet up if you're free soon.*

I scroll Instagram and Eric's just posted a photo of his shirtless godlike abs and body in the mirror at the gym. He's sticking his tongue out and I can feel myself stiffening in my pants as I hit like on the photo.

Eric: *News? What is it?*

Me: *I want to tell you in person to see your reaction. I also miss you, btw. I feel like we haven't really hung out since before that shit happened at your bday.*

Eric: *Yeah sorry just been a lot going on*

Eric: *I miss you too x*

Me: *Soooo maybe come over soon? Xxxx I can tell you the news and we could do some 'study' together...*

Eric: *Yeah, I miss studying, it's like one of my favourite things x*

Me: *I'd study with u right now if I could x*

Eric: *When's good for you? x*

Me: *U free after school? Got the house to myself till after 5 Xx*

Eric: *I can't sorry Rita invited me over to have dinner with her family*

Me: *Are you dating her or something*

Eric: *No lol she said she had something she wanted to talk to me about*

Eric: *I thought we been through this x*

Me: *Yeah, I just don't know how you could get with a girl, can't fathom it*

Eric: *Lol don't worry we will meet up again soon x*

Me: *Ok good x*

We arrive at the black-fenced fortress that is Carraway's Point High School.

'Farewell, my sons,' Dad says as me and Lewis get out of the car.

'Farewell, Father,' me and Lewis say at the same time as we close the doors. Lewis pulls his hood over his head and speeds through the gates looking at his phone. I trail in behind him and turn towards the science block, where my roll-call class is. I spot my best friend Amber waiting at the bottom of the stairs for me, like she always does. She's staring at something on her phone. She's trimmed her brown hair shorter and now it's just a bit less than a bowl cut. Amber was always one of the weird girls, but we became friends because we work together. And when I came out as gay, she was the only friend who felt *real* anymore.

'Hey, Short-legs,' I say.

'Hey, Gay-boy,' she says back. We both work at the cinema and a few months ago, these three drunken men came in around nine o'clock trying to get into the movies without a ticket. Me and Amber were the only ones in the lobby, so we had to kick them out. In return, they called me *gay-boy* and Amber *short-legs*, and for some reason, we call each other those names now and it's funny.

Amber goes into the building ahead of me. Along the corridor, I see Eric entering the classroom about five doors down. He gives me a smile and a nod. There's something about the way Eric smiles at me. It makes me feel sexy, like I'm not this gay loser with only two friends in the world.

I readjust my glasses on my nose as I smile back.

TWELVE

When I get home from school, Sophie's barking at the laundry door. I let her in and give her some pats, but she's quick to rush past me and climb onto the couch.

I have two hours in the house alone, and all I do is lie on the couch scrolling TikTok. Eric finally texts me and my heart beats a little faster, like it always does when his name pops up on my screen.

Eric: *Whatchu doin x*

Me: *Just chillin on the couch, you? x*

Eric: *Getting ready to go to Rita's*

Me: *Why you even going over there if yous aren't dating or anything haha*

Eric: *She probably just likes me or thinks we're gonna get together or something. I'll let her down gently*

Me: *Good cause your mine x*

Eric: *Lol x*

Just after five p.m., Dad's Laser pulls into the driveway. Josie bursts inside. She rushes to the TV like her life depends on it, puts on Netflix and starts her cartoons before Dad's even in the front door.

'How was school?' I ask Josie, joining her on the couch.

'It was fine,' she replies, not even looking at me. Dad walks in, wearing his national parks uniform, boots thudding on the lino floor. He closes the door behind him and drops his keys into the bowl on the little desk by the door.

'Where's Lewis?' Dad asks.

'He went to Dylan's after we got off the bus,' I say. Dad nods. 'You know what he's getting up to with his mates?' I ask. Like, I know Dad hasn't really had his head in the game for a while, but surely he's noticed his fourteen-year-old son has been spending more time out with his mates than at home.

'Jordy, he's all right,' Dad says. 'You know it hasn't been easy on him. He'll figure it out.'

Love that. Love the way Dad says it hasn't been easy on Lewis – *it* being my mother's death last year. Like it's been hard on Lewis and soooo easy for me.

'I know he's been hanging out with Dylan a lot,' I say.

'At least we know where he is, then,' Dad says. No, it's not a big deal at all. Dylan drinks and smokes and roams the streets late at night with his group – kind of like a gang – but Lewis hanging out with him isn't a big deal. Plus, everyone knows what happens to Koori boys who hang out with Dylan. I worry that Lewis is gonna get killed by a cop one night, too. I picture his coffin, a shining wooden case, like Brandon's was. I imagine Dad's voice as he struggles through the eulogy.

Me and Dylan used to be friends before high school, but he's a bad influence. I'm glad I got out of that friendship circle before he and Brandon went south.

'I'm meeting some of the fullas at the pub,' Dad says.

'But I have work tonight. I can't watch Josie.'

'You can drop her off at your nan's,' he says, then he's gone up the hallway and into the bathroom. The shower starts and the anger bubbles in my stomach. It's my best friend these days, the anger. It doesn't take much to get it simmering. I swear I'm the only person who thinks about anyone else in this house.

I sit with Josie while she watches her cartoons, biting into the apple she didn't eat at school.

As soon as Dad's out of the bathroom, he pivots to the kitchen and grabs a VB from the fridge. He walks back to his room and Sophie joins me and Josie on the couch. She lies on her stomach and rests her head by my thigh. I pat her and she looks up at me. With her eyes, she's telling me she knows how I feel, that she knows I'm sick of being the one everything falls to because Dad and Lewis want to go out and do whatever the hell they want. She's telling me she's here for me, that I'm not alone, so I pat her again and whisper, 'Thank you'.

It's weird that Eric's going to Rita's for dinner. Something about it makes me feel uneasy in the stomach. It's nestled in there beside the bubbling anger – a worry that something bad is happening right now that's going to hurt me.

No. I tell myself I'm overthinking. That's something I do quite a lot.

Dad races back up the hallway, dressed in jeans and a shirt, which he tucks in. He stops at the small mirror on the wall by the front door and checks himself out one last time.

'Farewell, my children,' he says.

'Farewell, Father,' me and Josie reply.

He leaves to walk into town on foot, and I open my phone and navigate to my contacts. I tap on Lewis's name and send him a text: *I'm working tonight. Are you gonna be home soon?*

In the bathroom, I place my phone on the bench and play Kylie's 'I should be so lucky'. Lewis texts back: *Nah.*

That's it. *Nah.*

I shower and change into my work clothes – red long-sleeved shirt and black pants. I slip on a hoodie and take Josie's red jacket from the coatstand in the hallway.

'But Nan's is so far away,' she complains as I hand her the jacket. 'And my legs are tired!'

'It's not that far,' I say.

She sighs as I turn off the television. Outside, the sun has set and the sky is a dark blue. The cars in town are rumbling in the distance, but it's quiet out.

It's a fifteen-minute walk through the neighbour-hoods and quiet streets until we arrive at Nan and Pop's orange-brick house. The chimney is spewing smoke and I'm hoping it's warmer inside.

Josie follows me through the wooden gate and up the stairs. I'm a little puffed when I reach the front door, knock and let us in.

'Who's that?' Nan asks from around the corner.

'It's Jordan,' I say. Josie follows me into the lounge room where Nan is resting in her recliner with her feet up. The news is on TV, and she turns down the volume.

'My favourite grandson and granddaughter,' Nan says, extending her arms. Josie rushes over for a hug and I follow her lead. There's a curry cooking. Pop comes in from the kitchen with a wooden spoon dirty with the rice he's been stirring.

'Jordy and Josie,' Pop says.

'Hey, Pop.' I shake his hand. His beard is trimmed short and the last of his grey hairs have been shaved off the top of his head.

'You off to work?' Pop asks.

'Yeah, just dropping off Josie. Dad's gone to the pub and Lewis is with his mates.'

'Are you staying for tea?' Nan asks. Josie hops up on the couch and her legs dangle over the edge.

'Nah, gotta run. I'm closing tonight, so Jose might have to crash on the couch,' I say. I give Nan a hug and a kiss on the cheek.

'You're almost finished school now, aren't ya?'

'Yeah, just a few weeks to go,' I reply. 'Then it's exams.'

'You'll be the first one in the family to finish Year Twelve,' Nan says. 'You should be proud of yourself.'

'I am,' I say, turning for the front door. I spot a photo on the entertainment unit above the television: Mum nursing a baby bump when she was pregnant with me. She looks younger, healthy, happy, with a big smile and freckles across her nose. 'I have to go,' I say. 'I'll drop in next week.'

'All right, son. Love you.'

'Love you too. Bye, Pop.'

I dash out the front door and unzip my jacket because the warmth of Nan's fireplace has brought on a sweat.

It's a short walk out of the hilly neighbourhoods and into town. The main street of Carraway's Point is pretty boring. At the far end is the cinema where I work, and to me it's the only interesting place here. Inside, there are a few people lined up to see the next movie.

'Hey,' I say to Amber behind the counter.

'Right on time,' she says, sounding all surprised, like I've never arrived on time in my life.

'Always,' I say.

Our boss, Emilio, is sitting at the computer, typing up next week's roster.

'Evening, Jordy,' he says. He's a thirty-something guy with an amazing moustache, which he flicks at the ends. I think he thinks the moustache is cool but it's giving *I don't read books, I read literature* vibes. I hang my jacket on one of the hooks. 'Have you heard back from the acting school?' he asks.

'Yeah,' I say. 'I got in.'

'No shit?' he says, holding out his palm for me to slap it. 'My maaaayn.'

Friday nights are usually busy at the cinema, but by ten o'clock, the place is dead. I've been alone behind the counter since the four people who came to the nine-thirty session in cinema one bought their tickets. This is my favourite night to work though, because Friday nights are Classic Movie Night in cinema two, and usually it's quiet enough after nine-thirty for me to sneak in and watch. People rarely come to Classic Movie Night, unless it's a horror movie. Last week was *The Shining*, so we had a nearly full house, but tonight it's almost empty.

I send a text to Eric, asking how dinner with Rita went.

I leave the counter and slip inside the cinema. *Dog Day Afternoon* is playing and there are only two people in the cinema, which is a shame because it's a great movie.

I take a seat in the middle of the fifth row. Just like hanging out with Amber and being with Eric, watching movies helps me take a break from this life where my mum died and my dad and brother are spiralling and I worry and worry and worry about shit all the time. I guess that's why I love acting so much – it's a kind of holiday.

I love Al Pacino in this. I want to be just like him when I become an actor. I want to have the presence he has when he's on screen. I love the way he stares and I've been practising my own stare in the mirror. As part of the acting school application, I had to do a short audition video, which Dad helped me record. I performed a scene from *Heat* – the scene where Al Pacino and Robert De Niro are talking in a restaurant. Dad fed me the De Niro lines.

As I watch *Dog Day Afternoon*, I imagine it's me in Pacino's role. I imagine it's me pointing the gun at the bank teller, panicking at the predicament I'm in, creeping to the window and looking out to see the police have me surrounded.

At the end of my shift, I slip on my hoodie and leave the cinema. It's colder now, but heat has filled my body. I put in my earphones and start my favourite Kylie song, 'Sleeping with the enemy'. It's easily her best, but it was a bonus track on her *Kiss me once* album, and it isn't even on Spotify, which makes no sense to me. It should have a music video at least, but instead, it's a download in my phone's files. Good old YouTube2MP3.

When I listen to Kylie, it stops me thinking about all the bad things that could happen to me as I walk home at night.

I know it takes me thirty-four minutes to get home, so I won't be in bed until after eleven. It'll take me thirty to forty minutes to fall asleep, so I won't get to sleep until just before midnight, and that's if I'm lucky. My body always wakes me before my alarm, so I'll wake up before seven, meaning I'll get about six hours' sleep, and then I'll have to get up and make me, Lewis and Josie breakfast, after Nan and Pop drop her off, and probably put away the beer bottles Dad might have drunk when he got home from the pub.

The thought comes to me like the cold creeping into the sleeves of my hoodie: this period of my life is only temporary. I've just been accepted into acting school, and soon I'll be getting the fuck out of Carraway's Point. I won't live and die in this town after all.

THIRTEEN

It's lunchtime on Friday and I walk to the canteen with Amber. Two Year Seveners ahead of us are talking about what kind of porn they prefer. I want to pinch their ears and tell them to soap their eyes. Little Year Seveners make me feel so old. I'm feeling extra annoyed because I've texted Eric every day since last Friday, and he hasn't replied at all. He hasn't even heart-reacted a message or anything – just straight up ghosting me, and I don't know why.

'So, when do you move to Sydney?' Amber asks.

'It'll be late January,' I say.

'That's too soon,' she says. 'I decided I'm taking a gap year. Alyssa wants me to go travelling with her.'

Travelling sounds great, but only *some* people have the privilege of taking a year off from life.

Me and Amber arrive at the front of the line and we both order chicken burgers and chocolate milk. We join the rest of our friends on the picnic table near the oval.

The sun is hidden by grey clouds today. They look almost black in the direction of the beach.

'Reckon it's gonna rain?' I ask.

'Fuckin' hope so. Imagine all the drenched buff footy boys over there,' she says. She points to the oval where a mix of boys of all years are playing touch footy. Eric and Mitch are there. Kallum too; he's slipped right back into the group since his mysterious return. I used to be one of them. It feels like a dream now, that there was a time in my life I was pretending to be straight and playing rugby league and being *one of the boys*.

'Did you guys watch *MAFS* last night?' Hamish asks the group. He's a Greek kid who started at school last year; he used to be homeschooled. His new glasses are too big for his head and it's hard to look at him for longer than a second without wanting to laugh.

'Oh. Em. Gee. I lost my shit at the end,' one of the girls says.

'I will never watch that trash,' I say, biting into my chicken burger. With each bite, my glasses slide further down the bridge of my nose. I push them back into place.

'It *is* trash,' Amber says, 'but that's why it's so fun.'

'I refuse.'

A group of popular girls walks past in their short skirts and made-up faces. Rita is one of them. I don't know if I actually hate her or if I'm just jealous because I know she's been with Eric. I mean, I know me and Eric aren't an official couple, but it still feels like she's trying to steal him from me. Eric said she seduced him after his party last month, when everyone had been kicked out because of the fight and he was depressed and drunk. I wish I'd stayed there, so I could have stopped her from getting her thin white fingers on his body.

'Oh, did you hear about Rita?' one of the girls asks, whispering. 'Stacey told me she's pregnant.'

My heart plummets.

'She's pregnant?' I ask.

'Apparently. Stacey said Rita's gonna keep it.'

'Do you know who knocked her up?' Amber asks.

'Nah, Stacey said she wouldn't tell her.'

'Why are you talking to Stacey, anyway?' Amber asks. 'Probably just spreading rumours.'

They continue talking, speculating as to whether Rita fucked this boy or that boy, if she's actually pregnant or if it's just gossip. The interest in the topic dissipates pretty quickly and the conversation turns to muck-up day being banned.

I take out my phone and send a text to Eric.

I need to talk to you. I've got a free period 5. Meet me at the senior area?

In period five, I'm sitting alone in the seniors' area. There are a few students hanging out under the shelters, watching things on their laptops and laughing with each other. It's beginning to sprinkle rain as the dark grey clouds roll over school.

I open my phone. Eric hasn't replied to my last text. I sit at the picnic table, watching the door where he'll come from, if he comes.

I'm scared and my brain is going to a million different places. If Eric is going to have a baby with Rita, he won't want anything to do with me. He'll be scared that if Rita finds out he's been seeing a boy secretly, she'll never let him see his baby. She'll be disgusted with him. She'll out him. He'll lose his mates. He'll want to stop seeing me and talking to me altogether. It'll be over. For good.

Maybe I'm overthinking things again. Maybe he isn't even the guy who got Rita pregnant. Maybe he's just stressed because she might think he is, and he's scared so that's why he's not talking to me. Maybe he can get a DNA test and it will prove he's not the father and we can finish school, he can come out, and we'll move to Sydney together, just as planned. I'll go to acting school and he'll play footy and we'll be in love – we'll be together and we won't be hiding anymore.

The bell rings to signal the end of fifth period and Eric hasn't come. I take out my phone as the other students walk back inside. I send another text to Eric: *Can I please see you? It feels like something bad is happening.*

Four minutes later, a text returns from Eric: *I'll call you later*

———

After school, I arrive at the bus zone with Amber. All the other students are rushing away. I feel like I'm going to throw up. On the bus we sit together and share Amber's AirPods, and she plays Billie Eilish as the bus fills up.

Lewis walks into the aisle, and behind him three of the footy boys step on – Mitch, Tom and Kallum. They used to be my mates too, in my closet-life.

I'm sitting in the aisle seat. As they pass me, their muscles are easy to see under their short sleeves.

'Faggot,' Mitch says, pretending to cough.

'Really?' Amber asks him. 'Homophobic slurs? That all you got, pretty-boy?'

'Whatever,' he says.

'It's getting old, lads,' I say, rolling my eyes.

They keep on walking to find a seat near the back.

'What fucking arseholes,' Amber says.

'Thanks,' I say. 'You're a social justice warrior.'

Amber turns the music up and rests her head on the window with a sigh. She reaches to hold my hand as the bus begins to move.

The bus drops me off at the end of Chopin Drive. Kallum has powered ahead, and Dylan steps off with his hoodie pulled up. Lewis is last off the bus with me and takes out his earphones.

'Why didn't you smack those fuckers on the bus?' he asks.

'What?'

'You shoulda smacked 'em. If anyone called me a fag, I'd smack the shit out of 'em.'

'Don't say that word.'

'I'm just sayin', if you don't smack 'em when they say that shit, they'll never stop.'

I roll my eyes. It's almost a reflex these days – my eyes just roll themselves. I've fought with Mitch before and it wasn't fun. I was drunk then, and I wasn't thinking things through like I usually do. I don't want to get physically hurt again. Mitch is way stronger than me. If I start throwing punches, I'll get hurt, maybe die. And besides, they're just words. At least, that's what I tell myself.

Me and Lewis arrive home and we both go to our bedrooms and close our doors. I stand there, drop my backpack from my shoulders. The tears are rushing to my eyes. I hate the tears and I hate Mitch. I wish I wasn't so scared to stand up for myself. I wish my brain didn't think of all the worst outcomes before I do anything. Maybe I wouldn't feel so defeated if I was punched in the face. At least I'd get some hits in too.

I take out my phone and send a text to Amber: *Thanks for sticking up for me*

She replies instantly: *No worries x*

Then I play 'Tightrope', by Kylie. As the song reaches the chorus, my phone begins to vibrate. It's Eric calling.

I want to tell him I've been accepted into the acting school, to hear his smile through the phone and the sound of his voice when he says he's happy for me, but there's this feeling in my stomach, like a churning that's gonna make me sick. The feeling tells me this call isn't gonna go the way I hope it will.

'Hey,' I say, holding the phone to my ear.

'Hey,' he says. His voice sounds shaky, like he's crying. I sit on the corner of my bed and study the white paint on the wall. I listen to his breath through the phone, like he's whispering in my ear. I can feel shakiness coming to my own throat in the eternity of silence between us. 'Are you breaking up with me?' I ask, finally.

He sniffles. 'Yes.'

'Because of Rita?'

'Do you know already?' he asks.

'That she's pregnant? Yep.'

The white-painted wall of my bedroom breaks away like dust in the wind and I imagine I'm on the top of a cliff. I stare into a violent, dark sea below where the waves are raging and beating against rocks like it's their mission to break the cliff apart. I stare into the black, to a place where I'm not feeling my heart ripping into a million pieces.

'What are you gonna do?' I ask.

'I have to be there for her,' Eric says. 'I mean, it's *my* kid.'

I imagine the waves raging louder below me on the cliff. The spray shocks my face. But it's not the spray off a howling sea – it's tears.

'I don't want this to end,' I say, crying now.

'I know,' Eric replies. 'I'm sorry, Jordy.'

I want nothing more than to keep seeing Eric, for nothing to change between us, but I know it can't go on.

I hang up, turn my phone off and drop it to the floor with a thud. Maybe a bit dramatic, but I don't care.

I surrender my head to my pillow, and the tears come like a tsunami of *this-is-the-shittest-I've-felt-since-Mum-died*. I take deep breaths, in and out, imagining I've fallen from the cliff, sinking deeper beneath the dark waves, and I look up to see the white water breaking above me.

FOURTEEN

It's been two weeks since Eric ended things, and he's still dominating my mind. I'm on my bed, waiting to see if Dad's stayed sober enough to come home and take me to my driving test.

When Eric and me first started meeting up in secret, I had a feeling it was never meant to end well. When he told me he wasn't sure of his sexuality, I warned myself that I might just be an experiment for him, but we kept seeing each other. When I came out, he told me that we weren't in a relationship, that we were just having fun, and lowkey threatened me not to tell anyone.

Loved that for me.

From then, I prepared myself for it to end at any moment. But a year later, we were still meeting up, and it wasn't just grinding and kissing anymore, it was cuddles and long talks, late-night texts that didn't stop until one of us fell asleep. It felt like love to me – at least what I thought love was meant to feel like.

Maybe the best way to get over Eric is to move on to someone else.

I open my phone and start downloading Maneatr. I've heard about it online – an app gay men can use to hook up with each other.

When the download finishes, I open it up. The first thing I need to do is create a profile. I'm seventeen until the second of December, so I put my date of birth back a year.

I need a fake name. *Ben* is the first one that comes to mind. There's a section that says, *What are you looking for?* I write: *Looking to meet and date.*

No, that's too weird and desperate.

I delete the text and write, *Discreet fun.*

The next step is to upload a photo. I angle the camera to get just my eye and some of my hair, and the rest of the frame is filled with the white pillow beneath my head. The flash goes off and I upload the photo to my page.

My profile is created, and a grid appears on the screen. There are two squares that are actual photos of men's faces, but most of them are either blank or pictures of cars or motorbikes. One is a picture of the ocean.

'Now what?' I whisper to myself.

I tap my thumb on the blank profile next to mine. There's no name, just the eggplant emoji. In their profile it says: *Looking for now.*

My phone pings and a red dot appears over the envelope symbol at the bottom of the screen. Someone has sent me a message and I didn't even have to do anything.

I open my messages and I've received one from a guy called YNG.

It's a simple *hey*, but someone has messaged me.

My heart is racing as I close the app. I'm absolutely terrified, but at the same time, this feels exhilarating. Naughty, secretive and thrilling.

At midday, I hear Dad's Laser arrive in the driveway. My time lying here thinking of doing silly things is over because I have to get out of bed now. I have my driving test in half an hour.

I don't have time for a shower, so I just get dressed, put on my glasses and brush my teeth. Then I'm in the car with Dad, heading into town. It's raining lightly today, which is fabulous. I envisioned doing my test on a clear, sunny day. Love that for me.

'Remember your head checks,' Dad says. 'Do them every time. They'll fail ya on the smallest thing.'

'Yes, Father.'

The town is busy during the day. I thought most people would be at school and at work, but there are white people everywhere, sitting and standing in front of cafes, walking along the footpath with shopping bags, crowding the banks and the hairdressers.

We pull into the car park of the motor registry and I wipe my glasses clean with the bottom of my shirt. Dad messes up his reverse park and has to pull out again and straighten up, muttering *fucks* and *shits* to himself. I feel like Dad's more nervous than I am.

I *should* be nervous. This is a big thing. I'm going to sit in a car with someone who will evaluate my driving, someone who has the power to grant me my licence or deny it, and I'm not nervous at all. I guess I don't really care. I could take it or leave it.

'Remember your head checks,' Dad repeats as we walk to the entrance of the building. The sliding doors open for us and we join the line of people queued for the desks. It's five minutes before we reach the front. Dad tells the skinny guy at the counter that I'm here for my one-thirty driving test. He tells us to take a seat, so I follow Dad to the row of plastic chairs by the window.

There's an urge in my stomach – an urge to take out my phone and reply to the guy on Maneatr. Dad's right beside me, though. I would die if he knew I had created a profile on a gay hook-up app.

'Jordan?' I hear. A tall woman in a white business shirt and blue jeans walks out from behind a door. I raise my hand and stand with Dad. She comes to us, checking over forms on her clipboard. She wears big, black-framed glasses and has short blonde hair. 'I'm Lily. I'll be your assessor today,' she says. Dad shakes her hand but I give her a 'Hi'. Dad walks with us to the car and Lily checks the blinkers and brakelights.

'Good luck, son,' Dad says, shaking my hand. 'Remember—'

'Yes, I know. Head checks.'

Dad chuckles and leaves for the shopping centre. I return to the Laser where Lily is making herself comfortable in the passenger seat.

Now I'm nervous. She's going to fail me. She's probably racist. She's probably homophobic and can sense the gayness oozing from me like the perspiration in my armpits. She'll find a reason to fail me.

I buckle my seatbelt, adjust the mirrors and turn the car on. I press my foot on the brake, release the handbrake and put it in Drive. I ease out of my parking spot and turn the car towards the exit, doing no more than ten kilometres per hour.

'I know it can be nerve-racking,' Lily says. 'Just relax. I'm sure you'll do great.'

I know, Lily. You don't have to tell me to relax.

Lily instructs me to turn left. I flick on the blinker and do all the necessary head checks. As I turn onto the street, Lily begins going through her checklist. I try to peek at what she's doing, but she points forward and tells me to go right at the traffic lights, onto the main street.

As I wait at the intersection, I feel panic hit me in the chest like a knife. The panic comes because I will be moving to Sydney next year, which means I won't be at home anymore, and I won't be here to make Josie breakfast, or clean up Dad's beer bottles in the living room, or tell Lewis he's making dumb decisions. If I'm gone, it'll all fall apart. Shit will get much worse. Dad'll get liver disease or something, and he'll die. One morning when Dad's still asleep because of a hangover, Josie will walk out onto the road and get hit by a car, and she'll die. And Lewis will keep hanging around Dylan and get drunk and do drugs and get shot by a copper just like Brandon did. And Lewis will die too. Where will I be? At an institute trying out accents and standing on a stage in a costume pretending I'm someone I'm not.

Maybe I should stay here. Maybe that's the right thing to do... the *only* thing to do.

I hear Dad's voice in my head, once again telling me to remember my head checks, and I realise I'm literally having this panic attack in the middle of a driving test.

I take a deep breath and bring myself back to the car, feel the steering wheel under my grip.

The test continues. I do my head checks, a reverse park, a right turn onto the busy main street, then we're back at the registry.

I park perfectly in the parking space and follow Lily inside. Dad's not back yet.

'Take a seat, Jordan,' she says. 'I'll go calculate your results and give you your answer in a few minutes.'

I pull out my phone and navigate to Maneatr. I find the messages and see YNG's *hey*. I tap on his profile. He's thirty-four. He's too old for me. I block his profile and navigate back to the grid. As the screen fills with pictures, I hear Lily call my name.

I stuff my phone in my pocket and walk to the desk where Lily is sitting, staring at a computer. As I arrive, she turns her gaze to me and smiles. 'Jordan. Congratulations,' she says. 'You've passed.' She's happy for me, and it feels nice.

———

Dad agrees to let me take the car for a drive after I drop him back at work. I drive to the school and wait out the front for Amber to emerge at the end of the day.

'Jordy,' I hear. I turn to see Dylan arriving at my window. My first thought is, *What the fuck does he want?* His face is dark under his hood and he has bags under his eyes, like he hasn't slept much lately. 'I wanted to ask you something.'

'What?' I ask.

'Umm, well,' he begins. 'I'm making a short film. I heard you were going to acting school next year and I wanted to see if you would act in it. Jarrod's in it too.'

'You're making a movie?' I ask, genuinely surprised that Dylan does anything other than smoke weed and stay up all night walking the streets of Carraway's Point with his mates. And how did he hear I'm going to acting school? Someone must be talking about me.

'Yeah. I make movies all the time,' he says. 'But this one's important and I was wondering if you'd be in it?'

I sigh, wishing Amber would hurry the fuck up so I could get out of here. Dylan's always been weird; there was always something off about him, even when we were friends. I can't think of anything more unusual than making a short film with him.

'I don't think so,' I say. 'Sorry.'

'Oh, nah, that's okay,' Dylan says.

Finally, I see Amber's face appear on the other side of the road. She's smiling from ear to ear as she rushes to my car. Amber's had her Ps for six months already, and she's been on my arse about getting my licence. She cared about it more than I did.

'Did you hear that Rita and Eric told their parents about the pregnancy?' Amber asks as soon as she's in the car.

'Oh. Nope.'

'Yeah, apparently her dad told him he has to get a job and support her. Rita said Eric cried. Kinda makes me feel bad for them. I don't know why she didn't just quietly get an abortion. They're ruining their lives.'

'You reckon?'

'Yeah. Fuck that.'

As I turn on the ignition and pull away from the kerb, I hear Dad's words in my head. *Remember to stick to the speed limit... It's school zones as well... Take it easy and watch out for the blue boys... Remember to put your plates on.*

The excitement drowns out his words because I imagine I'm standing outside watching myself behind the wheel, in control of the ultimate weapon. No supervision.

I drive through town and Amber is giddy, singing Taylor Swift to herself. The anticipation has taken my mind off Eric completely.

Except now that I've thought of his name, my mind is back on him.

No. He will not ruin my first unsupervised drive.

It feels so weird to be driving without Dad – illegal somehow.

Amber connects her phone to the car's Bluetooth and starts Kylie Minogue's 'Vegas high'. We drive past the beach, singing at the top of our lungs.

I circle back into town and drive onto the main street, past the cinema, past the townspeople of Carraway's Point who don't care I've got my P's. I'm driving slowly, staying under the speed limit, because I feel like if I speed up, Dad will find out somehow.

'How do you feel?' Amber asks, turning down the music.

'Light as a feather,' I say.

Amber cracks up. 'What are you, high?'

'Feel kinda like I am.'

I slow down as we approach a roundabout. As I turn right, my back wheel bumps the side of the roundabout. Amber yelps, which makes me scream, then we laugh our heads off as I continue along the road. 'Jesus, Jordy,' Amber says, still laughing, but catching her breath.

'Did that count as a crash?'

Amber answers with more laughter.

I could very well be the worst mistake Lily from the motor registry ever made.

We drive through the south side of town and I pull up at the front of Amber's house. She gets out and taps the ground of her driveway with her hand.

'Safe at last,' she says.

'You were always safe,' I say.

Amber giggles and we say goodbye.

I take off again, thinking that I could literally do anything, go anywhere. But I check the fuel gauge and there's not a lot of petrol – just over a quarter of a tank – not enough to go anywhere interesting.

I drive back to Chopin Drive. I spot Eric's car at the end of the cul-de-sac, parked at Kallum's house. Amber said Rita's dad made him cry. A part of me wishes I could be there for him. Wishes I could give him a hug, and we could lie on my bed cuddling to make him feel better. He must be so scared. I know I would be.

No. I can't keep torturing myself with thoughts of Eric.

I pull into my driveway and shut off the car. I've gotta go pick Dad up when he finishes work, and then Josie from Nan's, but for now, I need to get inside.

The tears are bursting from my eyes before I even make it to my front door. Inside, I take two steps across the tiles and gently surrender myself to the floor. I lie flat, let the tears flow.

I cry hard. I miss him. I don't want him to have a baby with Rita. I want it to be us and only us. No one else. I don't want anyone else to matter to either of us.

We could have been so happy.

I must have been lying on the floor for an hour before the tears stop. My face feels hot, my throat is scratchy, and I've got snot clogging up my nostrils.

My phone vibrates in my pocket. I take it out to see a text from Dad, telling me he's just finished work.

I open Spotify and navigate to my four-hour Kylie Minogue playlist. I scroll the songs until I find the one I need to hear right now: 'A lifetime to repair'.

I play the song beside my head on the floor. I hum along at first, but when it gets to the chorus, I blast the lyrics like I'm breathing fire. The fire helps me roll to the side, plant my knees. My hands are cold and numb against the tiles. I get to my feet and wipe my cheeks dry with my wrists. As Kylie continues to sing, and me along with her, the decision comes to me.

I will never cry over Eric again.

FIFTEEN

It's Friday night and most people my age are probably hanging out, drinking or partying, driving to nearby towns or doing other stupid shit, while I'm at home in my current acting role: Dad 2.0.

Love that for me.

Josie's watching *The Simpsons Movie* on the couch as I pour the pasta spirals into the pot of boiling water. I stir like Mum taught me to make sure they don't stick to the sides and bottom.

Next, I break up the mince and drop it into the frying pan, where it sizzles.

'Fucker!' I shout as the hot oil splashes my forearm.

'You can't say swear words,' Josie calls from the couch.

'I can if I have a good reason,' I call back.

I use a fork to stir the mince and then pour in the bolognaise sauce. Lewis comes out of his room with his shoes in hand. He takes a chair at the dining table and slides them onto his feet.

'I'm headin' out,' he says.

'I just made dinner,' I say back. 'At least eat with us before you fuck off and poison your body.'

'Can you just save some for me?' he asks, standing up. He's wearing his blue jeans and black hoodie. He fixes his snapback on his head like he's going out in the sun instead of the night.

'Where you going?'

'Just to Dylan's,' he says. 'We're going round Jarrod's to play some Xbox. Maybe go to Rory's.'

'You know what happened at Rory's last year when Dylan and Brandon went there?' I ask.

'Bruh, he lives in a different house now,' Lewis argues back. 'It's chill. Don't worry.'

I want to tell him I can't help worrying, that it feels like I'm his father and I want to make him stay here. He thinks he's just going out to have fun, that it's *chill*, but bad things have happened to Aboriginal boys in this town.

But I'm not his father. Maybe Dad's right – at least I know where he'll be.

'Catch ya,' Lewis says as he leaves. Then it's just me and Josie and the mince I'm burning.

I dish out our spaghetti bolognaise into bowls. I wrap two bowls up for Dad and Lewis and leave them on the bench, then join Josie on the couch. Sophie curls up at the other end and watches the movie with us as we eat. I loved this movie when I was younger, but now it's kind of shit.

Josie falls asleep just past nine o'clock. She's lying on her side, her face lit by the television. She looks so calm and peaceful. I miss being her age – I didn't have to worry about anything back then. Mum and Dad did everything, and I was playing *Halo* at night, footy on weekends with my friends, going to school and coming home, not knowing how unhappy I would be one day.

At ten o'clock, the door jiggles open with the sound of keys and Dad stumbles inside. I shoosh him and he stops dead in his tracks when he sees Josie sleeping on the couch. He slips off his shoes and tiptoes across the floor.

'Hey, son,' he whispers. 'How's your night?'

'Fine,' I say. I take my eyes back to the TV, where *Grown Ups 2* is playing now. If Josie wasn't asleep near me, I might just scream my lungs out, tell Dad to stop fucking drinking so much and be home with us. He probably doesn't even realise how much he's failing at parenting.

'Goodnight,' he says, and passes into the hallway. I hear his door close and the thump of springs on his bed.

When the movie ends, I nudge Josie awake. She peeks through squinting eyelids at me and covers her face with her hands.

'Come on, I'll carry you,' I tell her. Still with her eyes closed, she reaches her arms out and wraps them around my neck. I carry her to her bedroom, passing the snores behind Dad's door.

Now everyone in this house is asleep but I'm not tired at all. In my room, I open my phone and navigate to Maneatr.

I want to do something naughty. I want to do something gay.

When I open Maneatr, the screen fills with the men nearby. I click on the first profile with a photo.

Dan. Thirty-two years old. He's 700 metres away. His bio says: *Looking for some fun.* He's got the hairiest chest I've ever seen and looks older than thirty-two, so I swipe back and click on the next square, which is a photo of a motorbike. *New* is his name. He's forty-one years old and his bio says: *Looking for hook-up right now.*

I swipe away and click on the next black square. This guy's profile name is the number *20*. His bio says: *Looking for some fun, up for whatever. Inexperienced.*

He's twenty. He's online. He's inexperienced, just like me. I tap the envelope symbol on his profile and start a message.

Me: *Hey*

20: *Hey, got any more pics?*

I scroll through the photos on my phone. There's a selfie I took a few days ago in my bedroom window at sunset. It looks kind of nice because the sun is hitting the right side of my face, but the left is in shadow, and my lips are separated slightly. It looks pretty sexy. I send him that photo.

20: *Cute.*

Me: *You got a pic?*

No reply. A minute passes. Then, another minute.

A ding – 20 has sent me a photo. He's four minutes late but I'm excited. My heart is thumping hard as I open the photo. He's got a cute face, puffy cheeks with blush. He's got brown eyes and his skin is pale. He's not wearing a shirt and he's got a strong chest, bulging pecs, abs coming through on his stomach. He's not bulky buff, but he's toned. The photo cuts off at the top of his underwear and his pubes peek out, just a tad.

Me: *Ur hot*

20: *Thanks. Top or bottom?*

Me: *I'm not sure really*

It's true. I don't know what I want, or what I like yet. I need to offer something, though.

Me: *I'm free tonight*

Another minute passes. My heart is racing. I'm looking over our messages, begging him to reply. Then, ding.

20: *Okay. I can host. Can you get to mine? I live near the bridge.*

Me: *Yep sure. Send your address?*

20: *118 North Street. It's a long driveway. I'll meet you at the gate. Text me when you get here.*

Me: *Okay, see you soon.*

I slip on my hoodie and pull the hood over my head. I walk out of Chopin Drive, into the backstreets.

I turn through a park, and follow a path alongside the river. It's a quiet walk and makes me wonder if the gay men of town ever used to cruise in this area. It'd be a good place to hook up with a stranger.

I come out into sleeping streets with quiet houses. I follow my phone's directions onto North Street, passing a little playground with swings and a slippery dip, monkey bars and a flying fox.

The tar is loose on the road as I walk along. I'm kicking rocks everywhere and it's louder than I would like it to be.

At the end of the street is the bridge that crosses the river and leads out of town.

I count the house numbers as I walk. 62. 64. 66.

My phone vibrates in my pocket. It's a message from 20. My heart begins to race again.

20: *You close?*

Me: *Yeah, about two minutes away.*

There's a nervous rumble in my stomach. Maybe he's not even the guy in that picture. Maybe he's an old man who likes to do weird shit to young guys. Maybe he's a homophobic murderer who lures unsuspecting gays on Maneatr and stabs them in the spine, drags them to a secret dungeon under his garage and cuts off their penises, which he then stuffs into their throats to choke them to death.

98...100...102.

I'm close. I step onto the nature strip.

My mind is firing like an assault rifle. What if he doesn't like me? What if he decides I'm ugly? What if I'm not good at anything and he laughs at me? I should turn back, delete my Maneatr account, pretend this night didn't happen.

114...116...118.

I'm here. The house looks pretty big – two storeys. None of the lights are on and it's dead quiet. All I can hear are my own footsteps and a truck rolling along the distant highway. I stop at the steel gate.

In my phone, I type, *I'm here.*

No.

I can't do it.

I'm not ready.

This is too much.

I close the app, turn around and start for home. A tear falls, and it feels like ice on my cheek in the night air. This isn't making me happy – it's making me feel like shit. My brain won't let me go through with it. It's showing me flashes of my death at the hands of a stranger. Maybe I'm just not wired for spontaneous hook-ups. All I want right now is to be back in bed.

I put in my AirPods and play Kylie's 'If only' on full volume.

As I walk home, I try to think of the last time I felt truly like myself. It was with Eric, when he came over after school and we kissed for ages.

But I can't be happy with Eric, so I try to think of the last time I felt happy without him.

It was acting in the local production of *A Midsummer Night's Dream* last year. When I was on stage, wearing a blue and green costume, reciting Shakespearean lines I didn't fully understand, I felt good.

I am happy when I'm acting. I need to act again.

SIXTEEN

It's the start of my last week of school ever. Mr Drawbler is talking about syntax, scribbling notes on the board, part of our recent series of refreshers for the HSC. I'm sitting with Hamish in the second row. He's chewing gum, smacking his lips together like he's deliberately trying to annoy me.

Kallum's down in the front row with Ebony. They're whispering something to each other, and Kallum covers his mouth to stop himself from laughing.

Once I stopped hanging out with Eric and Mitch and the rest of the footy boys, I became one of those kids who drift into the background, who don't really get noticed. From the background, you can observe other people better, notice things. I've noticed Kallum and Ebony hanging out a lot since he came back to town. They must be dating, or at least seeing each other on the down low.

Eric said Kallum got expelled from his school in Sydney for getting into a fight. I've been wanting to ask Kallum about it, but we don't really talk to each other like that. After he came with me and Dad to the national park, it was like we were friends again for a minute. Now, we're just two Aboriginal guys who happen to live on the same street.

After class, I walk with Hamish along the balcony and down the stairs. We walk through the square and to the seniors' area. I spot Dylan sitting with Jarrod, who's in Year Eleven, and two younger boys, one of whom is Lewis, even though I told him not to hang out with Dylan. They're sitting by the drama hall. Dylan's eating an apple, laughing at something Jarrod's saying, and I can't believe I'm about to do this.

'I'll catch up with ya,' I say to Hamish, and I peel off towards Dylan and his hoodlums.

'Dylan,' I say.

'Hey, Jordy,' he says. His voice is soft, like a feather slowly gliding towards the earth.

'Are you still making that movie?' I ask.

'Yeah,' he says.

'Well, I can act in it,' I say. 'If you still want me to.'

'Really? Yeah, cool. Thanks.'

'How much are you paying?' I ask, and Dylan's eyes widen.

'Umm...'

'I'm joking,' I say. Dylan blushes.

'Well, umm, if you want to come by my place after school, you can look at the script,' he says. 'I only printed one copy.'

'Yeah, okay,' I say. 'See you then.'

———

After school, the bus pulls up at the end of Chopin Drive. Dylan and Lewis wait for me outside.

I go with Dylan and for some reason Lewis is tagging along with us. We pass the first house, Brandon's, which I notice Dylan glances to.

The front lawn of Brandon's house is overgrown, and there's an overflowing red wheelie bin off to the side of the path leading to the front door. It looks like no one's lived there in years, but Brandon's mum's old hatchback is in the driveway.

'It might be a bit messy inside,' Dylan says, as we arrive at the front of his house.

'I have been in your house before,' I say.

'Yeah, true.' We walk through his front gate, which is fixed open and off one of its hinges.

Dylan flings open the screen door and it screeches like a dying bat.

'Hitchcock!' I hear a voice shout. Just inside is the living room, where Dylan's mum is watching some quiz show on TV. She's smoking a cigarette and spots me as she goes to ash. She's wearing dirty blue overalls. She's famously the only female mechanic in this town.

'Oh, Jordy,' she says. 'How are ya? How's your dad?'

'He's good,' I say.

'This way,' Dylan says. I follow him and Lewis through the kitchen, where dishes are piled up in the sink and empty pasta packets sit on the bench, above a full bin with fruit flies hovering about.

Dylan takes us to his bedroom. His room is pretty big – I used to be jealous of the size of it when we were younger. But it's changed a lot since the last time I was here. Now, there's a little TV and an Xbox, with the TV still stuck on a pause screen, an old couch with fabric that looks really itchy to sit on and a desk and chairs behind, against the side wall.

Lewis drops his backpack and falls onto the couch, where he picks up a controller and starts playing, while Dylan walks to the desk.

'Don't you have homework or something?' I ask Lewis.

'Nah,' he says.

I follow Dylan, who picks up a few pages held together with a paperclip. The front page has a paragraph on it.

'This is the script,' he says. 'That's a synopsis, kind of.' He points to the paragraph.

GUILTY

A ticking clock. A Twitter feed refreshing.
The boy is haunted by memories of his murdered friend. He waits in his bedroom. The verdict is coming at three o'clock. The clock ticks down the minutes. The boy refreshes his Twitter feed, waiting for the update of the local newspaper sharing the verdict...guilty or not guilty?

The first thought that comes to me is, *Does anybody use Twitter anymore?* The next thought is that this film is about Dylan and Brandon, about the trial coming up.

'There are two characters,' Dylan says. 'One's called *The Boy*, and the other is *Lost Boy*.'

'Right,' I say. Love those imaginative character names.

I flick through the pages. There are only six in the script, and it is formatted wrong.

Silence. The Boy is sitting on his bed, wearing court clothes. He checks his phone, looks to the clock. Ticking sounds. Suspenseful music begins to play.

Cut to: Lost Boy coming out of the water in the new world. He's scared.

Lost Boy: Hello? Is anyone there?

I've read scripts before, and this is not how any of them were written. But Dylan has written *something* – he's put in the effort. Now is not the time to teach him how to format scripts – now is the time for the actor to read.

I sit down and read it in full. It's a sad story about a boy waiting to find out if his friend's killer is found guilty of his murder, meanwhile, his friend's spirit is trapped in the world between life and death, running from the Darkness Monster trying to take him to hell.

Yep. This is so obviously about Dylan and Brandon.

Dylan shows me the digital camera he's using. I don't really know cameras, but it's a Canon, and looks like the ones we use in photography class.

'I've already filmed some stuff,' Dylan says, as Lewis explodes a grenade on his video game. Dylan takes his laptop out of his backpack. It's a little thing, not much bigger than an iPad. He opens it and navigates to the videos folder. There are five files. Dylan double-clicks on the first one and it begins to play.

The screen is black, then shaky as the light takes over. The image settles on a close-up of Dylan's mate, Jarrod.

His face fills the screen, from the bottom of his chin to his curly hair. Jarrod looks directly into the camera, trying to contain laughter. In the video, Dylan tells

Jarrod to look scared and exhausted, like he's just been running. Jarrod works himself up and then he puffs, his face changes to that of a terrified boy, and Dylan's voice instructs him to look all around the rim of the camera with just his eyes, not moving his head. The video looks great. It's moody, claustrophobic. Jarrod's got a good face for the screen, despite being sort of a loser.

'This is just a shot of Lost Boy in the bushes of the new world,' Dylan says. 'I know it probably doesn't look like much, but I've got it all in my head. It'll be good once I've edited it all together. And your character doesn't have any lines, so you won't have to memorise anything.'

'It's all in the face,' I say. 'It's a good challenge. I'm up for it.'

'Okay, sweet.'

The video ends and I read over the script again, trying to visualise it as Dylan's imagined it to be. I think this movie might not be so bad after all.

———

Dad's in the kitchen cooking up some stir-fry when I arrive home with Lewis. I'm shocked. Dad's being a parent. It's about five o'clock and this is an early dinner. Josie's at the table building a Millennium Falcon with Lego. I start for my room when Dad calls my name.

'Can you swing downtown real quick?' he asks. 'I forgot to grab milk when I was there. And a loaf of bread.'

I turn back to Dad and drop my backpack to the floor where all our shoes gather every night. I take the fifty bucks he's holding out.

'I'll come with ya,' Lewis says, rushing from his room, already changed out of his school clothes somehow. 'I want to get some apples.'

'Apples?' I ask.

'Yeah,' he says.

I take Dad's keys and Lewis follows me out to the car. I fix my P-plates to the front and back and connect my Bluetooth to play 'Can't get you out of my head'. I bop to the music and Lewis grips the handhold on the door while I reverse out of the driveway, like I'm speeding at a hundred kilometres an hour and he's holding on for dear life.

'Relax,' I say.

'Just don't speed,' Lewis barks as I ease along Chopin Drive. I'm not even hitting the accelerator yet because the road dips down a little to the end, so I can just ride the momentum.

'Did you know Dylan made movies?' I ask.

'Yeah,' Lewis says. 'He wants to be a filmmaker. He's trying to get this scholarship to a film school in Sydney. That's why he's making this one.'

'Really? Ya think ya know someone.'

'You don't know Dylan,' Lewis says, and I guess he's right. I don't know him anymore. When we went into high school, we stopped knowing each other.

The main street is busy as hell, as expected at this time of day. I turn into the shopping centre car park and it seems like most of the town is here.

As I stop the engine, a car pulls up beside me. It's a loud ute, dark green colour, dirt all along its side. Me and Lewis don't have to do any guessing – we both know that's

Terry's car. He's one of the rednecks who live out of town – he and his brother Trent, who's a year older than me – and word is they've been getting around with that copper who killed Brandon, like they're his bodyguards or something.

Trent gets out of the back seat of the ute and walks to my window. He waves to me with a wide smile. He's still in his school shirt. Then Terry gets out and so do two more guys. The others are all wearing high-vis singlets, cargo shorts and boots.

Trent walks away and Lewis goes to get out of the car.

'Wait,' I say. I watch the rednecks walk between parked cars and into the Target beside the supermarket.

'What? You scared of those dickheads?' Lewis asks.

'Just let 'em go away first,' I say. I don't want to have to talk to them, hear them say something racist to me. About a year ago, Trent and Terry were hanging out in front of a pizza shop and I was walking past. I had come out two weeks before and they wolf-whistled. One of them joked that they'd give me five bucks for a blowjob. I tried to ignore them, until Terry called out, *Reckon you could get disability pension now that you're a gay abo? Double handicap.* I ignored them and kept going.

One time in primary school, Trent told me Aboriginal people were lucky that white people came to Australia, otherwise we'd be living in caves and shacks, wiping our arses with gumleaves.

I try to avoid them altogether if I can. I wait till they're far enough away, then climb out of the car with Lewis.

SEVENTEEN

It's Friday morning, our Year Twelve graduation day.

I'm with Dad, whose mingling abilities are on point as we gather with the rest of the students and parents outside the hall. Dad and Kallum's father are chatting like old friends while me and Kallum are just standing awkwardly, both wearing our school uniform for the last time.

I spot Amber with her parents over by the barbecue that's waiting to cook us food after the ceremony.

'I'll be back,' I say to Dad. He hardly looks at me, still caught in a conversation about fishing or diving or something.

I start through the crowd, passing Dylan and his parents standing on either side of him, neither of them talking. Dad told me they split up a while ago but he wasn't sure why.

Amber gives me a hug.

'We actually did it,' I say.

Amber squeezes me tighter. 'We did.'

The principal comes out and tells everyone to enter the hall. I walk inside with Dad then split off from him: parents up the back, students in alphabetical order. Pieces of paper with our names printed on them rest on the seats. I find mine and sit down.

The assembly begins when everyone's seated. Eric's sitting three rows ahead of me and to the left. I can see the side of his face, his brown hair with faded back and sides.

The guest speaker takes the stage: former student and published author Greg Lawthum.

'You know,' he begins, 'when I left this hall at the end of Year Twelve, I never thought I'd set foot in this place again.' He's got short red hair and a clean-shaven face. He's pretty tall and he's got a beer belly. When I hear *published author*, I expect an old white lady with grey curls, so he surprises me.

'I graduated here in two thousand and five. The Pussycat Dolls had the number-one song on the radio and John Howard was still our prime minister.' A few of the teachers and adults giggle behind me. 'I was just a boy with a dream. I wasn't sure I'd achieve it, but I was okay with the act of *dreaming*. I *was* from Carraway's Point, after all. This small country town by the sea seemed like the end of the world to me for most of my teen years. But I dared to dream. Unsure those dreams would be realised, I dreamed them anyway.'

The writer's speech continues for what feels like an eternity, until finally our year advisor, Mr Humphries, takes the stage. He calls us each up to get our graduation certificates and a photo with the principal. He entertains the audience with insightful comments for each of us as we climb the stage.

Eric's name is called and he stands and shuffles along the row, dodging knees and chairs.

'Eric's our future NRL star,' Mr Humphries says. 'If any of the parents caught the local first-grade grand final this year, Eric is the one who scored the match-winning try. He's super talented, but he's also just a genuinely wonderful bloke. He's very helpful whenever required and we know he will continue to make us proud as he pursues his rugby league dreams at the southern rugby league trials next month.'

The crowd cheers and Eric climbs the steps. He takes his certificate and shakes Mr Humphries's hand, then poses for a photo with the principal by the school banner. He smiles a great big smile as the flash strikes him.

Mr Humphries slowly makes his way through names until he arrives at mine. When he calls it, I stand and shuffle across the row. 'Jordan's one of our proud Indigenous students here. At the end of his first term of Year Seven, I asked Jordan to say the Acknowledgement of Country at our end-of-term assembly. Jordan got so nervous, his hands were shaky. But he did it. He spoke in front of his whole year group, even though he was scared. And now he's off to Sydney to study acting. I'm sure one day we'll be seeing him on telly, maybe rubbing shoulders with those beautiful people on *Home and Away*.'

The crowd applauds as I accept my certificate on stage. Mr Humphries's hand is moist with sweat when I shake it.

I dawdle to Mrs Stallberry, the principal. She smiles with me for a photo and the flash shocks my eyes.

After the ceremony, we're all outside the hall while sausages cook on the barbecue. Amber tells me some people are going to Mitch's place tonight to celebrate. She asks me to go but it's the last thing I want to do. Mitch is an arse and I know Eric will be there. I'd be happy never seeing them again.

'Nah, I don't feel too good, to be honest,' I say, lying. 'Think I should just stay home.'

'Fair enough,' Amber says. 'This means I'll be hanging out with your enemies. You sure you're okay with it?'

'Yes,' I say. 'Go, have fun.'

'Okay,' she says. We hug again as Hamish and his parents walk past, listing the dates for the HSC exams. My Biology exam is the day the trial starts for that copper.

When me and Dad get home after midday, Dad's quick to remove an old photo of him and one our cousins from the frame, replacing it with my Year Twelve graduation certificate. Most of my fellow graduates are thinking about the exams coming up in a couple of weeks, but I'm thinking about being alone in my room.

Dad hangs the certificate on the wall in the living room. 'I've got to jet off to work, but I'm so proud of you, son. I know your mum would be too.'

Dad wraps his arm around me and squeezes. It might be the first time he's hugged me since I was ten or something. He plants a kiss on the top of my head and now I'm blushing with cringe.

'Okay, Father,' I say. He steps away from me, towards the door, examines me like I'm some amazing sculpture.

'I'll see you later.'

Dad leaves and I go to my room. Sophie's asleep on the foot of my bed, curled up in a ball. I sit down and pat her.

'I did it,' I whisper to Sophie, who stirs in her sleep, adjusting herself but keeping her eyes squeezed closed. 'I finished high school. Are you proud of me?'

Sophie doesn't do anything, but I think she would be proud if she knew – if she understood how I wanted to quit school after I came out but didn't, how my parents never achieved what I just did.

I rest back on my bed. Amber's going out tonight, Eric's going out tonight, everyone's having fun except me.

I take out my phone and open up Maneatr. There's an unopened message from 20 from three days ago: *Hey, haven't heard from you?*

I could message him back, tell him I'm free again. Instead, I open the grid and the screen fills with the men nearby, mostly blank profiles. I tap on a close-up of a blond guy. He's got stubble, long curls and sunburnt cheeks. He isn't smiling, but he looks nice. There's a green dot on his profile so I know he's active right now.

Name: *Joe*

Age: *21*

Bio: *Just trying things out*

He hasn't filled in any of the other details, but I can see that he's eight kilometres away.

My phone dings with a message – from Joe. He's messaged me before I could message him, and if that's not a sign, then I don't know what is.

Joe: *Hey there. Ur cute.*

Me: *Hey, thanks! Not too bad yourself.*

Joe: *Think I've seen you around town before. I'm Joe* 😊

Me: *Nice to meet you! What are you looking for?*

Joe: *Umm I guess I'm just kind of experimenting. Never been with a guy before. You?*

Me: *Just some fun. You've never been with a guy before?*

Joe: *No I haven't. I've always been attracted to guys but nvr did anything about it.*

Me: *I get that. Carraway's Point isn't exactly a LGBT haven lol.*

Joe: *Defs not LOL. I'm home alone tonight if you're free.*

I hesitate a moment after his last message. He seems nice enough, but last time, I got cold feet. I might get scared again and let him down. But he's never been with a guy before. Maybe I've got more experience than him.

Me: *I'm not really looking for anything hardcore right now. You okay with going slow?*

Joe: *Yeah defs. I want to take it slow see how it goes.*

Me: *Okay, I'm free. What time? Send me the address.*

Joe: *8 or 9 would be good. I'll send it to you later x*

My heart is racing with excitement again, just like it did when I first messaged with 20. I'm going to meet Joe tonight, the sexy, blond-curled boy with stubble.

———

Lewis gets home at three-thirty and Dad gets home with Josie at five, but I've already showered thoroughly. I've cleaned every inch of my body with hot water and soap and brushed my teeth twice.

Lewis leaves the house after dinner, saying he's going to Dylan's. Dad doesn't protest. He cracks open a stubbie of Tooheys New and sits on the couch to watch the footy.

'Can I borrow your car later, Dad?' I ask.

'Where are you going?' he asks.

'I told Amber I'd get her home from a party.'

'Well, that's nice of you. Yeah, you know where the keys are. Just no speeding.'

'Of course.'

I listen to the sounds of the rugby league commentary from my bedroom while I scroll Instagram. Eric's posted a video of Mitch downing a beer-bong while Kallum, Tom and their other friends cheer him on. I quickly close it because I'm beginning to wish I was there so I could be with Eric – but that's old news.

And besides, I've got a hook-up tonight.

As soon as eight o'clock hits, I message Joe asking if he's ready for me to come over. His profile says he hasn't been active for two hours. I hope he's not getting cold feet like I worried I would. I've cleaned myself too long and hard for this to turn into a night in my bedroom alone or, god forbid, on the couch watching the footy with Dad.

Five minutes pass.

Ten minutes.

Fifteen.

I give up and join Dad on the couch. The Roosters are beating the Tigers, 28–12. Dad's onto his second stubbie. I take my mind from Joe and think about next year instead – January – when I'll be arriving in Sydney to start a new chapter of my life. I wish Eric was coming with me like we planned, but I think I can finally accept that he has to stay here. I think we were just never meant to be.

My phone vibrates and it's a message from Joe.

Joe: *Hey, sorry, was just out shopping, ready for u now*

Me: *All good. Send me your address and I'll head over?*

Joe: *77 Ravenswood Rd. It's a bit out of town. Follow the road through the gate and up to the house.*

I put his address into my phone and see that he lives out in the ranges near Terry and Trent and all the rednecks. I study Joe's face again, trying to remember whether I'd seen it with them. His face isn't familiar. He's probably not associated with them at all. I'm over-thinking this.

Me: *Okay, see you in about fifteen minutes x*

'I'm off,' I say to Dad as I stand from the couch.

'Amber's ready?'

'Yep.'

I grab Dad's keys from the bowl on the kitchen table and leave. I reverse Dad's Laser out of the driveway and cruise out of Chopin Drive, playing Kylie's 'Better the devil you know'. I'm pretty sure I'm not allowed to have my phone connected to the Bluetooth but nothing is coming between me and Kylie.

I follow the main street out of town until it becomes the highway. The night is black so I switch on my high beams when I leave the streetlights behind.

I have to drive through heavy bush for a while, and I worry a kangaroo might spring onto the road unexpectedly and I'll have to explain to Dad why I fucked up his car out of town instead of picking Amber up.

The bush ends and I climb the hill that overlooks Carraway's Point, then turn onto Harrison's Road, which leads into the ranges and farmlands. The hills are winding and rough as I slow my speed through a light fog. I haven't passed another car the whole trip. Dad needs to get his lights changed or something because I'm leaning forward over the steering wheel to see better.

I arrive at the turn. Wire fences line the sides of Ravenswood Road. I can see the silhouettes of cows and horses and sheep as I drive by. The bitumen road turns to rough gravel and the inside of Dad's Laser rattles like coins in a dryer. The noise is deafening and I can hardly think, so I turn the radio down.

I check my phone. It's not far now. Five hundred metres, on the left. The road rises and dips and passes over a small, narrow bridge. In the black distance, I can see the lights of houses, all spaced out.

No next-door neighbours out here.

I reach number 77 and pull to the side. There's a big steel fence blocking the entrance to the property. I climb out into the freezing September air. The fog drifts across the beams of my headlights as I powerwalk to the gate.

Before I begin to push it, I realise I'm pretty sure Joe said that the gate would be open and that I could just follow the road onto the property.

I pull out my phone and I've only got one bar of reception. I try to load the Maneatr app but the connection is too shit. I can't get into my messages and my heart is beginning to race.

I should go home. This doesn't feel right.

I go back to the car and my phone vibrates in my hand when I climb inside. It's a message from Joe: *You still on your way?*

I try to load the app again but it's so slow. Even though it's freezing, my hands and armpits are sweaty.

Screw it. I'm not backing out this time. I never take risks. I always get to this point and my stupid brain makes me stop and run to safety.

I return to the gate, slide it all the way open and drive onto the property, up the rise and around a hill. The house emerges in the darkness, resting at the top where the ground flattens.

There's a white ute near a shed, so I park behind it. I take a deep breath then pull my hood over my head to shield my freezing ears.

On my way to the house, I open my phone and try Maneatr, but yet again, it's not working. I can't even message Joe back.

I climb the creaky wooden steps onto the verandah and take a breath before I knock on the door.

My nose is becoming runny. A light flicks on above the door and it opens. There he is: Joe. He's tall, wearing a jumper and pyjama pants.

'Hey,' he says quietly – louder than a whisper, softer than an outside voice.

'Hey.'

He opens the screen door and lets me inside. The lights are dim and warm – very moody.

'This way,' he says. I follow Joe into a hallway where one door is open, bleeding light into the darkness.

Inside Joe's bedroom, my heart is thumping in my chest. My body is jolting with every thump as I gaze over the double bed. The bed is made, with a grey doona and pillows. There's a rack holding various jackets of different colours and styles – like all the people Joe pretends to be when he's not the gay guy in this room.

Joe slides off his jumper and exposes the white tank top underneath. He sits at the foot of his bed, gestures for me to sit beside him, so I do. His tank top shows off his shoulders, his broad chest. His chest hair peeks through the top at his neck. There's a bulge in his pyjama pants.

'Do you live alone here?' I ask.

'Nah,' he says. 'I live with my aunt, uncle and cousin. They kind of adopted me.'

'Oh.

'Your name's not Ben,' Joe says. 'You're that Jordan kid.'

'You know me?'

'You used to play footy.'

Joe moves to the side of the bed and begins to play some music from his Bluetooth speaker. It's a Madonna song from the eighties. I recognise it but I don't know what it's called.

Joe returns and I feel his heat enter my space, cutting through the cold of the bedroom. He lifts his arm over my head and relaxes it on the back of my shoulders. His armpit is hairy – so manly. He wears Brut deodorant.

His warm hand gently falls onto the back of my neck. He spreads his fingers through my curly hair and I know where he's trying to push my head.

'You cool?' he asks.

'Yeah. Umm...I just...Can we kiss for a bit first?' I ask. My palms are sweaty again and the voice in my head is telling me to bolt out of this house and escape.

'Yeah, we can kiss.'

I turn back to Joe and he kisses me. His lips are dry at first but, before long, both our lips are wet and my jaw is getting sore. He's a pretty good kisser, though, better than Eric. I'd be happy if kissing was all we did.

I hear shifting in the wooden walls, then the clang of keys and voices entering the house.

'Oh, shit,' Joe says. He springs from the bed.

'They reckon he's looking at twenty years,' an old man's voice says. While Joe is panicking, saying how they were meant to be out until late, I'm listening to what the unexpected intruders are saying.

'No way,' a younger man says. 'Miles'll never see the inside of a cell.'

'Not like he did anything wrong,' a woman says. Her voice is sharp and loud. 'One less dole bludger on the street.'

'He was a kid,' the younger man says.

'A *future* dole bludger then.'

'I heard they got a witness,' the older man cuts in. I'm still standing like my feet have been cemented to the floor.

'Terry's gonna take care of that,' the woman's voice says. 'They aren't going to say anything.'

They're talking about Brandon. They're talking about the copper who killed him – Miles Higgins. They're talking about Terry *silencing* the witness ahead of the trial.

'You home, Joseph?' the woman calls from the living room. 'You got a girl over? Saw the car.'

'Don't talk,' he says to me. I zip my lips shut with my fingers. The last thing I want to do is say a word when we leave this room.

Joe opens his door and I follow him into the hallway.

'Hey, aunty,' he says. An old white woman, an old white man, and a younger white man are sitting in the living room opening beers around the coffee table. 'Sorry, this guy was just buying something. He's leaving now.'

They all stare as Joe ushers me past. He opens the front door and stands aside to let me out.

'Buying something?' I ask. Seems like a stupid excuse for me to be here.

'Just go,' he says. 'Make sure you got cash next time.'

I don't argue. I leave as they begin asking him what I was buying. In my car, I reverse quickly onto the driveway. I speed back down the hill and around bends, replaying the words I heard through the walls over and over.

I heard they got a witness.

Terry's gonna take care of that. They aren't going to say anything.

I know who they're talking about – everyone knows who was in the room that night: Dylan. I pass through the open gate and back the way I came, the car rattling on the rough road.

EIGHTEEN

The hot shower is so much more soothing at six in the morning. It's six days since I graduated Year Twelve and today, I'm heading off to our Aboriginal graduation camp. I hate camping. I hate not having a working toilet with a flush system, and I hate being out in the bush because you never know if you'll have reception or not. Not to mention the bugs, the mosquitos, the goannas that sneak in to steal food, and the cold.

As much as I'm not looking forward to camping, I'm also thinking about last Friday night, when I heard those white people saying Terry was going to *take care of* the witness in Brandon's murder trial. I thought about going to the police, or telling Kallum's mum, cause she's a cop, but I know they wouldn't be able to do anything about it, cause I'm just an Aboriginal boy who says he heard something. They wouldn't believe me, or worse, they wouldn't care because they're all on Higgins's side.

Maybe the only thing I can do is warn Dylan. I know those boys – they talk a lot of shit. Maybe Terry wouldn't even do anything, and I'd be putting Dylan on edge for no reason.

Out of the shower, I step into the wind of the small fan heater plugged in at the corner. Heaters – another thing I'll miss at camp. I dry myself and step into the hallway. I can hear Lewis snoring through his bedroom door and Dad's in the kitchen boiling the kettle.

The clothes I've picked out for today are laid out on my bed – my plain black shirt and blue jeans, my dark blue hoodie, my jean jacket and my warm bed socks.

I get dressed and Dad drives me to the pick-up point at the school. A white minibus is waiting for us where Glen and Ivy are having a laugh with an older white man.

'Okay, have fun, son,' Dad says. 'Call me tonight?'

'I will.'

I close the door and cross the road. It's freezing and my jeans are doing nothing to warm my legs. Love that.

The fog looks pretty heavy down the hill where Dad is driving off.

Everyone's shivering just as much as I am at the bus stop. Dylan's got his hoodie over his head, tightened at the front to cover most of his face. Kallum's resting against the school gates with Elijah and Corey from Carraway Catholic. The girls from there, Doreen and Maddie, are standing near the bus. Kallum's got his fingers beneath his mouth and he's blowing his warm breath on them. Billy from our school arrives and joins me against the wall.

A blue Ford Territory pulls up and two girls get out. I assume they're the students from Belrose.

Two more cars arrive with Jasmine and Kaz, and Glen clears his throat.

'Gather round, boys and girls,' he says. He's basically yelling and it's cutting right through the dying fog. 'It's a long trip and it'll be a full bus, so no complaints about having to sit next to anyone. All right?'

It takes a moment before everyone starts filing into the bus. I get on behind Kallum.

'Do you know how long the drive is?' I hear Corey ask.

'I think it's two hours,' one of the Belrose girls replies. This bus is about a quarter of the size of a regular school bus, but there is a TV screen at the front, behind the driver and the passenger.

I climb onto an empty seat towards the front while everyone pairs up. I take off my jacket and rest it on my lap.

'Bro,' Jasmine says to Kaz behind me. 'I can't fit my arse onto this tiny space.'

'Oh.' She shuffles against the window and Jasmine slides in.

The heater is on and I can feel the warmth blasting through the little air-conditioner above. The seats are tall and I can rest my head back.

Ivy boards the bus and takes the seat beside me. Glen sits in the front passenger seat and gazes over us.

'All right, mister driver,' he says. 'Time to hit the road.'

'Before we go, I have an extremely important question,' Ivy says. Then she holds up two DVD cases. '*Chicken Run* or *Spider-Man: Into the Spider-Verse*?'

'*Spider-Man*,' everyone says in unison. Ivy slides the DVD into the player.

I don't feel like watching the movie. I put in my AirPods and start 'The one' by Kylie Minogue.

The door swooshes shut and the bus rumbles out of town onto the highway. We are finally on our way to camp. As the movie begins, I can already hear snoring somewhere behind me.

———

The two-hour journey passes quickly. We turn off the highway onto a dirt road. Out the window, the bush is thick and tall. I look up and can hardly see the sky behind the leaves and branches. The bus bumps and rocks.

'I feel like we're in a washing machine,' Elijah shouts behind me. Even though he's yelling, it's difficult to hear him over the rumbling road and the roaring engine.

I check my phone and there isn't any service. This is the way all horror movies start – a bunch of teenagers travel into the woods where they can't get a phone signal and then they all get butchered by some killer with super-human strength.

Out my window I spot a kangaroo, its ears perked, watching this roaring vehicle pass by.

The road becomes smoother as we begin to pass through clearings where other campers have set up tents.

'Fuck, that was fun,' Elijah shouts.

'Language,' Ivy shouts back.

There are grassy clearings everywhere now. A small building, like a one-bedroom unit, sits on its own. A man and a woman, both wearing national parks outfits, wave to us. We pass the sign:

Welcome to Camp Kamble.

———

As we make our way towards the shelter covering barbecues and picnic tables, Ivy hands us printouts of a map displaying our cabin assignments. All the boys are in Cabin B, and the girls are in Cabin C. Each cabin has six bunk beds. The adults are staying in Cabin A. Cabin A is on one side of a fire pit, and Cabins B and C are on the other side.

Everyone's got a friend they're talking to except for me and Dylan. We're both loners. I decide to go over and stand with him.

'Hey,' I say.

'Hey.'

'How's the movie stuff coming along?'

'Good. I need to start shooting again soon cause the deadline's in November,' Dylan says. 'You still keen?'

'Yeah, why not.'

After lunch, we follow a pathway through the bush towards the cabins. I can hear the rolling waves of a beach somewhere out there.

Kallum, Elijah and Corey enter the boys' cabin and the fight for top bunks begins.

'I swear to the Seven, if you don't give it to me...' Elijah says to Corey, who's sitting atop the bunk against a wide window looking out to the bush.

Billy has claimed the top bunk above Kallum and there's only one set left, so that's for me and Dylan.

'You want the top or bottom?' Dylan asks me.

'I'll take the top.'

I sling my backpack up there and climb the short ladder. The mattress isn't the thickest. I can feel the springs. The pillow is very fluffy, though. In fact, it's almost too fluffy. Why didn't Dad remind me to bring my pillow? Oh well.

'Over here, boys,' Elijah says, waving us all to his bunk. Me and Dylan are slow to get off our beds but we gather with everyone around Elijah. He's unzipping his duffel bag, and pulls out a rolled towel.

'I reckon we sneak down the beach for a nip tonight,' he says.

He unwraps the towel to reveal a full, unopened bottle of Wild Turkey.

The last time I drank alcohol, I got in a big fight with Mitch at Eric's party. Something bad always happens when there's drinking.

NINETEEN

After an afternoon of high ropes and bushwalking, then a barbecue dinner and showers, we are all gathered at the yarning circle between cabins.

The yarning circle is really a square and I don't think anyone has pointed that out to Glen or Ivy.

A couple of girls arrive from their cabin with Ivy. I pause the Kylie music playing in my ears – 'Say something' – and Glen starts playing the didgeridoo. He plays for five or six minutes without stopping as the campfire flickers on everyone's faces.

Dylan's sitting across the fire from me. He's got his elbow planted on his knee and his chin in his hand. I hear those words again – the words I heard that night at Joe's. Terry and his goons talk a lot of shit, but Terry's not a nice person. Maybe he actually would do something to Dylan. Maybe I should tell him, even if there's nothing to worry about – at least he'd have a heads-up.

When Glen finishes playing the didgeridoo, Ivy leans forward and her eyes drift over all of us.

'Well,' she begins, 'you're all done. Year Twelve has come to an end and this year we have the highest number of graduating Indigenous Year Twelve students the region has ever had. That's a fact you should all be extremely proud of.'

A bird begins singing somewhere in the black. The trees are blowing in a light breeze, their leaves jostling each other quietly.

'It's important that as you go out into the world,' Ivy says, 'you remember who you are and where you come from. You're all strong, resilient, Aboriginal people. You're all descended from warriors, from survivors. As you go into adulthood, you'll be going in as Aboriginal people.'

'Being Aboriginal isn't just a label,' Glen says. 'It's not just a *word*. Being Aboriginal is something deeper. It's a spiritual thing that connects us with each other, with this ground beneath our feet, with that bush singing behind you. You all have it in you, like Ivy said. It's in your blood. It'll run in your children's blood. Whatever you do in life, you'll only be as strong as your connection to your Ancestors. Connection to Culture is the way forward. It's the only way out of darkness. When you stray from the path, Culture will bring you back.'

Glen stands with Ivy. Ivy takes her bowl and she and Glen make their way around the circle, painting symbols on our faces.

Glen paints Kallum, Elijah and Corey. Dylan reluctantly raises his chin and closes his eyes as Glen's big fingers stroke his cheeks and forehead.

They arrive at me and Glen takes his thumb to the bowl. He brushes it along my forehead, then on my cheeks. I close my eyes. This is the most *Aboriginal* thing I think I've ever done. Culture has never been something I was desperate to learn. I've got a million other things to worry about, like Eric ruining my life and acting school and Dad's alcoholism, and being one of the only out gay kids in town. Oh, and my dead mother.

'Who do you want to be?' Glen asks, his eyes moving to each of us. 'Who do *you* want to be?'

He sits down and I feel like he wants us to answer.

'That's what I want you to think about during this camp,' he says. 'I want you to think about the person you want to be, the person who will make your people proud of you.'

What I want is to be happy. I want to be away from Carraway's Point and happy. I want to love someone who loves me back, who isn't ashamed of me and who wants only me. I want to be a good big brother to Lewis and Josie. I want them to know they can always come to me about anything. I want to be proud of who I am.

I make my way to the cabin at bedtime. Glen is still sitting at the fire pit with one of the camp workers.

The lights are off inside and I use my phone torch to guide myself. Elijah's watching laggy TikToks on his phone in a tank top and sweatpants. Corey's playing some game on his phone above him. I climb onto my top bunk and rest my head on my pillow. It's freezing in here, so I pull my hoodie over my head and wrap myself in my blanket.

After some time, Elijah gets up. The bed creaks like an unoiled tinman. He tiptoes in the darkness, across to the front door.

'They gone, boys,' Elijah says with a sharp whisper. 'Fire's out. Lights are on in their cabin.'

Corey lands on the floor with a thud. He pulls on his shoes as Elijah slips on his. He loads the towel-wrapped bottle into his backpack. Suddenly, we're all up except for Billy, who says he's going to sleep. We're moving about the darkness of the cabin in silence.

Kallum is testing his phone's torch, and Dylan is off his bunk, pulling on his hoodie. I never thought I'd be sneaking out and drinking with Dylan, especially not after all the trouble he's gotten into, yet here I am, at a camp to celebrate Aboriginal graduates, sneaking out in the middle of the night to drink.

TWENTY

Elijah leads us – me, Kallum, Corey and Dylan.

We tiptoe across the gathering area and into the bush, but my footsteps feel loud as thunder. We start down the trail, using our phone torches.

It's the dead of night, but the bush is alive. Chirps and clicks and rustling leaves surround us. It's full-on surround sound, like sitting in the middle of a cinema. It's cool, but not freezing like it was when I got out of the shower this morning.

Normally my brain would be taking me to the worst places, telling me all the bad things that could happen, but tonight it's quiet.

Dylan's also quiet beside me as we begin to fall behind the rest. He probably doesn't want to be here, like me.

'Lewis told me you're trying to get a scholarship,' I say to Dylan. 'To go to film school in Sydney?'

'Yeah,' he says. 'That's the hope.'

'I never knew you wanted to be a filmmaker,' I say.

'Well, we don't really hang out anymore.'

'True. I'm moving to Sydney too. Aunty Lisa is gonna put me up for a bit at her place. If you need somewhere to stay, I could ask her for you.'

'Yeah? That'd be good. Thanks. See if I get the film done and get the scholarship first.'

Back in primary school, me, Dylan, Kallum and Brandon used to walk to school together. At lunch, we owned the long bench beneath the big oak tree – that was our spot. We'd eat quickly and join in the game of footy on the oval every day, and we never got sick of each other. High school changes you, I guess. We went different ways.

'You know that copper's trial's coming up?' Dylan asks.

'Yeah,' I say, remembering the conversation I overheard on Ravenswood Road.

'Brandon's mum, Kathy, and a lawyer came over the other day. They asked me if I could give evidence in court about what happened that night.'

'Are you gonna do it?'

'I dunno. I'm told them I'd think about it, but they said they could get some *order* to make me do it if they thought it was needed.'

My heart beats faster and a heat rushes over my body. I have to tell him what I overheard.

'Hey, Dyl,' I say. 'I…I need to tell you something. I was out on Ravenswood Road a few weeks ago. I overheard some people talking about Brandon and…they said Terry was gonna *take care* of the witness. They don't want that copper convicted.'

'Oh.'

'So . . . I guess just be careful.'

The rolling waves grow louder, and they feel more ominous in the darkness, like mountains rumbling towards us.

Soon, the dirt beneath my feet turns to sand.

We climb down towards the beach and Elijah plants his arse with the dune at his back, like he's sitting on a lounge. I sit beside him with Kallum, Dylan and Corey.

Elijah flings his backpack off his shoulders. The end of the towel flaps out of the opening and he pulls out his big, full bottle. With Kallum's light shining on it, the liquid looks like tea.

Elijah unscrews the lid and chucks the protective plastic strip to the sand. He takes a swig, then passes the bottle to Kallum, who also takes a swig. He passes to me and I take a big sip. It tastes like petrol. It's on fire in my throat. As it travels to my stomach, I feel it warming every inch of body, from the belly out. Corey and Dylan take a sip each, much smaller than mine, then Elijah takes the bottle back.

'You reckon our ancestors were sitting right 'ere one time?' Elijah asks me. 'I reckon a couple of 'em were sittin' right 'ere. There were a bunch of 'em fishing in the water there, while the others sat 'ere and watched. Maybe they told stories to each other to pass the time.'

Elijah stands up suddenly. He's lit by moonlight as he takes off his shirt and pants until he's down to his underwear.

'What you doin'?' Kallum asks.

'Goin' for a dip,' Elijah says. He takes another big sip, then hands the bottle to Kallum. He asks Kallum if he's coming in.

'Not a fucking chance,' Kallum replies. Corey follows Elijah and as soon as he hits the water, he screams so loud, I can hear him from all the way up the beach.

Elijah and Corey disappear into the black water. They can only be spotted when they rise from the waves and their wet shoulders are caught in the persistent moonlight.

'It's fucking freezing!' Corey shouts. 'I love it!'

I didn't notice he'd got up and left, but Dylan is walking along the wet sand near the shore, slowly making his way up the beach.

Kallum takes a swig from the bottle of Wild Turkey. We've drunk almost half the bottle already. He plants it in the sand beside my feet. I'm keeping my shoes on because it's a cold night, but Kallum takes his off, stuffs his socks inside, digs his toes in the sand.

'You must be keen,' I say. 'Those footy trials are coming up soon, yeah?'

'Oh,' Kallum says. 'Yeah. I don't know if I'll go, hey.'

'Why not? You gonna try out the park ranger thing?'

'Yeah, maybe.'

He's different to the Kallum I remember from a couple of years ago, the one who was footy mad and started working out with *the boys*. This Kallum seems a bit quieter, more guarded. He used to be loud, confident, joking all the time. Now, it's like he's seen some shit that changed him, like a young guy who comes home from war.

'So, what's Sydney like?' I ask. 'I'm moving up there in a few months. Any advice?'

Kallum looks to me, rests his chin on his shoulder.

'It's loud,' he says. 'Bit chaotic. Always cars and people everywhere.'

'It's a big place, isn't it?'

'Yeah. One time we went to the Blue Mountains for an excursion,' he says. 'Seems like you can drive for nearly two hours and still be in Sydney. The buildings are massive, which was pretty cool to see.'

'Did you go to the Harbour Bridge? Opera House?'

'When I first moved there,' he says. 'It's pretty neat, but it's mostly for tourists, I reckon. The glam wears off.'

'The *glam*?'

'I dunno,' he giggles. 'What's new with you since I last lived here?'

I was a bit more comfortable hearing about the glam of Sydney. If I was an arsehole with no soul or conscience, I would tell Kallum about how my relationship with Eric started not long after he moved away, if I could call it a relationship.

'Well, I decided I want to be an actor,' I say, pushing my glasses back along the bridge of my nose. 'I got into an acting school in Sydney, so that's why I'll be moving there in January.'

'Really?'

'Yeah. I can't wait.'

I look out to the sea, the rolling waves of black and white. It appears endless, but I know there's an end — there's always an end to everything.

'So what actually happened in Sydney?' I ask. 'Did you get kicked out?'

'Yeah. Expelled.' Kallum sighs.

'Why?' I ask. 'If you want to tell me, anyway.'

Kallum brings his knees to his chest. He looks to the clouds for a moment then screws the lid off the bottle, steals another sip, and plants it back in the sand.

He rests his chin on his shoulder, kind of looking to me, kind of looking to the waves. 'Can I ask you something?'

I nod.

'Was coming out scary? I mean, is it *hard* being out? Everyone knowing? Seems kinda like a personal thing to me. Something that's no one else's business, you know?'

'Yeah, it's really no one's business.' I chuckle. 'Sometimes it's hard. Like, sometimes I'll be out somewhere and someone at a shop will look at me funny, and it makes me wonder if they're lookin' at me funny because I'm Aboriginal or because they can tell I'm gay. I don't really know if people can tell.'

'Nah,' Kallum says. 'It's not that obvious.'

He's completely avoided the question about why he got expelled.

'I kind of wish it was,' I say. 'I thought a gay person only had to come out once, but I've done it at least fifty times. Sometimes I'm glad everyone knows now, so I don't have to come out so much. Sometimes...I dunno...I feel kind of exposed.'

A big wave beats the shore in a violent crash and the impact sends spray all the way to us. It shocks me into a shiver, but Kallum stays still, like he wasn't startled.

'Does it feel different?' Kallum asks.

'Different?'

'Yeah, like…does it feel different, or worse…being able to be *yourself* now?'

'Umm,' I say, looking to the clouds covering the moon. 'I was very sad and angry with myself before. I was very scared of it. Now, I guess I'm just…cruising along. I mean I'm still angry about things, but *different* things. I don't have to pretend anymore, I guess.'

'Did you feel like there was this version of yourself… a version that wasn't really you?' Kallum says. He's asking a lot of questions, showing way more curiosity than the small-minded athlete I thought he was. 'Did you feel like you were *acting* all the time, even when no one else was around?'

'Yeah,' I say. He's hit the nail on the head, as Dad would say. 'That's exactly it. I was always hiding something, a part of myself, I guess. No one could ever really know the real me because I never let anyone see it.'

I look out to the water. The figures are black and even with my glasses on I can't tell who is who.

'Right,' Kallum says. He takes another swig from the bottle. I feel like he's trying to tell me something.

I look at him, focus on the side of his cheek that is caught in the moonlight. He's kind of dark, mysterious, pretty. He looks to me, a slight smile growing on his face. His eyebrow furrows and it would be hard to see in the darkness if I wasn't wholly concentrated on it. Maybe he'll kiss me. Maybe I'll kiss him first.

'Is that how *you* feel?' I ask. 'Like you're a version of yourself that isn't the real you?'

Kallum looks away, shows me the back of his head as he peers towards the other side of the beach. The clouds are rolling fast across the moon, like they're racing each other.

'It's why I got expelled,' Kallum says. 'I got catfished by some dickheads.'

'Catfished?' I ask.

'I thought I was meeting a boy,' Kallum says.

'Oh.'

I get it now. He's telling me something that's hard to say. I feel a warm, invisible orb growing around us, and we can tell each other anything while we're inside.

'I went into, like, proper survival mode,' Kallum says. 'I nearly killed him. So, they kicked me out...the *angry black kid*.'

'That's not who you are, though,' I say.

'You won't tell anyone, will you?' Kallum asks.

'Of course not.'

Kallum looks back at me and smiles. My phone starts to vibrate in my pocket. It's Dad calling. I tell Kallum I'll be right back. I start along the sand towards where Dylan's standing, staring out to sea.

'Hey, Dad,' I say, holding the phone to my ear. I shield the breeze from the mic.

'Son, I thought you were gonna call me tonight,' he says. 'I got worried.'

'Oh. Sorry. Yeah, reception's pretty shit here.'

'What are you up ta? Sounds like you're outside.'

'Yeah, just at the beach with a couple of the boys. Don't tell on us.'

Dad chuckles. 'I won't. Just be careful, yeah? Don't get in trouble.'

'I won't.'

I hear Dad take a sip.

'You having a beer?' I ask, and suddenly my chest feels heavy.

'Yeah, just having a couple.'

'I'm worried about you,' I say, and I can hardly believe I said it. Somehow, it's easier to talk to him over the phone about the important stuff.

'What you worried about me for?'

'It's just... you've been drinkin' a lot,' I say. 'You never used to, but now you drink nearly every night.'

'Well, yeah,' Dad says. 'I suppose I drink a bit. It's nothin' you need to worry about.'

'But I do. I feel like all the worrying is left to me,' I say, and my eyes are beginning to sting. 'I worry about Lewis, I worry about you, I worry about Josie. I just... I feel like everything is gonna fall apart at any moment. If I move to Sydney, I don't know what'll happen. It makes me not want to go cause I'm scared of what'll happen if I do.'

Dad sighs – it's a long sigh.

'I'm sorry, son. I know I haven't been the best dad since... since your mum.' Dad sniffles. 'Don't you worry about moving to Sydney. That's your thing. You get to go out and start your next chapter. And you're right. I know I drink a lot. I told myself I'd cut back eventually, but it starts now. And Lewis...your brother'll be right. I need to pay more attention to him, *and* you and Josie. I'll stand up again. Everything will be okay.'

I wipe my runny nose, brush away an escaping tear with my thumb and readjust my glasses on my nose.

'You promise?'

'Yes, son. I promise. Don't you worry about us. I know a lot has fallen on your shoulders these last couple of years, but you don't have to carry that anymore. You can go on and everything will be good. Trust me, son. It's *your* time, now.'

'Thanks, Dad.'

After I hang up, I start back for Kallum up the beach. He's sitting there beside the bottle planted in the sand. He smiles at me.

'You okay?' he asks. He must be able to tell I've been on the verge of tears.

'Yeah.'

In the silence, I can feel Kallum's eyes on me. 'I miss us hangin' out,' he says. 'Wish we still did. Wish we never stopped.'

I place my hand on Kallum's knee, gently, like it's a helicopter landing safely to ground. Kallum's knee is cold, but it begins to warm under my hand. I think for a moment that I've done the wrong thing, but then Kallum covers my hand with his, trembling. I never thought I'd feel Kallum's hand over mine. I never looked at him in that way. But right now, it feels like the beginning of something.

'I wanted to tell you,' Kallum says. 'I was sorry to hear about your mum.'

'Oh. Thanks,' I say.

'You're such a strong person, Jordy.'

'You too.'

Kallum squeezes my hand gently. 'I'm here if you ever want to talk about your mum, or anything.'

'Thanks,' I say. 'I don't...I'm not really ready yet. To talk about it, I mean.'

'That's okay.' Kallum smiles.

In my head, I'm playing 'Get outta my way' by Kylie Minogue, as Kallum gazes back out to the waves, where Elijah and Corey are swimming. They can't see that we're kind of holding hands. In this moment – this brief moment – it feels like everything's gonna be okay.

Love that for me.

DYLAN

TWENTY-ONE

It's a cold Thursday evening and I'm walking into town with Jarrod after we've done some filming at the river. Neither of us are talking about it, but in the paper this morning there was an article about the copper who killed Brandon a year and a half ago – something about how hard a police officer's job is. Miles Higgins's trial starts next week and I know we're both thinking about it. At least Jarrod doesn't have to give evidence in court like me.

As we step into the shopping centre car park, white spray-paint on the orange brick wall catches my eye. Two council workers in high-vis shirts are on ladders, scrubbing away the words: *WHITE POWER*.

I guess I expected something to happen, given the article today. I'm feeling the same unease I felt when they announced that the copper was being charged with Brandon's murder four months after it happened. I felt like there were people watching me walk around, people who wanted to hurt me. I knew that Higgins would have support in this town, that a lot of people thought him killing Brandon was justified, but I didn't imagine these two words would be spray-painted on the wall in front of my eyes.

Behind the ladders, a crowd of old white people and two Aboriginal men have gathered. The council workers scrub away as cars pull in and leave, and dozens of people stroll in and out of the supermarket, pushing trolleys and carrying groceries like white supremacy hasn't shown its face on the wall outside.

For most of this town, it's business as usual. And I'm standing here at the edge of the car park, pulling my black hoodie up because the voice in my head is telling me to hide. I'm Aboriginal, I'm black, just like my friend Jarrod beside me, who is also stopped in his tracks.

Jarrod leans forward with his phone, snapping a shot of *WHITE POWER* before the council workers can remove it all.

'Well, that's something you don't see every day,' Jarrod says. He posts the photo to his Instagram page with the caption: *Welcome to Carraway's Point.*

I unzip the camera bag looped around my shoulder. I take out my DSLR and aim it at the writing. I capture it, then stuff the camera back in the bag.

'Come on,' I say. We cross the car park, past the crowd gathered below the spray-painted words.

'I'm so ashamed,' a white woman in a blue jumper says.

'This is not what our town is about,' a white man in a brown business suit says.

'I'm honestly shocked,' the Aboriginal man says. 'Never thought I'd see this in my town.' He spots me passing the white woman and we lock eyes. I turn away quickly, hide my face behind my hood as me and Jarrod head for the ramp. I don't remember his name, but he's Jarrod's cousin. He works for the Carraway's Point Council in their Aboriginal education department or something. I don't know the details, but I know he's pretty close with the big white people in town, and that Dad calls him a *coconut*.

Jarrod's cousin says he never thought he'd see this in his town, but he knows who did it, just like me, just like Jarrod. It was those rednecks from the hills. They race each other along bush roads and hunt boars. They have hunting guns and muscles and blue jeans and cowboy boots. They get together on weekends and do stupid shit, like chase Koori kids in their cars and throw bricks at houses. When I was in Year Seven, they threw a half-drunk can of beer from their car window at me. It exploded on the footpath and sprayed beer all over my legs and school shoes. They shouted *white power* as they sped away.

'Dylan. Dylan?' Jarrod says.

'What?'

'Did you hear what I said?'

'No.'

'I said Brandon would lose his shit if he saw that on a wall.'

'Yeah,' I say. Brandon *would* lose his shit, because he would know those redneck boys wrote that because of him, because of the copper. Dad made me stop hanging out with Jarrod after what happened, but that only lasted a few months and then Jarrod was back around our house, letting himself into the fridge and pouring himself glasses of Coke like he was part of the family. And when Mum kicked Dad out six months ago, Dad couldn't tell me what to do anymore. He's been living at the caravan park up on the highway since the big fight.

I try not to think about Brandon too much, but Jarrod has put him in my mind. When I think of Brandon, I usually see his face as it was the last time I saw him – as I wish I'd never seen it. There was a spatter of red on his chin, mouth opened but no sound, his eyes blinking slowly as his brown cheeks turned pale.

I don't like to think about that face.

Heading into the shopping centre, it feels like all the white people are watching us, because they know *WHITE POWER* is written on the wall outside. When they see us, they see two Aboriginal boys with backpacks, hoodies over their heads – me with a camera bag, and Jarrod with his new bright white Nikes.

Jarrod gets his chocolate milk and we start for home.

It's a long walk back to our neighbourhood on the south side. Jarrod lives two blocks from me in a white weatherboard house, where his dad's late nineties Hyundai Excel is resting with long grass growing beneath it.

Wood smoke is in the air, drifting from chimneys across streetlights. It makes me think of Nan's house, when Mum and Dad would drop me there with my older sister, Bree, to watch the footy while they did other things, whatever they were. Smoke makes me think of sitting on

Nan's couch while she commentates the footy and my pop shouts about his bet that is about to fail.

Pop died years ago, and Nan's old now. Smoke makes me sad those days are over.

'When are you filming with Jordy again?' Jarrod asks when we stop out the front.

'Saturday. Hopefully I'll finish the editing before the deadline on Sunday. It'll be done before the trial starts.'

'True. Hope they roast him,' Jarrod says. 'I wish I was in the room too, so I could take the stand with ya. It'd be the two of us, then.'

'Yeah.' I wish he saw everything too, so I wouldn't be the only eyewitness to what happened. I wish it was him in that room instead of me.

Jarrod crosses from the street onto his lawn, examines his tin mailbox then starts towards his front door. 'Catch ya tomorrow.'

'Catch ya.'

I head for Chopin Drive. Our front yard is a paradise compared to Jarrod's. The lawn is mowed short and the garden beds are maintained with neat edges.

When I walk inside the smell of roasting pork hits me immediately. The lights are off in the living room, where Bree is sitting on the couch. She's still in her Coles shirt, and has her feet up next to her like a mermaid, her eyes fixed on the TV. I kick off my shoes next to Mum's steel-capped boots.

Mum is taking the pork out of the oven. She's still got her work pants on, blue overalls with the shoulder straps hanging down at her waist. Mum's the town's first female mechanic. She's also the best cook in the world. Literally.

'Hey, Dyl,' Mum says. 'How'd the filming go with Jarrod?'

'Good. Just got one scene left to film with Jordy on the weekend,' I say.

When dinner's dished up, Mum and Bree sit at the table while I land on the couch. The news is on. Some old white woman is telling us about a hurricane in Queensland, while we all eat quietly. It never used to be this quiet. Dinner times used to be loud and there would be arguments and laughter and conversation. Ever since Dad moved out, it's like we're just people who live together.

'Some dickhead spray-painted *white power* at the supermarket,' I say.

'I saw it on Facebook,' Mum replies. 'Remember when they tried to get us to go to that Australia Day thing last year? Maybe now they can see why we said no. This town has always been racist, but they want to pretend it's not.'

'It's easier that way,' Bree says. 'To pretend they don't see it.'

'They can't pretend they didn't see that writing. It's all over the community page.'

'You know *why* they're writing that shit now, though,' Bree says, lowering her voice like she doesn't want me to hear.

'Yeah, cause the trial's on next week,' Mum whispers. They're the worst whisperers on earth but they stop talking after that.

After dinner, I wash the dishes while Bree dries them. Mum steps out to the backyard for a cigarette, like she and Dad used to after dinner. I watch her from the kitchen window, off to the side under the back light. She looks lonely. I wonder if she misses Dad. I don't think they've talked for a few weeks.

'How you feelin'?' Bree asks.

'What?'

'The paper today...' Bree says. 'The trial next week...'

'It's fine.'

'So...are you okay?'

'Yeah.'

I pour myself a glass of water and leave the kitchen.

'I'm here if you wanna talk about it or anything,' Bree calls after me.

'I know.'

In my room, I close the door and fall onto my bed. My phone is vibrating in my pocket. Dad's calling.

'Hello?' I answer.

'Hey, son, how's it going?' Dad asks.

'Good,' I say. If I said I was terrible, I wonder how he'd react.

'I wanted to see if you could come round to Nan's tomorrow? Help me fix up the house a bit.'

Nan's getting older every day, and Dad helps her out every now and then. I've usually been able to get out of it, using Year Twelve as an excuse, with all the important assignments and study to do, plus a film to make, but my lucky streak has run out.

'Yeah, all right,' I say.

'Good,' Dad says. 'How's Bree and ya mum going?'

'They're fine,' I say, as I plug my camera into my laptop. I want the call to end so I can get to my film again. It makes me feel like shit, a little bit. I don't see Dad much these days. The past couple of months, he's been scarce. Last time I saw him, he was clean-shaven, saying he was gonna convince Mum to take him back.

'Glad to hear,' Dad says. 'I'll pick you up in the arvo.'

'Sounds good.'

After he hangs up, I load the last video we filmed. It buffers slowly, but I like it: the lens brushing through the trees to simulate Jarrod's character's point of view.

It's dreamy, scattered, just like the nightmares that come every now and then. I haven't had one for a while, but they're always dark and disjointed, and Brandon's always there. I'd see him being chased through a deserted Carraway's Point by this *thing* that looked like a shadow with a crown on the top of its head. I hate those nightmares. They make me feel awful, and the awfulness lasts the whole day, like I've been struck by lightning.

After I get in bed, I hear scratching at my window screen. The light is off and there's nothing but blackness behind my curtain. The scratching comes again so I sit up. I pull the curtain away and see Simba, Brandon's cat. He's mostly white, with an orange strip along his back and over his head and tail. He's loitering on my windowsill. I watch him trot to the end then jump off. I want to open the window and let him in, but he's already gone. I hadn't seen him since the last time I went to Brandon's house.

TWENTY-TWO

It's just after one o'clock on Friday and I'm waiting for Dad to come and pick me up. It's a sunny day but clouds are starting to blow in. Chopin Drive is quiet. Usually there are some kids playing in the street, like me, Jordy, Kallum and Brandon used to, or a pair of neighbours chatting on their front lawns, but it looks like everyone's inside at the moment.

I'm thinking about the district courthouse, which is in Gerring, thirty minutes up the highway. Gerring is a small city, and Carraway's Point and Koolum and Belrose are like its outer suburbs. It's where everyone goes to do their Christmas shopping at the big shopping centre. I haven't been there in a while, and I hate it cause there's always too many people and too many cars.

I don't like to think about this.

I think about my film instead. It's almost done. It's a story about an Aboriginal boy who is haunted by the memories of the night his friend was killed by police.

Jarrod plays the Darkness Monster chasing Jordy's Lost Boy.

Jordy is also playing The Boy waiting in his bedroom to find out if his friend's killer is found guilty of murder, but when he's that character, he's wearing a blue cap. I begin to worry that it might be too obvious that Jordy is both characters, or worse, it might be a little too real. But it is political. It's topical. It'll get attention. And if I can pull it off, it'll go to film festivals.

The story is contained, tense. I found some great sound effects and music to build the tension. It'll be amazing when it's finished. I'm sure of it.

Soon enough, I hear Dad's faulty muffler. He pulls up in his Hilux and I get off my seat on the front steps.

Dad turns down the radio and asks me how I'm going. I swear he never used to ask me how I'm going. Maybe now that he doesn't see me much, he actually cares to know.

'Good,' I say, just like I said on the phone last night. He flicks down his sunglasses and the greys in his five o'clock shadow look white under the sunlight beaming through the windscreen.

We head towards town. Dad's lawnmower is in the back, and the inside of the car smells like mowed grass and sweat and cigarette smoke. His seat covers are tattered and there are empty Coke cans everywhere. I make a remark to Dad about how he always tells me and Bree to clean our rooms, but he clicks his tongue and says, 'Respect your elders, son.'

On the floor of the passenger seat, there are random pieces of paper ripped from a notebook, each with scribbles and sentences written in blue and black pen.

Dad's a writer – at least that's what he tells everyone. He wrote a book before I was born, when it was just him, Mum and Bree living in a two-bedroom unit on the other side of town. His book sold pretty well and he won some big award for it. Ever since then, he's been *working on* his second book, but he's also had another kid, changed jobs, and finally settled as a horticulturalist for the council.

I pick up one of the papers and read: *Clarence is the killer. He moved the body in a golf cart from the course to the beach. The tracks don't match Daisey's car because they belong to the golf car.*

'Don't mind that,' Dad says. 'Old ideas. The manuscript's evolved since then.'

'So, it's coming along?'

'Yep,' Dad says. 'Four thousand words deep.'

It's been a good eighteen years since his first book, so I don't know if he'll ever finish his second.

We stop at a traffic light. On the other side of the intersection, revving its engine, is a dark green ute: Terry and the rednecks.

Terry's driving. His sunburnt face turns to our car as he sees me in the window. A wild smile grows across his face – the kind of smile that says *I could kill you and eat your heart.*

As we cross the intersection, Terry's arm slings out of the window and he raises his middle finger at us – at me. In the back seat, his friend is yelling something.

I can't make out the words, but I don't need to hear them because I still remember what Terry said when I came back to school after Brandon's murder.

He was picking up Trent, wearing a dirty denim jacket. As he passed me, he said, 'Your boy probably got what he deserved.'

I swear I changed in that instant, like a Transformer. I turned into a rocket.

I launched at his body. My forearm was raised like a shield.

Terry lost his balance and fell back. His mates rushed onto me like flies on shit and I was so hot with anger, I didn't even feel what they were doing to me.

Terry's car and his redneck friends speed away.

'The fuck was his problem?' Dad asks.

'Dunno,' I say. I think it's better not to tell him about Terry, about his brother Trent and how he once said to me and Jordy that Aboriginal people should be grateful white people came to this country, or how Jordy told me he heard Terry was going to silence the witness in Brandon's murder trial.

I've been on edge walking around town since then. Whenever a ute comes by, my heart begins to thud like a drum and my hands get sweaty because I think it might be Terry. I don't know what he's capable of. Maybe it was nothing but hot air when he told whoever it was that he was going to *take care of* me. But maybe not.

The neighbourhoods on the west side are different from the rest of town. The lawns are unmaintained and the houses are old, except for the odd one here and there that looks like new. The streets and driveways are stacked with old cars – bombs, Mum and Dad call them. There's a bare park in the middle of the housing estate, where a swing set and slippery dip remain unused over tanbark. There's an old community centre with its windows boarded up and its walls vandalised with holes and writing – people's names and *FTP*. The houses sit behind wire fences.

There are a couple of kids riding bicycles along the road, wearing caps instead of helmets. There are a few people sitting on the concrete slabs between their front doors and their lawns, smoking cigarettes and yarning.

Nan's is the red-brick house with a garden full of dead flowers. The windows are dark and the white wooden front door is dirty and looking more brown these days.

Dad parks in the driveway. Nan's little Toyota Corolla from twenty years ago is sitting there, its tyres all flat and red paint stripped with sun damage. There are cobwebs on the side mirrors. Nan had her driver's licence taken from her nearly two years ago because her eyesight got too bad and her car hasn't moved a centimetre since.

The sunny day has disappeared and storm clouds are rolling in, big and dark. As we approach the house, I can hear the footy playing on TV. It's loud because Nan's hearing ain't what it used to be.

Dad taps the screen door three times before he screeches it open.

'Who's that?' Nan's voice calls from inside.

'It's Dylan and Dylan junior,' Dad says.

'I'm no *junior*,' I whisper.

Dad giggles. 'Well, I'm no senior.'

I follow Dad inside. The smell of old cigarette smoke lingers in the air and on the walls, like it's become a part of the paint. Nan quit the ciggies a few months ago, which is evident by the patch on her arm as she waddles around the corner of the kitchen. There's a steaming cup of tea on the bench.

Nan's a small woman. We used to see her all the time, have sleepovers at her house, come to watch the footy because she had Foxtel, go for drives to the beach. She was this bubbly, fierce, round Aboriginal woman, but a few years ago she got lung cancer. She's changed so much. She's lost a lot of weight. Her eyes are tired now. The skin on her face droops like it's hanging from her cheekbones by a thread. Her cancer was declared in remission the day before Christmas last year, but it's taken its toll. When she walks, her steps are small, with her head always ahead of the rest of her body.

'Hello, Mum,' Dad says. Nan's eyes are wide and red.

'Oh,' she says. 'Big Dyl and little Dyl. I just made myself a cup of tea. Youse want one?'

'None for me,' Dad says.

'I'm good,' I say. Nan smiles and takes a few short, straight steps towards me.

'Give me a kiss, son,' she says. I lean down and give her a kiss on the cheek. She hugs me. She's smaller than she was two years ago. Her hair never fell out but she doesn't dye it anymore – now she has flowing grey curls.

Dad opens the fridge and examines it as Nan walks back to her cup of tea. She takes the cup slowly back to her lounge, where she puts it down and then falls into her seat. An old footy replay is on. She reaches for the remote. Her fingers are trembling as she turns the volume down.

'How's the Meals on Wheels been?' Dad asks.

'The what?'

'Meals on Wheels,' Dad repeats, louder.

'Oh, that shit. I only eat it because I'll die if I don't.' Nan turns to me. 'What's been going on in your life, Dyl? Come over here so I can see you.'

I walk to the side of the couch and stop at the edge of the mat, where a small glass coffee table sits with her cup of tea on top.

'Not much,' I say. 'Finished my HSC exams. I'm making a short film to try to get a scholarship to go to film school in Sydney.'

'What was that?' Nan asks.

'I'm making a short film,' I say, louder this time.

'Oh. Still makin' movies, ay?'

'Yeah.'

'Have you got yourself a girlfriend yet?'

'Nah,' I answer. 'I'm a lone wolf.' *Just like how I'll be all alone on that stand in court*, I think to myself.

Nan smiles.

'We don't want any grannies just yet,' Dad interrupts, scribbling onto a piece of paper with a pen from Nan's bench.

'Your time will come,' Nan says to me. 'Don't get tied down with girls right now. You've got your whole life ahead of you.'

Dad mows the lawn while I help take out all Nan's rubbish and make a start on weeding the garden. All the while, Nan sits inside watching us from the window. I wave to her and she waves back. She's fragile now. I never thought of her as fragile before.

Before we leave, I cook a big pot of chicken soup. I dish a bowl up for Nan and place the pot in the fridge, which is near empty.

'Thanks, son,' she says to me.

'Don't worry about it.' It feels like a weird thing to say. Nan blows gently on the soup.

When we're all done, Dad loads the lawnmower into the back of the car and we reverse out of the driveway. Nan waves to us from the front door.

An aching sadness comes over me. It's hard to see her as an old woman.

The shopping centre car park is pretty empty when we arrive, considering it's three o'clock on a Friday afternoon. Dad parks close to the entrance, facing the wall where *WHITE POWER* was written and some smudges of paint remain. A raindrop falls onto the windscreen, then another.

Dad sends me in with some cash to get some groceries for Mum. I think he's still trying to win her back.

I manage to get from the car to the entrance of the supermarket without getting wet. I grab a trolley and study the list Dad handed me.

When I have everything, I decide to go for the human-manned checkout rather than self-serve, because I can't be fucked bagging all this shit myself.

As I join the queue behind an older woman and her

young daughter in a soccer jersey, I see an Aboriginal woman. It's Kathy, Brandon's mum, walking towards me with an orange basket half-filled with groceries. There's a younger girl walking with her, carrying a pack of laundry detergent.

Kathy looks tired, her hair unbrushed, but her eyes spark to life when she sees me.

'Little Dyl,' she says. My heart is racing and I'm not sure why. I haven't really spoken to her since Brandon's funeral. 'This is my niece, Alira.'

'Hi,' I say.

'Hey,' she says back.

Kathy places her basket on the ground and wraps her arms around me. The hug is tight, and she smells like flowers and cigarettes. She's a small woman. Her head rests on my chest as she holds me for a few seconds longer than feels comfortable.

'How are you?' I ask.

'Oh, I'm all right, son,' she says. Her voice is croaky. 'Got all the mob up at the house to talk about the trial.'

'Yeah? I seen some cars out front.'

'Cousin Betty got some shirts printed,' she says. 'When we go to that courthouse, we'll be wearing Brandon's face. That's how we make sure those whitefullas remember he was a person, ya know.'

'Sounds like a good idea,' I say.

'How you feelin' about taking the stand?' Kathy asks.

'Bit nervous,' I say.

'You just tell the truth. That's all that matters. You're

a good young man, just like my boy…all you boys from Choppin Drive.'

Kathy's the only one I've ever heard pronounce the name of our street *Choppin Drive*.

She picks up her basket and moves along with the young girl. I feel the bottoms of my shoes catch fire. There's a force in my chest telling me to run – to abandon the trolley, get back to Dad's car and make him drive as far away as we can on whatever amount of petrol is in the tank.

It's the anxiety – the trial starts next week. The anxiety makes that night flash in my brain.

The music.

The laughter.

Brandon belting out 'Livin' on a prayer', lying on the kitchen floor.

The knock at the door.

The blue uniforms.

The shouting.

The gunshots.

TWENTY-THREE

Dad drops me back at home and the rain clouds seem to have moved on. I get out with all the groceries he bought for us.

'You kids coming to visit for my birthday on Sunday?' Dad asks.

'Yeah,' I say. 'I think Bree's got you a present from us.'

'Good. See if your mum'll come.'

'I'll try.'

I spend the rest of the day helping Mum wash clothes, then waiting for her famous spaghetti meatballs. Her secret ingredient is a few sprinkles of Keen's Curry in the mince.

Mum and Bree steal the couch and TV to watch some reality show. Jarrod's usual Friday-night text arrives just after eight o'clock. He's asking if I want to do something. Sometimes *something* is drinking in his shed watching the footy. Sometimes it's going out to someone's house for more drinking. Sometimes it's going for a Maccas run on foot.

I go to my room and get changed into my black jeans. I take my grey hoodie to carry because it's a bit warm outside tonight.

'Where you off to, Dyl?' Mum asks as I slip on my shoes at the front door.

'Just going to see Jarrod.'

'I want you home by twelve.'

'Okay.'

It's still a little light out. I pass Brandon's house and see Simba sitting in the front window. He's loafing, with his paws beneath his front, staring at me. I notice the two cars parked in the driveway. Kathy is at the boot of the rear car, loading big sheets of cardboard into it with the younger girl, Alira, I saw her with earlier. I can't make out the writing on the cardboard but I can see photos of Brandon's face – his Year Nine school photo. It's the only one he actually smiled for, teeth and all.

Kathy glances over her shoulder to see me leaving Chopin Drive. I wave and she waves back, then returns to her packing.

I walk around the corner to Jarrod's house.

There's music playing inside and I hear footsteps rushing to the front door. Jarrod's dad, Kenny, opens up.

'Dylan,' he says. 'Jarrod's out the back with your other mate.'

'Thanks,' I say. I head inside, dodging toys scattered all over the floor. Kenny starts cleaning up as I pass through. Jarrod's mum is spoon-feeding his younger sister in a highchair, the radio's playing in the kitchen and there's a footy replay on TV on mute.

I walk through the back door and follow the extension cords attached to other extension cords leading to the shed.

Inside the shed smells like a mixture of weed and stale alcohol, and the concrete is sticky beneath my shoes. Jarrod's lying on the couch, playing Xbox with Lewis, Jordy's little brother.

'Oi,' I say. They both turn to me. Jarrod flings his feet off the couch to make space for me. I sit down, gaze over the coffee table, which is home to a half-drunk bottle of Corona, a glass bong and a small bowl of chopped weed.

'Thought you stopped smoking?' I ask.

'It's Dad's,' Jarrod says. 'I been stressed lately.'

'Stressed?' I giggle.

'You want some?'

'Nah.'

They're playing a basketball game. Lewis's player shoots for a three-pointer and lands it.

'We was just boutta head to Rory's,' Jarrod says, pausing the game. Rory's the local dealer who thinks he's cool because he hangs out with teenagers and buys us grog when we ask. Ever since Brandon died, I've been trying to stay away from him – it was his house we were at that night. Jarrod still likes him for some reason. He gets up and grabs another Corona from the mini fridge and hands it to me.

I don't really like the taste of beer. I always thought it would be this amazing thing because Mum and Dad drank it most nights, that it would be better than Coca Cola.

It's not good at all but I take a sip anyway. Me, Jarrod and Brandon used to drink a lot – mostly Jim Beam or Jack Daniels. I was fourteen when the three of us were in this shed with our first longnecks of VB – which Rory bought for us for a ten-dollar tip. We were having a sleepover, playing Xbox and eating Doritos. We waited until midnight, when we thought Jarrod's parents were asleep, then we opened the longneck and took turns taking sips. It was warm and tasted like poison, but after I got through the disgust, it made me feel like I could do anything. It made me want to tell Jarrod and Brandon how much I loved them, how they were perfect friends for me, and it made me want to drink more.

But ever since what happened with Brandon last year, drinking doesn't appeal to me anymore. It's not fun without him. It feels kind of sad.

I plant my beer on the table after a big sip. Jarrod pulls on his shoes and his Nike snapback.

'You want to come to Rory's?' he asks, switching off the Xbox and TV.

'Nah, I'm pretty tired,' I say.

'You not finishing that Corona?' Lewis asks.

'Nah.'

Lewis picks it up and takes it with him as we leave. Part of me wants to go with them to Rory's, to make sure they get home okay, but I don't know how late the night would end.

We walk to the end of the street. It's dark out now and dogs are barking in backyards nearby.

'What you gonna say in court?' Jarrod asks me.

'I don't know,' I say. 'The truth, I guess.'

'I wish *I* got summoned. I'd tell the judge I saw him do it all.'

'But you didn't,' I say. 'It was just me in that room, except the cop. They got bodycam.'

'True,' he says. 'Doesn't matter what we say though.'

'What you mean?'

'Cops get away with everything. This won't be no different. Thought he was reaching for a weapon. Bullshit.'

Jarrod has a point. Maybe it doesn't matter what anyone says on the stand. Maybe it's all just a waste of time. That copper will walk free, Brandon's mum will be heartbroken, and we'll go back to our shitty lives in this shitty town where people spray-paint *WHITE POWER* on the walls of the supermarket.

Or maybe they'll lock him up and he'll be the first copper jailed in this country for an Aboriginal death in custody.

Jarrod and Lewis are going one way and I'm going the other. 'Take it easy, you two,' I say.

'Have a good sleep, Dyl,' Jarrod says.

Back home, Bree is still on the couch watching a movie – *Sweeney Todd: The Demon Barber of Fleet Street*. In the hallway, I can hear Mum's voice through her bedroom door. She's on the phone and her pitch is going to extremes, followed by chuckles, so I know she's having a good gossip about something.

In my bedroom, I crawl under my blankets, but before I can fall asleep, I hear a rustle in the bushes outside. I can't see anything through my curtain.

Then there's a scratching on my windowsill. I sit up and pull the curtain away. It's Simba again.

'Simba, what you doin'?' I ask, as if he's going to respond. I unlatch the window, then slide it up. The cool air rushes inside my bedroom. Simba turns towards me. I hold out my hand, stretching my thumb towards his face. He sniffs my thumb, then meows. It's a quiet meow, almost a whisper.

'You okay, Simba?'

Simba meows again. I push my window open a little further, so he has more room.

'Do you want to come in?'

Simba peers into my room.

'You can come in if you want.'

Simba meows again, then turns away from me. He walks back to the edge of the windowsill, staring at the dark and narrow path along the side of my house.

'You good, Simba?'

Simba makes a moaning sound. It's not a meow, not a cry. It's the kind of sound that tells me he's thinking about something, the way humans go *hmm*.

Then he jumps from the windowsill and disappears into the dark.

It's strange. As I close my window and lie back in bed, it almost feels like Brandon's been here.

TWENTY-FOUR

It's Saturday night, just after eleven o'clock, when we arrive at the funeral home to film the final scene of my short film. Jordy's been rambling with worry since we left Chopin Drive.

'What if there are cameras or alarms?' Jordy asks.

'I told you,' I say. 'I scoped it out already. It's fine.'

'I hope so, or I'll kill you myself.'

I know what Jordy thinks of me – what most people think when they see me and Jarrod walking around town. They think we're wannabe gangsters, out of control, delinquents. They think we're always up to no good. Maybe that was me for a while, but things changed after Brandon died.

Even though we are about to break into a funeral home in the middle of the night, I think I've changed Jordy's mind about me. I think he knows now that I'm still the same me he used to be friends with.

Jordy follows me along the driveway, which dips down to a locked garage door and a carport with a hearse in it. The light turns on above the front door as we walk past. Jordy gasps, but I know it's just the motion sensor.

'This is a bad idea,' Jordy whispers behind me as we walk through the backyard area of the funeral home.

'Relax,' I say. Jordy takes a breath as we step onto the back patio. We pass a big coffee tin filled with cigarette butts and stop at the back door. I begin to shimmy the window to the side of the back door, and it slides open.

'I can't believe I'm doing this,' Jordy whispers.

'It's okay,' I whisper back. 'I'll take the blame if we get caught.'

The window space is no bigger than an A3 piece of paper, but I weave my body inside. The window rattles as my legs pass through and I land on my shoulder when I hit the tile floor. Inside is all dark, except for moonlight shining in the open window. I unlock the door and let Jordy in.

'It's freezing,' Jordy says, folding his arms.

'I suppose it's the ghosts of all the dead people who've come through here.'

'Fuck off.'

I lead him through the small room and into a hallway. There's an office at the far end, but we walk towards the reception area, where couches and an empty desk sit in darkness, then another room with a kitchenette. Jordy follows me down a set of stairs beside an elevator door.

I use my phone to light the way. The stairs seem longer than I remember.

At the bottom, I open a door into a corridor that looks like a hospital. The smell of sanitiser lingers in the air.

We turn into a big white room where the cold hits me harder. I pull my hood over my ears.

'This is like the fridge?' Jordy asks. 'Where they keep the bodies?'

'Looks like it,' I say. 'Do you wanna see one?'

'Fuck no.'

'As if I'd do that,' I chuckle. Brandon's was the last dead body I ever want to see.

I flick the switch and white light fills the room. There are tables in the centre and benches with tools and hoses and jars on them. The place has been cleaned recently and I can smell the disinfectant.

'So, where do you want me?' Jordy asks.

'Well, this is the end of the nightmare sequence. I want a shot of you standing by the bench, and a shot of you lying on the table, and then one of you crouched in the corner. So, I guess we'll start with you standing?'

'Okay.'

I walk with Jordy and place him beside the bench. I pull out my camera and take a few steps back. I frame the shot and tell him to look at the bench, then around the room, but to keep his feet planted.

'Look scared, but not too scared,' I say.

'Oh, okay, sure,' Jordy says, unfolding his arms. 'What should I do with my hands?'

'Just keep them by your side.'

I start recording. It's a wide shot of Jordy, standing a little off-centre in the frame. His lips tremble and his eyes widen as he looks around the room. I record for two minutes then stop.

Next, I get him to lie on the table, which is a silver slab that they must put dead bodies on. I imagine it is Brandon on the table instead of Jordy. The image flashes in my mind – a body on a silver slab. This is where his body would have been after he died. He would have been in this room, laid out on this slab while his body was prepared for the funeral. I see his face where Jordy's is – the face he wore after those shots rang out and he lay on the floor. I feel heat in my chest. It burns through my body like wildfire and finds my hands. The camera shakes in my grasp.

'This is ice-cold,' Jordy says.

The flash of Brandon goes away, and it's Jordy on the table again. I feel the fire simmer down and I'm back in the room. I feel the ground beneath my feet, stretch my toes against the wall of my shoes. 'It's okay,' I say. 'Just hold still.'

I frame him side-on and hit record.

'Wait, am I still scared?' Jordy asks.

'Yes, but be still.'

Jordy settles back and I move in closer with the camera, slow steps along the hard grey floor. I bring the camera to the side of his face. There's a tear trickling from the corner of his eyelid. I bring the lens to the tear and track it slipping down towards his ear, until my body casts a shadow over him.

Next, I order him to the corner of the room, beneath the drawers where bodies are stored.

'This feels so creepy,' Jordy says.

'It's fine. So, for this one, I'm gonna start with a wide shot again, then come in for another close-up. Keep those tears coming. Remember, scared but not hysterical.'

'Scared but not hysterical? Mmkay.'

Jordy holds his knees and tries to get himself crying again. I frame up the wide shot and hit record. I record for forty seconds then move into the close-up. I stop in front of Jordy and crouch, capturing just his face and shoulders. I keep filming as his tears begin to fall. I move in slowly, focus on his eyes.

'Look around the room a bit,' I whisper. Jordy's eyes dart around. In the frame, I can see both his eyes and the bridge of his nose, and the beginning of his hairline. It looks good – cinematic. A calm comes over me. It's okay that I'm in here, it's okay that Brandon's been in here too. This film is for him, and I'm telling the story he won't get to tell.

I've been recording for two minutes when I hit stop.

Jordy gets up and wipes the tears from his eyes.

'You happy with it?' he asks.

'Yeah, it's great.'

'Cool. So can we get out of this icebox now?'

I pack up my camera and lead Jordy out of the cold room. We climb the stairs and I lock the door when we leave the funeral home. The sensor light comes on again as we rush back up the driveway.

Jordy's puffing when we get back to the road. He shakes his head and looks at me with narrowed eyes.

'You're crazy,' he says. 'You know that, right?'

'It'll be worth it,' I say.

We turn onto Barker Street, towards the south side of town where we live. Jordy kicks a rock along the road and the rattle when it hits the gutter is the only sound I hear, apart from our footsteps. Carraway's Point is notoriously quiet at night, unless you're on the main street where the pubs are.

'When do you finish at the cinema?' I ask Jordy.

'Christmas Eve,' he says. 'I know it's a *job*, but I think I'm really gonna miss working there.'

'Maybe you can get a job at a cinema in Sydney.'

'Yeah, maybe.'

There's the rumble of a car engine somewhere nearby.

'So,' I begin. 'How was your date the other night? Didn't think there were many gay guys round here.'

'You'd be surprised,' Jordy said. 'Where there are people, there are gays.'

'Right.' I giggle.

'The date was good. It was our one-month anniversary.'

'Did you do anything special?'

'Nothing extravagant,' Jordy says. 'Just ice-cream in bed and *Big Bang Theory*.'

'Nice. So, you gonna tell me who he is, or what?'

It's dark but I can tell Jordy's blushing.

'Nooooo. He's not out yet, and I'm moving away. We're not sure if it's gonna last, but I dunno. It's exciting, for now.'

'Fair enough.'

'What about you?' Jordy asks. 'Any girls or guys in your life?'

'Me? Nah.'

'No one?'

'No one. I don't think relationships are for me, right now.'

Headlights turn onto the street. They shine at our backs, casting our shadows long in front of us. As the car grows closer, the rumbling engine roars louder.

The brakes squeal as the car pulls up beside us. I turn to see a dark ute. The doors swing open and three men get out. It takes me less than a second to realise who it is: Terry and Trent Harlen, and their redneck friend Gus. Terry's got a dark beard.

'Oh, fuck,' Jordy says.

'Knew we'd catch ya roamin' round late at some point, Dylan,' Terry says.

They surround us, closing in.

'We wanna show ya somethin',' Terry says. 'Come with us for a drive.'

'Fuck off,' I say. Terry stands close to me. When I raise my arm to push him back, Trent grabs it. Suddenly, Terry's got me as well and is shoving me in the back of the car.

'You can come too, gay-boy,' I hear Gus say. I'm shifted to the far seat when they jostle Jordy in beside me, with Gus coming next. I try to open my door but it's locked. I try to buzz down the window but it's not budging as Terry accelerates away with us.

TWENTY-FIVE

Blackness surrounds the car as we speed onto the highway. Terry's got the music up at full blast, playing some country-rock song. Jordy's shouting for them to stop and let us out, but Gus pulls a switchblade from his pocket and holds it to Jordy's throat.

'Shut your fuckin' mouth,' Gus orders. Jordy stays quiet after that.

I feel like I'm in a horror movie. I've been kidnapped. Jordy warned me that Terry would *take care of* the witness and that's what's happening right now. I tell myself that as soon as I'm out of the car, I have to run, but I can't leave Jordy behind. And we can't plan an escape because Gus's got a knife on Jordy.

There's nothing I can do but sit and wait as we drive further out of town. Outside, all I see are wire fences, the black bodies of cattle and other animals watching us blaze past.

We turn onto a dirt road, towards Brown Mountain. The tyres flick rocks into the sides of the ute. It's dark and remote. No one will see what they do to us. No one will hear us if we scream. I have the same feeling in my chest as I did the night Brandon died. It's a pressure that burns and makes it hard to breathe.

After what feels like an hour, Terry slows down and turns onto another road. It's bumpy but his engine roars as he drives up a hill. Trees close in around us. We're out in the bush somewhere – probably the far end of Carraway's National Park. Me and Jordy can't run away out here. We'd get lost. We'd freeze or starve to death.

Terry slams his brakes and takes another sharp turn. He avoids a boulder in the middle of the track and I swear the car is gonna roll over. The road is so narrow, if a car was coming the other way, there wouldn't be enough room.

Terry turns down the music and leans forward. He slows and pulls onto a grassy shoulder, turns off his engine.

Terry's out of the car, then my door swings open and he pulls me out. He keeps his arm around my shoulder as the others pull Jordy out, then he walks me to the other side. He grips my shirt as he presses a blade to the side of my neck. There's no way I can get away.

Trent has a smile on his face and his eyes are beaming with excitement. He flicks on a big camping torch and leads us down a dirt path into the bush.

Terry forces me forward and Jordy and Gus follow.

'You're not gonna make me use this, are you, Dyl?' Terry asks, pressing the blade harder into my skin. He's about to cut me.

'No,' I say. 'Just let us go.'

'We will, if you play nice,' Terry says, and he sounds a little like Steve Irwin. 'You must be havin' a hard time remembering what happened that night, hey?'

'What?'

'That night your dumb mate died,' Terry says. 'I know you were there. When you see things like that, it becomes this thing called *trauma*. Trauma makes you forget things the way they were, sometimes it makes you remember different. You must be havin' a hard time remembering exactly what happened.'

'No,' I say.

We arrive at some bushes and then Trent leads us through them, off the path. I can't see shit, apart from where Trent's shining the torch. The ground is littered with fallen leaves and rocks and I'm pretty sure I'm walking through spiderwebs.

Trent has stopped and shines his torch downwards. Terry eases the blade off my neck and I try to shrug away when I see what the light's shining on: a hole in the ground with a shovel beside it.

'Fuck off,' I say. Terry grabs my shirt and wrestles me down, then Trent's on me as well. My cheek stings on the rocky dirt. I'm trying to get him off, struggling as much as I can with his weight on me.

'Cut it out!' Terry yells. 'Stop fightin', ya stupid motherfucker!'

Jordy is shouting for him to let me go. I worry they'll kill Jordy too, or make him watch me die, so he'll be haunted by me forever like I am with Brandon.

They drag me to the edge of the hole and their weight pins me to the ground.

'Please! Please! Please!'

'Shut up!' Terry yells again. 'You won't be goin' in there *tonight*.'

I calm down, though tears are burning my eyes.

'Like I said,' Terry shouts. 'You won't be goin' in there tonight. But you will be if you say anything on Wednesday that sends our mate to jail. You understand?'

'What?' I ask, wondering if they'd really kill for their *mate*.

'You prolly don't remember everything as it happened,' Terry says. He forces the weight of his knee harder into my back. It feels like a sledgehammer breaking through my spine. 'You can't remember what happened, can ya?'

'Jordy!' I shout. 'You still there?'

'Yeah!' Jordy shouts back. His voice is hoarse, like he's been crying. Gus is holding him. We're both fucked.

'Dylan, for fuck's sake,' Terry says. 'I need you to focus. I know you got a smaller brain an' all, but I need ya to focus for a fucking second. You don't remember much, do ya?'

I'm panting. I try to slow my breathing, but it's hard to breathe at all with Terry on top of me. I dig my fingers into the cold dirt. I clench dead leaves in my fist, crush them. I can't say I don't remember what happened, because I do. I remember all of it.

'You can go on that stand and tell all your lies if ya want,' Terry said. 'But if you get Miles sent to prison, you'll be right in this hole. We won't even kill ya before we bury ya. No one will ever find ya. Not your mum, or your frigid sister. They'll never find ya. So, why don't you just admit you don't remember anything? Don't be dumb like your dead mate.'

I scream. Pressure on the back of my head pushes my face into the ground and I've got dirt all over my lips. It turns into mud in my mouth.

'How much do you remember, Dylan?' Terry shouts.

'Nothing!' I shout back. And I begin to cry. I cry hard, because I've just betrayed Brandon. No one will ever really know what happened that night because I won't say a thing. I'm sure of it. I don't want to die in this hole in the middle of nowhere.

'So,' Terry says, sighing. 'When you get up there, and they ask you questions about that night, what'll you say?'

'I don't remember!'

The pressure releases from the back of my head, then Terry climbs off.

'Good boy,' Terry says. 'And just in case you're thinkin' of telling your lies still, know that your boyfriend here will be joinin' you in that hole.'

I hear laughter.

'Were you and Jordy makin' some gay porn or something?' Terry asks. I glance up and he's taking my camera out of its bag. He powers it on and then throws it like a baseball. I hear the crash as it lands on a tree trunk. I close my eyes again and rest my face back in the dirt.

'Come on,' Terry says. I hear their footsteps crunch over the debris of the bush. After a while I hear the engine start, then tyres spin dirt and the sound of the motor fades. A hand on my shoulder shakes me gently.

'Dyl,' Jordy says. 'You okay?'

Slowly I get to my feet. The tears have stopped but my back is killing me. I wipe the dirt from my face with my shirt. I pull my phone from my pocket, power on the torch and start for the tree where Terry threw my camera.

I find the broken lens among the leaves. Pieces of glass are lost to the dirt and my camera is destroyed. I stuff the pieces into the camera bag. I hope the memory card is okay and I can salvage my footage at least.

'I'm sorry, Dyl,' Jordy says.

I shine my light around. Beyond is absolute darkness, and within it, the sounds of insects and night birds.

'Do you remember the way to the path?' I ask.

'I think so,' Jordy says. He pulls his own phone out and turns on the torch. 'No reception. We gotta call the cops.'

'What? No, Jordy. We can't.'

'Seriously? They just kidnapped us and threatened to kill us.'

'We can't go to the cops. *They* killed Brandon, not those dickheads.'

Jordy sighs and begins leading us back to the path. We follow the road for a hundred metres and when we get to a rise, Jordy says he has a bar of reception.

'I'm gonna call Kallum to come get us,' he says.

'What? No.'

'Why? We can't walk all the way back into town.'

'Not him. His mum's a cop.'

'She's not a *bad* cop, Dyl. Jesus. Kallum won't tell.'

'Why wouldn't he?'

'He wouldn't. I promise.'

I stop walking and sit on a boulder on the side of the road. I check my phone. It's got one bar of reception as well. I don't really know Kallum anymore. He became a footy arsehole then moved away on his fancy scholarship, like he was so much better than the rest of us. And his mum's a cop. He's not like me and Jordy.

I don't have any other option right now, though.

'He can't tell anyone anything,' I say. 'Or I swear to god, I'll kill him myself.'

'He won't,' Jordy says. He brings his phone to his ear and I hear the ringtone in the silence. 'Hey, Kal. I can't really explain, but can you come pick up me and Dylan? Yep. I just need you to come get us, please. Okay...yeah, we're okay...I'll send you my location. Okay...thanks...bye.'

Jordy taps on his phone screen for a minute and I rub the back of my neck. I can still taste the dirt in my mouth, stuck between my teeth. I spit it out and feel my chest, which is as sore as my back.

Jordy takes a seat beside me on another boulder and sighs. He folds his arms, shivering, but I'm hot. My blood feels like it's boiling beneath my skin. All I want to do is hurt Terry, Trent and Gus. To them, Brandon was nothing, but he was a person. He had dreams, he made jokes, he got sad sometimes. Sometimes he got angry and paced around the room like he was about to explode. He was my friend. To them, he wasn't even human.

'I'm sorry,' I say to Jordy.

'It's not your fault, Dyl. I'm okay. I just can't believe they actually did that.'

'I can.'

'So what are you gonna do?' Jordy asks. 'Are you gonna say you don't remember when they ask you in court?'

'I don't know,' I say, and I really don't.

It's a long wait in the cold and dark before Kallum arrives in a Toyota Yaris after two o'clock in the morning. When he picks us up, he asks again what happened, and Jordy tells him he'll explain later. We sit in silence all the way back to Carraway's Point, while I try to think about what other evidence they might have to put Higgins away for Brandon's murder. I wonder if they really need my testimony, if everything else might be enough. All I know for sure is that I can still see the shallow grave that was dug for me. It's burned into my mind like a tattoo.

TWENTY-SIX

When I wake up and check my phone, it's two o'clock in the afternoon and there's dirt all over my sheets. I climb out of bed and my back is so sore – it feels like there's a big bruise on my spine.

After a shower, I put my sheets in the wash and Bree passes me in the laundry.

'What happened to you last night?' Bree asks.

'Nothing,' I say. 'Just filming stuff.'

'Mhmm.'

Back in my room, the first thing I do is take my broken camera from the bag and pull out the SD card. The film is due by midnight and my heart is racing because it might be all gone.

I slide the SD card into my laptop. It takes a few seconds, but the memory loads up – it survived the crash. I copy the files and see the stuff me and Jordy filmed last night. I cut the parts of the clips I want to keep and edit them into the sequence. Now it's time to add the music and sound effects I found.

But I'm still thinking about last night, how Terry held a blade at my throat, how he pinned me against dirt at the edge of a shallow grave that I'll be buried in if I tell the truth.

I'm thinking about how this movie could get me a scholarship and get me the hell out of this town.

Today's Dad's birthday and he's expecting us up at the caravan park. It's six o'clock and I'm in the supermarket with Bree, heading into the bakery section to get the cake. Mum's waiting in the car.

'Mum *so* doesn't want to be doing this,' Bree says.

'Yeah. She could've said no.'

'She did, multiple times. But I think it's better this way. I think they can be friends again if they don't live together and aren't romantically attached anymore.'

'What you mean?' I ask.

'They were always fighting,' Bree says. 'I swear, they hated each other. I think once they both accept that the romance is off the table, they'll actually get along again.'

'Did they ever get along?'

'Yeah,' she says. 'You remember. It was like ten years ago.'

I don't remember. I don't remember ever seeing them kiss or talk cutesy. They hugged once, years ago, but that was because Dad went away for some writer's retreat for two weeks and Mum hugged him when he came home. I don't remember them ever being a *happy couple*. Maybe

Bree's right and their break-up might be a good thing. It doesn't feel like that big a deal, though, because right now, there's a hole out in the bush waiting for me.

We get a chocolate mud cake and some candles, and as we get back to the car, I yawn for the fifth time in an hour. I'm so tired today. Even after I made it to bed last night, my blood was still rushing until five a.m.

Mum drives us to the caravan park on the outskirts of town, and when she stops the car, she speaks. 'Now, when we get in there, I don't wanna hear no comments 'bout me and your father getting back together.'

'Of course not,' Bree agrees.

We follow the footpath through the caravans with our eight-dollar mud cake, Mum carrying the boxed and wrapped bottle of rum she bought Dad.

This place is its own little town. There's a kiosk where you can buy takeaway food and soft drinks, a bathroom block, a little pond and a swing set and slide for kids to play on.

We arrive at Dad's caravan, deep in the heart of the park. Dad opens the door with a smile on his face. His hair is still wet from the shower. He's wearing a new black polo shirt tucked into his blue jeans, and he's bathed in a pool of cologne that smells like oranges.

'Welcome,' he says.

'Happy birthday,' me and Bree say at the same time. Dad thanks us and lets us in. Bree begins by asking Dad what he's been up to today, if he's been celebrating.

I take the cake to the bench and put on the candles while Dad tells Bree he's spent the whole day cleaning and watching Netflix because our visit was the thing he was looking forward to the most today. All the while, Mum is quiet. She takes a seat on one of his two small couches and crosses her legs.

'How are you, Vanessa?' Dad asks her.

'Fine,' she says. 'Oh, forgot. Happy birthday.' She hands him the present.

'Thank you.'

I take the lighter from the kitchen bench as Dad unwraps his rum bottle. I bring over the cake with two lit candles on top. Together, me, Mum and Bree sing 'Happy birthday'. I place the cake on the coffee table in front of Dad and he smiles.

'Hip, hip,' I say.

'Hooray,' Mum and Bree cheer back.

Dad blows out his candles and then it's time to eat. In the kitchen, Dad takes chicken nuggets out from the little oven while Mum gazes around the caravan. This is the first time she has seen it. It's small, but homey. It's got the couches, a double bed, a kitchenette with the tiniest sink ever, and a little TV. Dad told us the only real downside, apart from being away from me and Bree, was that he has to take his shits and showers in the block ten metres down the road.

After the nuggets, Mum cuts the cake while Dad and Bree talk life. They're discussing her friend, whose little brother, Eric, is having a baby with Rita. Apparently it's stressing her friend out bad, but she's excited to be an aunty. Dad tells her about how there was a fight at work at the Aboriginal health centre, between an elder and the new CEO because they don't like each other. Dad's talking about how the new CEO is a micromanager and no one feels trusted at the moment.

'Why don't you just quit?' Bree asks. 'Get a job somewhere else.'

'Well, I got my book as well,' he says. 'I'm almost done with the first draft. I think it's gonna be a killer. It's a crime mystery. I'm *actually* gonna finish this draft. I can see the end, just gotta get the words out.'

'Good on you,' Bree says.

'Yes, very good,' Mum interrupts, arriving with plates of cake. She plants two on the table, then brings the next two over. They're not small pieces.

Our mouths are full of cake and we're eating together in silence like a normal family. I've never thought of our family as *normal* before. We don't sit around the table for family dinners, we never say *I love you*, and we never go on family holidays, but in this moment, it feels like home again.

It's about nine o'clock when Mum tells us we need to get going. Dad polishes off the last of his second slice of cake and walks us back towards the car.

'How's work going?' Dad asks Mum.

'It's fine, Ken,' Mum replies, almost sighing. Me and Bree are walking behind them.

'Just showing a bit of interest in your life,' Dad says.

'You had twenty years to show interest in my life,' Mum says back. 'Why start now?'

'All right, all right.'

The rest of the walk is silent, apart from the TVs playing in caravans, and people having cigarettes and chatting outside.

When we get back to the car, me and Bree say happy birthday to Dad again and he thanks us once more. Mum is already starting the engine.

As we reverse out, I wave to Dad through the window. He smiles, but I feel like he's sad. He has to watch us leave him on his birthday. I know Bree's right, and that they weren't good together, but I wish he was still there. At least then we could pretend everything was okay.

Back at home, I go straight to my room and bring my laptop to my bed. I watch my film through again, making little edits as I go.

It's near eleven o'clock when I feel like it's ready for submission. I export the file and open up the film school website. I navigate to the high schooler's scholarship page and open my submission. I've already filled in most of the details except the specific ones about the film.

Title: An Unfortunate Incident

Story: An experimental story of a young Aboriginal boy waiting to hear the verdict from the trial of the police officer who shot and killed his friend. Inspired by a true story.

Hmm. It doesn't sound that interesting, but that's what it is.

It needs something more, so at the end, I add *Guilty, or not guilty?*

That's better. I copy the download link into the form and go to click submit, but I stop myself.

This is a big deal. If I get this scholarship, if my film is good enough, I'll be moving to Sydney. I'll leave Carraway's Point behind, as well as Mum, Dad and Bree. I'd be leaving Jarrod behind, and Brandon's mum.

My throat is dry as fuck, and my head is killing me. I feel like I'm out bush again with Terry, staring into the shallow grave as I hover my finger over the trackpad.

I hear the bushes rustle outside my window. It's Simba, sneaking along my windowsill. He stares at me for a moment, then jumps into the darkness.

I feel like Brandon just told me to submit this motherfucker.

TWENTY-SEVEN

The trial started today. The lawyers will be at court in Gerring, but I'm on my way to their office anyway.

As I walk through town, I can't help but turn my head to every car that passes by. I imagine Terry patrolling the streets, watching me, making sure I'm doing what he says.

The office is on the second floor of a tall building beside the cinema. The receptionist at the front desk asks how she can help me.

I pull out the business card the lawyers gave me just before the graduation camp. 'I was hoping to speak to someone about the Miles Higgins trial. I met Graham and Lisa before. Graham Barton and Lisa Toolan.'

'They're both in court right now,' the receptionist says. 'I can take a message?'

'Oh. Nah. I need to speak to someone today. It's pretty urgent. Can you call them or something?'

'I can try. Give me a moment.'

I take a seat in one of the comfy chairs beside the desk. It's cold in here. The air-con is on full blast. I hold my hands in my lap. My palms are sweating so I wipe them on my shorts.

After a minute, the receptionist dials another number and holds the phone to her ear.

'I'm getting the voicemail again,' she says to me. 'What's your name?'

'Dylan Keenan.'

'Do they have your number?'

'Yeah, I think so.'

The receptionist leaves them a message, telling them I visited the office and need to talk to them urgently.

'Thanks,' I say. I leave the office and step into the lift again. When I arrive at the ground floor, my phone starts vibrating in my pocket.

'Hello?'

'Dylan,' she says. 'It's Lisa Toolan. I just received a message that you need an urgent chat.'

'Oh, yeah,' I say, clearing my throat. 'I, uh, I just needed to say...umm...I don't think I can take the stand anymore.'

'Why is that? Did something happen?' she asks.

'No, I...I just don't think...I can't do it.'

I'm in the lobby of this office building, staring out the glass doors at the traffic rolling by on the main street. I feel like I could crumble into a million pieces.

'Dylan, I'm gonna be honest with you,' she says. 'Right now is not the time to be backing down. Your police statement and your witness testimony are the strongest weapons we've got. In simple terms, we need you and I really can't afford to let you back down.'

'I get it, but...'

'Is it nerves? I totally understand being nervous about this. But I thought it was important to you, to do this for Brandon?'

'It is.'

'So why are you now saying you don't want to do it?'

'I...' My heart is about to explode in my chest. 'I'm sorry,' I say. Tears are pooling in my eyes.

'Dylan,' Lisa says. 'We need you. Really. I know you can't see me right now, but imagine that I am on my knees in front of you, begging you to do this. Don't do it for us. Do it for Brandon. Do it for Kathy. Do it for those who knew Brandon, those who miss him. I really, really don't want to pressure you, but you are the key here.'

'I just...' I almost tell her that Terry threatened to kill me, that he took me and Jordy out bush and showed me the hole he intends to bury me in if I testify and send Higgins to prison. I can't tell her. Instead, I start to cry. I back against a wall and slide to the floor, wiping my tears away with one hand and holding the phone to my ear with the other.

'Dylan,' Lisa says, her voice softer now. 'I apologise. I'm being very stern right now. It's been a big morning here. We've just presented our opening arguments. We're going the hear the defence's soon. You are scheduled for Wednesday and it's really important that you attend court. I wouldn't press so hard if it wasn't so important to our case.'

I think for a moment. There's no way I can get out of this. I have no choice but to go through with it and say what Terry wants me to say: that I don't remember anything.

'Okay,' I say. 'I'll do it. Sorry.'

'Don't apologise, Dylan. I'm glad you—'

I hang up and press both my palms to my eyes. I press them hard until the tears have stopped. I'm thankful no one has walked in while I've been slumped on the floor in this mess.

I need to see my mum. I've never wanted to see her so bad.

It takes me fifteen minutes of navigating backstreets until I arrive at the mechanics where she works.

Inside, there's a car up on the hoist. Mum's underneath it, tinkering away with some tool she has to use both hands for. It smells like petrol and fumes in this place.

'Dylan?' Mum spots me from behind the car tyre and wipes her hand on the rag attached to her belt as she approaches me. 'What're you doing here?' she asks.

'I was just around,' I say. 'Thought I'd come see you.'

'Okay,' she says. 'So nothing bad's happened? With your sister or father?'

'No, nothing like that,' I say.

'Good. Well, umm, give me about fifteen minutes and we'll go grab a feed? Fish and chips?'

'Okay. I'll wait in the office.'

The office is air-conditioned. There's an old man sitting across from me on the other couch, wearing glasses that rest on the tip of his nose, reading something on his phone.

On my phone I navigate to Brandon's Instagram. His last post was two weeks before he died. It was a pic of a stack of empty beer bottles on the plastic table in his back shed, with the caption: *Soooo this is why I'm hungover today #alcoholisbad*

We were drinking that night. He was drunk when he died.

'Let's go, Dyl,' Mum says from the doorway.

We climb into Mum's car and drive the five minutes to the fish and chips shop by the pier, next to the pizza place. Mum orders a seafood box and the fish and chips lunch deal for me.

We sit with our food at a table outside. It's a sunny day and the seagulls are stalking us from across the road, perched on the top of wooden posts, waiting for us to drop a chip their way.

'What were you doing in town?' Mum asks.

'I just went to the lawyer's office but they were in Gerring.'

'How you feelin' about Wednesday?' Mum asks, biting into a prawn cutlet. As I dig into my chips, the salt burns the corners of my mouth.

'Okay, I suppose,' I say. 'I just want to get it over with.'

'You nervous? I had to get asked questions in court once, and I was so nervous, I was shaking.'

'You had to speak in court?' I ask.

'Yeah. One of my friends got into a fight with this other woman at a club and it ended very badly. I had to answer a few questions about her. It was the longest twenty minutes of my life.'

'Great.'

'Not trying to scare you,' Mum says. 'I can't imagine what you're feeling right now, Dyl. I don't know if I could handle it, if I was you. You're a strong boy. Tell me how you're feeling. I'm your mother. I know you the best out of everyone.'

'I don't know how I'm feeling,' I say.

Mum scoffs down some chips.

'We don't talk that much anymore,' Mum says. 'You used to tell me everything. I miss that.'

'Well,' I begin. 'Why did you kick Dad out? What happened?'

'Oh,' Mum says. 'Nothing *happened*. It's just...we started dating when I was twenty. I had Bree when I was twenty-two, then you when I was twenty-five. I spent all my twenties and thirties being a wife and a mother. You and your sister are the best things that ever happened to me. I wouldn't change that, but I can choose what happens now, you know? I never got to go out, date people, try new things, go travel somewhere on my own for the hell of it. Those years when I could've been doing those things...they just went by. I lost them. I loved your father, but I just...I haven't been happy. Not for a long time.'

A tear escapes from Mum's eye, and I suddenly feel bad for asking the question.

'I mean, I *do* love your father,' she says. 'But I was still figuring out who I was when I met him, when I had you kids. I need some time to find out who I really am, you know what I mean? Probably doesn't make much sense.'

'Makes sense,' I say.

Mum sighs, finishes off her chips while I start digging into my fish.

'We keep a lot of secrets from each other in that house,' Mum says. 'Too many things. We don't talk to each other like I want us to. I don't want it to be like that. I want you to know you can talk to me about anything. There's nothing I don't want to hear.'

'Okay,' I say.

Mum leans forward and I feel like I'm about to be asked something important.

'You never talked to me about that night,' she says. 'We're not very good at *talking*, are we? We're going to that courthouse on Wednesday. You're gonna be asked a lot of hard questions. It'll bring back all the memories.' Mum reaches across the table and places her hand over mine. She holds it and I feel the lump in my throat returning, because I can't remember the last time my mother touched me.

'Ever since that night,' she says, 'I feel like I've been watching you fall away, like you've buried pieces of yourself. I watched the light leave your eyes and I haven't done anything, have I? I've been a shit mum. We used to laugh so much and we don't anymore. You're still trapped in that night, Dyl. I can see it suffocating you. Please let me help now. I want to help.'

I'm still, but tears are leaking down my face. I wipe them away with my wrist, sniffle back my runny nose.

'It's...hard,' I say.

'Just try.'

I take a breath, and then I tell my mother what happened the night Brandon died.

I don't know if they're the same words I'll say in court on Wednesday.

TWENTY-EIGHT

It's seven on Wednesday morning and I'm exhausted. I hardly slept at all. I've been thinking about today for a long time.

I texted Jarrod last night to ask if he wanted to come with me to court today. He said he felt too anxious, that being at the courthouse and seeing Miles Higgins would be too much for him to handle at the moment.

I wish I could say that too, and crawl back in bed.

I'm in my bedroom fixing my tie in the mirror, and the Aboriginal boy I am staring at looks like he's going to a funeral. I'm wearing black pants and a white dress shirt that Mum got me from the op shop yesterday. The jacket hanging on my doorknob is black too.

There's a knock at the front door. Worry streaks down my spine as I imagine that it's Terry at the door, and when Mum opens it, she'll be shot with a sawn-off shotgun and Terry will kill me and Bree, to make sure none of us say anything.

I leave my room with my black dress shoes in hand. Mum's opened the door but it's not Terry on the other side – it's Jordy and Kallum. They're both dressed in nice collared shirts and jeans, like they're going to a dinner with white people.

'What are you lads doing here?' Mum asks.

'We wanted to come with Dylan today,' Jordy says. 'For moral support.'

'If that's okay,' Kallum adds.

Mum turns to me and lets me decide. 'Okay, sure,' I say.

'Great,' Mum says. 'The more, the merrier.'

I sit at the kitchen table and Mum goes to finish getting ready.

I pull on my shoes while Jordy and Kallum stand awkwardly by the front door.

'You really don't have to come,' I say. 'I'm sure you got better things to do.'

'No,' Jordy says. 'We want to come. I know we haven't really been friends in a long time, but we're here for you.'

'We were kids when we said that,' I say. 'We didn't know anything.'

'True,' Kallum says. 'But we're here anyway. Don't want you to go through this alone.'

I look at them. They're not the boys I knew when we were playing cricket with a wheelie bin as the wicket in the cul-de-sac. Dad would put on his brimmed hat and pretend to be the umpire and Jordy's mother and mine would sit on Jordy's lawn and drink cans of beer while they watched us. We've all changed, gone different ways, but they're here now, and it feels really nice.

'Thanks,' I say.

When Mum gets back, she's wearing a black dress and high heels. It's the first time I've seen her in make-up for years. She's still putting in her earrings as we leave the house and get in her car to drive to Gerring.

My stomach feels sour, like I need to do a massive, diarrhoeal shit, but I know it's just because this is all real now. I'm gonna have to sit in the courtroom and face the cop who killed my best friend. Then, I'm gonna have to lie and say I don't remember most of it. It's gonna disappoint Brandon's family, his mother, the lawyers, but only Jordy will understand why.

When we arrive in Gerring, the place is crawling with people. Mum always grips the wheel with two hands when she's stressed, and she's gripping it now.

There's a gathering of people outside the court – mostly Aboriginal people – Kathy among them. They're holding signs, wearing those black t-shirts with Brandon's face on them. There's some guy standing there talking to them – a white man in a plaid shirt. He's holding his phone to Kathy's mouth and she's talking into it. I suppose she's doing an interview for the paper.

The air is warm here. There's no cool breeze to soothe me and I feel like I'm gonna throw up.

'Ready, Dyl?' Mum asks, as she, Jordy and Kallum join me on the footpath.

'Ready as I'll ever be,' I say.

The courthouse is a big white building with automatic doors and tinted windows. I'd expected to see pillars out the front, like the kind you see in photos of ancient Greek temples.

My heart is like a kick drum in my chest and my throat feels tight. It's getting harder to breathe as we walk up to the automatic doors.

We pass through the security screening and go to the desk with a sign saying COURT ASSISTANCE.

'Hi,' Mum says to the woman behind the desk. 'My son is a witness. He's giving evidence today.'

The woman directs us to a waiting room upstairs. It's a big space with chairs in rows. The morning show is playing on a TV, but I don't hear it. There must be thirty people in here, all silently waiting to give evidence in different cases.

We check in with the clerk, then find a corner where no one else is sitting. The seats are comfortable at least.

'Now, we wait,' Mum says.

It's a long time before Graham Barton and Lisa Toolan arrive to chat with me. They tell me to remember to only answer the question being asked when the defence lawyer cross-examines me, like we practised a month ago. They remind me not to talk about things I didn't see with my own eyes or hear with my own ears. They tell me I can have my mum come into court with me, but Jordy and Kallum have to stay outside.

After they leave, my stomach is rumbling. Then the lunchtime break rolls around and me, Mum, Jordy and Kallum get sandwiches from the delicatessen across the road.

Kallum and Jordy fill Mum in on their plans for next year – Jordy's moving to Sydney for acting school, Kallum's staying in Carraway's Point to work at the national park and wants to study environmental-something later.

'Did you apply for that scholarship?' Jordy asks me. 'Finish your movie in time?'

'Yeah, it's all done,' I say. I don't want to talk though. I just want to get this over with so I can go home, maybe sleep for a few days.

When we cross the road back to the courthouse, Kathy is out the front smoking a cigarette with one of Brandon's aunties.

'Can I bum one?' Mum asks the aunty. She hands her the packet with the lighter stuffed into the plastic casing. I can't look Kathy in the eye because I'm gonna lie soon, and she's gonna hate me.

'How you feelin', Dyl?' Kathy asks me. 'And Jordy-boy? Kallum?'

Kallum and Jordy say they're good, and ask how Kathy is doing.

'This is a punish, I tell ya,' Kathy says. 'No mother should have to go through this. It's good to see all you boys 'ere, though. I remember when youse and Brandon were playin' round with my car and accidentally rolled it down the driveway.'

Jordy laughs. 'I dove out the passenger door while it was moving,' he says.

'Yeah, and left me, Brandon and Dylan inside,' Kallum adds. 'When we hit the gutter, felt like we crashed.'

I remember Kathy came out and started yelling, so we got out of the car and ran away from Chopin Drive. We hid behind a tree at the park around the corner until dark. Brandon said when he got home that night he got a good smack. We were probably ten or eleven then. I'd forgotten all about it. I've forgotten so many of the good times.

'Dylan,' Kathy says. 'We're gonna do a silent march through Gerring next Friday, after closing arguments. Do you want to come? I know Brandon woulda wanted you there.'

I lift my gaze from my shoes to Kathy's shirt, Brandon's face printed across her chest. He was too young to die. He shouldn't have died.

'Yeah, maybe,' I say.

'Well, it's one o'clock,' Mum says. 'Better get back in there.'

The afternoon rolls on and my palms and armpits are still sweaty, but I'm more tired than nervous now. Who knew sitting and waiting could be so tiring? Mum leaves to go to the bathroom and Kallum does the same, leaving me and Jordy sitting here. We're both quiet for a while, then Jordy clears his throat.

'So, what are you gonna do?' he asks, whispering. I hear the words in my head, spoken in my own voice: *I don't remember.*

'I don't have a choice,' I say. 'Do I? It's not just me I have to worry about, you know? It's my parents, my sister, you.'

Jordy nods, leans forward and looks to his shoes. 'I'd be okay with you telling the truth, Dyl. He can't get away with it. He can't.'

'I don't know.'

245

'But if you don't, that's okay too. You don't ever have to beat yourself up about it,' he says. 'I wouldn't hold that against you.'

Before I can say anything in response, Kallum walks back into the room. Jordy said he would be okay with me telling the truth in court, but if I do, and Miles Higgins gets convicted, Terry will pick me up one day, maybe Jordy too, and I'll be buried in that hole in the bush. My parents will never know what happened to me; they'll never find my body.

In my head, I say sorry to Brandon again. Mum returns and sits beside me.

Not more than thirty minutes later, I hear my name over the speakers.

'Dylan Keenan to courtroom one,' the voice says. 'Dylan Keenan to courtroom one.'

My heart starts racing again and the sour feeling in my stomach returns like a shark to a bloody carcass. When I stand from my seat, I swear I'm about to shit my pants.

'Good luck, Dyl,' Jordy says. He gives me a nod and a warm smile – a smile that says *it's okay, I know why you're going to say what you're going to say.*

'Yeah, good luck, brother,' Kallum adds.

'Thanks,' I say, then I walk with Mum out of the witness room, along the crowded corridor and to the tall white doors of courtroom one.

TWENTY-NINE

When we walk through the doors, a chill comes over me, like I've just walked on Brandon's grave. He's angry at me for what I'm about to do.

The courtroom is long, and filled with people facing away from me. When they hear the door close, they all turn to see me – the scared black kid in a jacket and tie whose legs are quickly turning to jelly.

Mum takes a seat in the back row, and all I can think is that this courtroom doesn't look like I imagined it would. The floors are blue carpet. The chairs are hard black plastic. Ahead, the judge is on a high bench looking down on everyone. There's a table at the front where people in suits are sitting and there are more people at the side of the room, between the judge and the watchers.

A lady in a blazer comes to me and I don't even register the walk from Mum's seat to the witness box. I swear an oath to tell the truth but it feels like a bad dream, like the words didn't really come out of my mouth but someone else's.

After the oath, I glance to the judge. She's a large woman with white skin, wearing a black robe and reading something in front of her. It's so quiet in here as I turn my gaze to the long table my chair is facing. I feel like I'm a thing on display in this small wooden box with a tiny microphone in front of me.

At one end of the table, Lisa and Graham are looking over some documents. At the other end, two men in blue suits are sitting with a man in a black suit: Miles Higgins. He looks smaller from here. He keeps his eyes on his lap as Lisa stands from the desk and crosses the carpet towards me.

'Hello, Dylan,' she says. 'Thank you for being here. Could you please state your full name, age and where you live?'

'Okay,' I say, clearing my throat. 'Dylan Royce Keenan. Eighteen. I live on Chopin Drive in Carraway's Point.'

'Do you live on the same street as Brandon Long did?'

'Yes.'

'Next door, right?'

'Yes.'

'Were you and Brandon friends?' she asks.

'Yes,' I say. I can feel everyone's eyes on me.

'How long were you friends?'

'Since we were little,' I say.

'Since primary school?'

'Before,' I say. Lisa takes a look back to the people across the room, the jury.

'Dylan,' she says. 'Were you with Brandon on the date that he died? At seventeen Blackmore Street?'

'Yes.'

'Could you tell us what happened that night?' Lisa asks. 'From when you arrived at the address until you were removed at two a.m.?'

All the memories of that night rush to the front of my brain, exploding like flashbang grenades before my eyes. I glance to the watchers. In the front row, I see four Aboriginal people in black shirts with Brandon's face on their chests. I see Kathy looking up at me.

The words are right there: *I don't remember.*

They're easy words to say.

I don't remember.

I don't remember.

I don't remember.

I can't say them, though. If it was me who got killed, and Brandon was up here, he would tell the truth – every word of it – no matter the consequences.

Brandon was brave – braver than me. Brandon was funny. Brandon was compassionate. Brandon wanted to be an Aboriginal health worker. Brandon had plans of one day moving to Townsville to attend every North Queensland Cowboys home game.

Brandon was murdered.

Brandon's life was stolen from him.

Brandon deserves justice.

Instead of saying what I thought I was gonna say, I start describing when I arrived at Rory's house on Blackmore Street. I tell the court about the rap music that was playing from the TV speakers, an artist I didn't recognise, how Rory was dancing with two girls in the dark living room. I tell them how me and Jarrod found Brandon in the kitchen making a toasted sandwich. I tell them how Brandon was bragging about the cops wanting to talk to him about a stolen sound system, how he said he was *a wanted criminal now*. I tell the court about how we drank Canadian Clubs at the kitchen table, played king's cup with Rory and the girls before they left around one o'clock to go drink with some older people at a house nearby. I tell them how Brandon was in the middle of a fit of laughter at something Jarrod said when he got a text from Rory saying the cops had stopped him up the road and told him they were looking for Brandon, and that one of the girls told them he was at Rory's house. Rory told him to get out of there, *jump fences*. I tell them how loud knocking began at the front door while we were figuring out what to do, how Brandon ran into a bedroom to hide, and me and Jarrod turned off the music and tried to hide the rest of our alcohol in cupboards. I tell them how two cops barged in, how they searched through the house and found Brandon hiding under a bed. I tell them how I followed the cops and yelled at them that they were hurting Brandon when they pulled him by his ankles, how I saw his phone fall from his pocket, how I heard the thud on the carpet as it bounced near the edge of the bed when they pulled him out. I tell them how Miles Higgins started wrestling with Brandon on the floor, how Higgins put his forearm on Brandon's throat and wouldn't take it off even though Brandon was shouting that he couldn't breathe.

I tell them how when Higgins got him to his feet, Brandon spat in Higgins's face and got free, how he knelt, reached for his phone, which was visible on the floor. I tell them how the loud bangs shocked my ears into deafness, how I dropped to my knees and held my hands to the sides of my head.

I tell them how Brandon fell to the floor, about the blood I saw – bright red – pooling where Brandon was lying. I tell them how Brandon was still blinking and I was yelling at Higgins to help him but instead, he picked me up and shoved me stomach-first into the wall, told me not to move. I tell them how the other cop was shouting at Jarrod to stay where he was outside the room, how he came in and looked for the *weapon* Brandon had reached for under the bed but only found his phone, how the two of them stood in the doorway to the bedroom talking about it for what felt like ages before Higgins went to check on Brandon, how I yelled and yelled for them to do something and how I was too scared to go to him myself in case they shot me too. They told me to shut up and called an ambulance. When the ambulance officers arrived, they called Brandon's name, but he didn't say anything back. He was still as a rock. He wasn't breathing anymore.

THIRTY

It's a long drive back to Carraway's Point. I smell like I've run two marathons and forgot to put on deodorant before. Jordy and Kallum are quiet in the back seat, Mum's turning up the radio, but I'm replaying the questions that Higgins's lawyers asked me and the answers I gave them after I told the courtroom what happened.

I'm thinking about how they asked how much I drank that night and I finally used the words I had been preparing to say over and over – *I don't remember.*

How they asked if Brandon had ever been violent, and I told them I had seen Brandon in two fights at school and one fight at a party, but he was always just defending himself.

How they asked me if I was aware that alcohol intoxication can cause lapses in memory, and how I said yes.

I just want this fucking day to be over. I don't even

care if Terry comes along and takes me back to that hole in the bush. I'm no longer scared of it.

It's about five o'clock when Mum pulls into the Maccas on the highway, which sits halfway between Gerring and Carraway's Point.

The Maccas is pretty busy. Jordy and Kallum place their orders on the self-service machine, then I order a double McChicken meal with a Coke. We find a table near the window looking out to the car park.

Traffic is rolling by on the highway. With every car that passes, I'm looking for Terry's ute. He'll know I've told the truth, that I didn't say I didn't remember anything, like I said I would. He'll know by now for sure, and be planning how he's gonna grab me. He can do what he wants, because I told the truth and I didn't let Brandon down like I thought I would.

Once we've got all our food, Mum scoffs down her chicken and cheese burger. I dig into my chips first, eat half of them and then move onto my burger – my usual routine when eating burgers and chips.

When Mum goes to the bathroom, Jordy says, 'We have something to tell you.' He and Kallum both have red faces, and I don't know what this is about, but if it gets my mind off the courtroom, I'm happy to hear anything.

'Well, go on,' I say, because a few seconds have passed and there's nothing but awkward, blushing smiles between us.

'Well,' Kallum begins. 'We are actually . . . gay.'

Kallum looks to Jordy, as if he's asking him to finish this.

'Everyone knows Jordy's gay,' I say, biting into my McChicken.

'Yes,' Kallum says. 'What I meant was...I'm gay too.'

'And we're together,' Jordy says. He glances at Kallum and they both smile and oh my fucking Jesus.

'We're together,' Kallum adds.

Kallum is gay. The bigshot footy prodigy is gay. He and Jordy are together. They're a couple.

'For real?' I ask.

'Yeah,' Jordy says. 'We were keeping it a secret, but when we were waiting for you at court we decided we should tell you.'

'Yeah,' Kallum says. 'You're our friend. I know we've drifted apart, all of us, but we'll always be friends, I think.'

'Unless you're super homophobic and planning on bashing us right now,' Jordy says.

I chuckle. I know Jordy's just being funny. I'm honestly happy for them, and it makes me feel happier knowing they've got each other now. They're together and they're both being who they are.

'How long have you guys been seeing each other?' I ask.

'Since that graduation camp,' Jordy says.

'No, that's when we started talking,' Kallum interrupts. 'We started seeing each other, like, in a gay way, two weeks after that.'

'Well, it was more like twelve days,' Jordy says.

I start laughing and they laugh too. It's been a long time since we laughed together, and suddenly it feels like no time has passed at all.

'Well, I'm happy for you,' I tell them.

'So, you're okay with it?' Kallum asks.

'Yes, of course. What do ya take me for?'

'Sorry,' Kallum says. 'I kind of thought it might weird you out a bit.'

Mum arrives back from the bathroom and we all eat our meals. Mum starts asking Kallum how his parents are going,

'Mum's good,' he says. 'She's hardly at home though. Always working.'

'Yeah, I can imagine a cop's life never stops,' Mum says. 'How's your father?'

'I'm not too sure, really,' Kallum says. 'We stopped talking for a bit after I told him I was quitting footy.'

'You quit footy?' I interject.

'Yeah. Long story, that one. Dad had the shits with me for a while, but things mostly went back to normal after I came out to him and Mum.'

'Oh, you're gay?' Mum says.

'Yes,' Kallum replies.

'And you two?' she asks, nodding to Kallum and Jordy. Kallum nods back.

'How did coming out go?' Mum asks, and it feels like she's fishing for gossip or something.

'I kind of expected it to be this big deal,' Kallum says. 'But they were pretty chill, said they weren't surprised, that they were proud of me, loved me, all that sappy stuff.'

'Did you cry?' Mum asks. 'Did *they*?'

'Mum, Jesus,' I interrupt.

'What? I love coming-out stories,' Mum says.

'I cried,' Kallum says. 'Mum cried, but Dad didn't.'

'I see,' Mum says. 'What about you, Jordy-boy? How's Dad and the sis?'

'Dad's all right,' Jordy says. 'Better, these days. Josie's good too. Actually, she told me the other day that she's got a boyfriend named Alan. My first thought was: who names their kid Alan these days? But also, I kind of want to meet this kid. Reassert my brotherly protection.'

'My god,' Mum says. 'Isn't she like six years old?'

'Seven,' Jordy says. 'I will die if she's already kissed a boy when it took me sixteen years to do it.'

'Kids are silly,' Mum says. 'They don't need to rush into any of that.'

We finish our food and return to the car. As we accelerate back onto the highway, I decide to check my emails. When I open the app, I see there's one from the film school.

'Oh my god,' I say, jolting upright in my seat.

'What?' Mum asks, like I've just scared her.

'I got an email from the film school.' I read on, thinking it's an email to say that I've won the scholarship, but it's not. 'They're just saying they've received my application and will let me know the outcome by the end of Friday next week.'

'Exciting,' Jordy says.

'Yeah, I suppose.'

'Come on. I was in your movie, so it's already a masterpiece,' Jordy says.

'Maybe.'

'Well, time will tell,' Mum says. She turns up the radio and I settle back in my seat. The film school emailed me, acknowledging my existence, which means they received my application. On top of that, Jordy and Kallum are a thing. And today I also told the truth for my friend in court. Maybe my testimony puts Higgins away, or maybe not. Maybe it doesn't matter what the black kid who wears a hoodie and walks the streets at night with his mates says. If Higgins isn't found guilty, maybe Terry won't try to kill me after all, or maybe he will. Maybe I'll actually get the scholarship and escape to Sydney with Jordy before Terry gets the chance. All that matters is I told the truth. Today wasn't such a bad day.

THIRTY-ONE

It's Friday morning; the closing arguments of the trial are today. I'm thankful that I don't have to be there anymore, that I can lie here under my blanket thirty minutes away in Carraway's Point. My mind is still there, though.

I've been lying in bed for a while, not wanting to get up. I hear footsteps in the hallway, then the coffee machine, then the morning show on TV. Rain is pitter-pattering on the roof.

Voices in the living room bleed through my walls and I check my phone. There's a text from Jarrod but I don't read it yet. It's just after eight o'clock when I finally slide my legs out from under the blankets.

Mum and Bree are in the kitchen looking at their phones, and I swear neither of them notices when I walk in and pour myself a bowl of Nutri-Grain.

'Morning,' I say, and as soon as I say it, there's a knock

at the door. Once again, fear streaks along my spine that Terry might be there with a sawn-off shotgun.

Mum opens the door and it's Kathy. She's wearing her Brandon shirt again and her hair is wet from the rain.

'Hey, Vanessa,' she says. 'I wanted to check in on Dylan, see if he wanted to come to the courthouse for the march this afternoon. We're marching at three o'clock.'

Kathy spots me inside at the kitchen bench with my bowl.

'I might come later,' I say. I don't really want to stand outside the courthouse in the rain all day, and I don't really want to be there when they march. I've never been in a march before and the thought of it makes me nervous. I imagine onlookers yelling racist slurs at us, people shouting *white power*.

'Okay,' Kathy says. 'I'll see you later, eh?'

'Yeah, maybe.'

'Good luck, Kath,' Mum says.

She leaves and a churning feeling grows in my stomach. It feels real now: today is the day.

'You right, Dyl?' Mum asks.

'Yeah,' I say.

Soon Mum and Bree leave for work together. I go to Jarrod's text on my phone.

Jarrod: *You going to Gerring today?*

Me: *I don't know. You?*

Jarrod: *Nah gonna go to Rory's for a bit*

I sit in front of Netflix all morning, refreshing a Reddit thread giving updates on the trial.

10:32. Prosecution have given their closing arguments.

12:00. Defence have given their closing arguments. Jury have left for deliberation.

I tell myself I don't want to be there today. I don't want to be in Gerring. I don't want to be a part of the march. I don't want to go because I'm scared.

But I know I *should* be there. I feel like I owe it to Brandon.

I don't really have a choice.

I text Jarrod that I'm gonna get the bus to Gerring. Jarrod texts back that he's smoking cones at Rory's. I want to text him something angry, tell him getting high is not as important as going to the march. Instead, below his name in my messages is Jordy's name. I text him that I'm going, ask if he'd be keen to drive there.

Jordy: *Can't drive, dad took the car to work sorry*

Me: *All good, don't worry I'll catch the bus*

Jordy: *Well I'll come with ya. I'll see if Kallum wants to come*

Me: *You don't have to*

Jordy: *Feel like I do*

Jordy feels like he has to go, just like I do. I shower and change, then pull on my hoodie and the sneakers with the smallest holes in the soles. The rain has eased a little, but I know I will end up with wet socks today.

I check myself in the mirror before I step out of my room. I'm not the same boy I was when Brandon died. I am older now. I have stubble. My hair is longer. I'm probably taller, too. Life has moved on for me. I wonder what Brandon would have looked like today if he was still here.

When I step out of the house, Simba is taking shelter from the rain on the doorstep near my feet. I bend down and scratch his head.

'You okay, Simba?' I ask. 'Come on, let's get you home.' I pick up the cat and he doesn't struggle at all – he rests in my arms like he belongs there.

I carry him across my front lawn and into Brandon's yard, place him on the front step. He's safe from the rain here. The front door is locked, but he's home.

'I'll catch you later, Simba. You can visit anytime.'

Simba meows and I feel like he's telling me I'm doing the right thing by going to Gerring to march for my friend, to show that he meant something to me, like he did for so many others.

'Ready to go?' I hear. It's Jordy and Kallum arriving – Jordy with a black jacket and Kallum in a white hoodie.

'Yep,' I say, and we begin the walk for the bus stop in town.

'The jury went into deliberations at twelve,' I say.

'Is that where they decide if he's guilty or not?' Kallum asks.

'Yeah. I'm a bit nervous about it.'

'Yeah, I feel ya,' Jordy says.

'Come on,' Kallum says. 'He shot him four times. There's no way he ain't goin' to jail.'

If he goes to jail, Terry will take me to that hole in the bush. I thought I didn't care about it anymore, but suddenly I'm jumping at every car that passes as we walk along the street. At least I've got Jordy and Kallum with me – we'll be able to put up a fight.

As the bus stop comes into sight, I see a bus parked there. When I realise it is bus 701, I tell them it's the one we need for Gerring and we start running. The 701 only leaves once an hour.

The footpath is slippery with rainwater and my shoes are sliding under me. Kallum's fast, powering ahead, but he's still twenty metres away when the bus turns on its blinker and pulls away from the kerb.

'Wait! Wait!' Kallum shouts. Faces turn to us along the street and I know it's no use. We've missed it.

We're all panting like dogs when we stop running and dawdle to the bus stop in defeat. We sit under the shelter and Jordy rests his hands on the back of his head.

'We'll probably miss the start of the march,' I say.

'This is fucked,' Kallum says. 'As if he didn't see us running up.'

I resign myself to sitting here for an hour, but I keep my eyes peeled for Terry's ute. I scan for my escape options, if I need one. My best bet would be to run into the shopping centre.

Aside from being anxious about Terry, I'm hungry as fuck now. There's a pizza shop across the road, so the three of us go buy a slice each and bring it back to the bus stop. It takes me back to a memory – we must've been about eleven or twelve on school holidays. The four of us were hanging out at the newly built shopping centre, and we got hungry so we came out to the pizza shop. Me and Kallum got a slice of cheese and bacon, Jordy got a pepperoni, and Brandon got a slice of Hawaiian. Kallum said something about how pineapples were an abomination to pizza, and that the ancient Italians would be rolling in their graves. Brandon picked off the pieces of pineapple and chewed them, licked his lips and rubbed his stomach. *Damn, that's some good pineapple*, he said, smiling while Kallum pretended to vomit. That became a regular thing – everytime we ate pizza, Brandon would savour the pineapple and Kallum would pretend to get sick. We were so dumb, then. We were just kids, sitting outside the pizza shop, thinking nothing would change and that we knew what life was about. We had no idea of all the shit coming our way when we got older. I wish we could go back to that – the four of us wasting our days in town during the school holidays.

'I'm glad you're both coming,' I say.

'Yeah,' Jordy says. 'Glad it's the three of us.'

'The whole thing feels kinda...wrong,' Kallum says.

'I get ya,' I say. That's exactly how it feels to me too: wrong. Like it shouldn't be happening, like none of this was meant to be. A big mistake was made in the timeline and now nothing makes sense.

'Did Brandon ever talk about us?' Kallum asks. 'Like, about the old days?'

'Sometimes,' I say. 'He used to bring up how he saved us from that dog, Zelda, all the time.'

'*You* didn't need saving,' Kallum says. 'I remember you abandoning us and jumping your fence.'

'I thought youse would follow.' I chuckle, remembering the fear I felt when that black dog came running at us, barking like she was about to tear us to shreds. When I realised no one else had followed me over the fence, I poked my head over and saw Brandon calm Zelda down, rub his hand between her ears before he walked her to her house. When he came back, Jordy and Kallum had already gone home, and I met him at the front of my yard. I told him the dog had scared the shit out of me.

Don't worry about it, he said with a smile. *I got you.*

He never made me feel bad for being scared. Whenever he'd bring up the story, it was always about how he was the dog whisperer.

The next bus to Gerring arrives at ten past two. We climb on after a bunch of old white people and sit on the back seat.

That yucky feeling is growing in my stomach again – the feeling like I need to take a massive shit. I haven't felt it since I stepped off the stand in court last week, since Terry took me and Jordy into his car, and now it's back. It grows stronger as we leave town and speed onto the highway, and stronger with every kilometre we draw closer to Gerring.

None of us talk on the journey. We just sit, watching the highway pass by. I thought Jarrod would be the one I'd march with, but I'm glad it's Jordy and Kallum. The three of us are connected again. We'll always be connected because of Brandon. Even though I've had Jarrod, I've felt kind of alone since Brandon died, like he was the reason for me and Jarrod to hang out. I'm not alone anymore.

As the bus rolls into Gerring just after three o'clock, I can see police cars blocking the road ahead. Bodies move beyond them – the march has already started.

The bus pulls over on the side of the street and the doors swish open.

'Sorry folks,' the driver says over the speakers. 'This is as far as we can go. Main street of Gerring is dead ahead.'

My stomach is in knots as I climb off the bus. We start for the march and I feel like I'm gonna throw up.

'Let's go,' Jordy says, picking up his pace. Then he and Kallum are jogging and I'm jogging behind them to keep up.

We arrive at the barricades and cross onto the footpath of the main street. We stop for a moment and view the march. We're at the tail end now, and there's only about twenty people still to pass by where we are standing. In the other direction, the crowd stretches for hundreds of metres. There's maybe a thousand of them.

'Come on,' I say, leading them to join the crowd, many of whom are carrying signs and posters with Brandon's face on them.

F#CK THE POLICE

JUSTICE 4 BRANDON

NO MORE BLAK DEATHS AT THE HANDS OF WHITE POLICE

STOP KILLING OUR KIDS

The march is silent, as Kathy said it would be. No one's talking. I don't know why I was so scared of being here – I feel like this is the right thing for me to do. I feel unity among these strangers, and among friends. We're all here for the same reason: for Brandon. There are a lot of Aboriginal people here, a lot of Aboriginal flags and shirts with Aboriginal designs on them, but there are also a lot of white people and people of other ethnicities. I don't feel as alone as I did when I saw the words *WHITE POWER* spray-painted on the wall of the supermarket.

I pick up the pace and we weave through the marchers. 'I wanna get closer to the front,' I say.

As we pass through the supporters, I see police cars parked beside barricades to block off the side streets, their blue and red lights flashing. Cops in blue uniform stand on the footpath; it must be every cop in Gerring and the whole district here to watch us. They're showing us that they're ready to pounce at any opportunity. I even see two riot squad cars that look like black tanks. I've never seen them in real life.

'So many people,' I hear Jordy say. He and Kallum are right behind me and we make it as far to the front of the march as we can before there are too many bodies to move further.

The rain has eased a little, though thunder rumbles in the clouds above, which are slowly growing darker. I'm getting wet, but I don't care because I'm doing something – I'm a part of something. I let down my hood and feel the rain coating my hair. I look up and allow it to run down my face.

It's close to four o'clock when the crowd comes to a standstill. Voices begin murmuring, until someone speaks through a megaphone.

'The jury have reached a verdict!' the voice shouts. 'We are going back to the courthouse! I repeat: they have reached a verdict! Back to the courthouse!'

My stomach is churning again, my heart is racing.

'That was quick,' Jordy says. 'I thought they'd take at least a couple of days. It's only been a few hours.'

He and Kallum turn around to walk with the crowd, but I'm stuck where I'm standing. They've decided already. This isn't just a march anymore, this is an outcome, an ending.

'You right, Dyl?' Kallum asks, placing his hand on my shoulder. I look up to him, and he looks back at me. I look to Jordy, too. He gives me a nod like the one he gave me in court before I took the stand. I'm terrified and my heart is pounding and threatening to bust out of my chest, but I've got my mates with me.

'Yeah,' I say. 'Let's go.'

We move with the crowd back along the main street of Gerring. This time, the pace is faster. The rain begins to fall more heavily and I pull the hood back over my head.

Everyone gathers in front of the courthouse. We're standing in the middle of the road, amid the body heat of strangers.

I spot Brandon's mum and a couple of people wearing the Brandon t-shirts making their way through the crowd. The activist from Brisbane, Shirley Gordon, is walking with them. They have their fists raised above their heads. People around me begin raising their fists as well, so me, Jordy and Kallum do the same. The crowd cheers as Kathy and a few others walk through the doors of the courthouse.

Thunder rumbles again. The sky has darkened, and it feels like it's past sunset already as we stand here, getting wetter and wetter. Voices speak around me in every direction but I can't make out what anyone's saying.

The sour feeling in my stomach has turned to dread. If the jury only took a few hours to make their decision, that means the outcome was clear to them, whichever way they chose to side. All of them were on the same page. Surely, they saw it clearly that Miles Higgins murdered Brandon in cold blood. Surely, they didn't think Brandon deserved to die.

It's just past five o'clock and my phone's almost out of battery. There's a text from Mum asking where I am. I text back that I'm in Gerring with Jordy and Kallum. I tell her we're outside the courthouse waiting for the verdict. She tells me she'll come pick me up in an hour.

The cops surround the courthouse, facing us. A blue wall has formed and they watch us like prison guards.

Soon, figures start to emerge from the courthouse. The crowd hushes. Some white people carrying briefcases walk out, and cops in suits with their copper name-badges on their chest – one I recognise from the night Brandon died. He has red hair and a goatee and he arrived at the house just after the ambulance got there. The trial must be over – the verdict must've been read.

Thunder booms in the sky like an explosion and Kathy comes out the front door with two Aboriginal women holding her arms. Kathy's walking slowly as a camera crew rushes to her and a man shoves a microphone in her face, all under the watchful eyes of the coppers at the front of the courthouse.

The activist, Shirley, steps to the front of the crowd with a megaphone.

'My people,' she says. 'The verdict was *not guilty.*'

A shock streaks through my body. My mind runs from it. I'm with Brandon, the four of us walking along the middle of Chopin Drive, telling dirty jokes, trying to best each other, laughing so hard I can't walk straight. Then I'm looking at his dead face as he lies on that bedroom floor, a speck of blood on his chin. Or is it my face, my blood? Me instead of Brandon. I feel the bolt of pain where the four bullets entered his body – my body – and knocked life out of us both.

He was just a boy – an Aboriginal boy – and now it's like he didn't matter at all.

Voices ring out through the crowd. The standstill turns into a surge of movement towards the courthouse. Me, Jordy and Kallum share a glance. Their faces are red, and I'm sure mine is too but I'm stuck here, can't move. The voices are a hum around me, growing louder into shouts and cries.

'On behalf of Kathy Long, we will not be accepting this verdict,' someone says through a megaphone.

'This is an unacceptable injustice, and we will not take it as truth!' It's Shirley. Kathy's beside her – she looks stuck where she is, like me. 'The justice system has failed us! We will not stand for the racist systems that protect murderous cops! The fight has only begun!'

People are yelling things and crying. An older Aboriginal woman near me is bawling her eyes out, held by an Aboriginal man and a younger girl.

Some people move towards the cops at the front of the courthouse. They're screaming at them, waving their arms.

A crashing sound bursts behind me and I turn to see a cop car passing through the crowd with a smashed windscreen. The lights are flashing as plastic bottles hit it and people bang on the doors and side windows.

Everyone moves around us, but me, Jordy and Kallum are still standing where we were this whole time. I don't understand. How can it be *not guilty*? How?

'This is fucking bullshit,' I say, and a rush of heat pulsates through my body. The heat brushes away the cold from my skin and I'm a ball of fire ready to engulf the world. Jordy's crying. Kallum's got tears in his eyes. They're sad but I'm angry. I want to smash something. I want to charge at every one of those coppers and throw my fists at them. I want to watch them hurt like we're hurting – like I'm hurting.

It's not fair. This is not justice. We follow the movement towards the courthouse and join the cries of the people around us.

'Fuck the justice system!' I shout. 'Fuck the judge! Fuck the jury! Bullshit!'

At the front of the crowd, marchers come face to face with the police, who stand their ground. The cops might beat them away with their batons, pepper spray them, shoot them like they did Brandon.

Not guilty.

I'm fully prepared to be arrested right now.

Not guilty.

I'm fully prepared to fight for my life.

Not guilty.

My fists are clenched at my side.

Tears burn my eyes as I shout at the top of my lungs. 'Fucking bullshit!'

I shout so loud and hard that I swear my throat is tearing. I thought I was so brave to speak the truth instead of lying to save my own arse, and it was for nothing. In my head, I'm saying sorry to Brandon – I'm saying sorry that my words weren't enough, that his killer gets to go back to his life like nothing ever happened.

More screams ring out behind me and at the courthouse ahead. Some of the cops have pulled up long shields to cover their bodies. They are pepper spraying the people at the front. The protesters scream and surge backwards. One man falls onto me, kicks my ankle hard, and I nearly go down. The pain in my leg shocks me back into my body.

I'm in a crowd where a stampede might happen.

We can't stay here. This is fucking chaos.

'Come on,' Kallum says. 'Let's get outta here.'

I follow Jordy and Kallum to the edge of the crowd and we head towards another street – a quieter one, though there are some people crying on the footpaths, cursing the cops and the lawyers and the judge.

We arrive at a corner shop and take shelter in front of it. The rain is bucketing down now. My feet are soaked and numb in my shoes.

'I can't believe this shit,' Jordy says. I shake my head. 'How could they? It's fucked up.'

'I know,' I say. 'I want to get drunk. Fuck this.'

Kallum's standing there quietly, like he's got nothing to say. I text Jarrod as my battery grows lower, asking if I can come over. He replies with a yes, that he's back at his place now, and I text Mum our location. She's already on her way to pick us up.

THIRTY-TWO

When I tell Mum that the verdict was not guilty, she sighs.

'Can't say I'm surprised,' she says. 'I'm sorry, boys.'

We're dripping water all over the floor of the car. 'That Shirley lady says she's gonna help Kathy appeal it,' Jordy tells her.

'Yeah, they'll keep fighting,' Kallum says.

I don't respond. I'm only thinking about getting shit-faced right now.

'Can you drop me off at Jarrod's?' I ask Mum.

'Jarrod's? Why?'

'So we can talk about what happened.'

Mum sighs. 'Okay.'

We drive out of Gerring with the wipers on full speed. Mum doesn't speak another word.

It feels like we're driving back to a different world. Or maybe it's the same world and I just didn't see it for what it really is: a world where a white cop can kill an

Aboriginal boy and face no consequences, a world where the only consequences are the sadness felt by those who loved them. And the anger – my fists are clenched in my lap. Mum turns up the heater and I didn't even realise I was shivering until the warm blast hits my face.

I relax my hands and rest my head against the window. Traffic is slow on the highway and the silence is deep. I'm still hearing the words coming through the megaphone and I'm still there, standing in the rain, hearing the news that my friend's killer was found not guilty.

When we get back to Carraway's Point, the rain has almost completely stopped. Mum drops me off at Jarrod's place.

'Don't do anything stupid tonight,' Mum says to me.

'I won't,' I say.

'Want us to come?' Jordy asks. I know they don't like Jarrod, and they'd only be coming for me.

'Nah, it's okay. We'll catch up later,' I say. 'Thanks for coming with me.'

'Of course,' Kallum says.

'Yeah, no worries,' Jordy adds.

'I know it's shit, and it's not what you wanted, but you just have to take a breath, okay?' Mum asks. 'It's not over yet.'

'Okay, Mum.'

When they drive off, Jarrod meets me at the front of his house. He shakes his head and I know we're both thinking the same thing: this is fucking fucked.

He leads me through the side gate and into the shed in his backyard. I don't want to hear any more words of wisdom from Mum, I want to be numb again. I don't want to feel anything.

I kick off my shoes at the door and leave my wet socks beside them. Jarrod pulls beers out of his fridge and hands me one, then we sit on the couch.

Jarrod puts on the news, wanting to see if there's a report about the trial. We watch for forty minutes and there's no mention of it at all.

'Why ain't the news reportin' on this bullshit?' Jarrod asks between sips of beer. 'People need to know.'

'They don't care about Brandon,' I say. 'They don't care about *us*. It's not news because no one cares.'

Jarrod downs the rest of his beer and gets us another. Before long, it's nine o'clock and I'm drunk. Jarrod suggests going back to Rory's because he's got people over, drinking their sorrows away. Instead of choosing to go home at this point like I usually would, I agree to go.

I put my wet socks and shoes back on. The world is blurry when we leave. It feels good. Rory's in a new house, so it's not the house Brandon died in that we're walking to. We're carrying the beer bottles we had left over in plastic bags. I want to forget today. I want to forget what it felt like to hear those two shitty words.

I'm thinking of Brandon, imagining him watching all that happened on a big TV. I imagine him watching the verdict read, watching his mother cry, watching me, Jordy and Kallum barely containing our anger. I imagine he can feel how I'm feeling. I imagine he'd want to help, tell me it's gonna be okay and that this is not the end of the world. But he can't do that.

At Rory's house, The Kid Laroi plays from speakers in the living room and everyone's out in the backyard.

There's Rory, three girls and two other boys sitting around one of those glass-top outdoor dining tables. On the table is a bong and a bowl of weed. The backyard needs a good mow – the grass is probably knee high.

Everyone's talking about the verdict.

'We gotta do somethin', eh?' Rory says. 'Like, a protest or fucking riot or somethin'.'

'What can we do?' one of the girls asks. 'We're just a few people. No one'll listen.'

I picture an angry mob in the streets of Carraway's Point, throwing bricks through store windows. Tear gas misting through the air. Coppers with batons. Aboriginal faces shouting for justice, crying, bleeding.

The images remind me of the nightmares I used to have.

I notice Jarrod's got a tear rolling down his cheek. It falls silently while the others talk loud and it feels like we're miles away from the conversation.

'You right?' I ask Jarrod, quietly.

'Yeah,' he says. 'It's just shit.'

He wipes away his tear and sniffles.

On the Saturday, a week before he died, Brandon got his red Ps, and he sped his mum's car along Chopin Drive, looping at the end of the cul-de-sac. He stopped in front of my house, blasting his horn. I knew it was Brandon because he'd texted me that morning saying he'd signal me if he passed the test.

It was a hot day, and the fans were on in the house. I looked through the curtain behind the TV and saw him sitting at the foot of our driveway.

Brandon was smiling from ear to ear. He had long curly hair that sat like a bush above his head, puffy and black.

Brandon always had chubby cheeks. He said they stayed chubby because his mum was always squeezing them, even though he was seventeen now. In the little two-bedroom house next door, it was just Brandon and his mum and his cat, Simba.

As I arrived at the car, I saw Jarrod sitting in the back seat. I opened the passenger door and climbed in the front.

'Why you sittin' in the back?' I asked Jarrod.

'Safest place to be,' Jarrod replied.

'He's a pussy,' Brandon said, turning to me. 'Seatbelt.'

He waited until I had buckled myself in before he put the car in drive, then his foot hit the accelerator and we zoomed back to the end of the street. Brandon hit the brakes hard at the stop sign and the tyres screeched.

'Okay, let me out,' I said, pretending to take off my seatbelt.

Brandon laughed. 'I'm just fuckin' with yas.'

He turned and drove at a reasonable speed into town. We went through the Maccas drive-thru and got a frozen Coke each.

'You're next, Dyl,' Brandon said as we received our orders from the window. Brandon was eight months older than me.

'I won't get my hours up before my birthday,' I said.

'Just forge 'em. Everyone does.'

'Dad would not let that happen.' I giggled.

As we pulled out of Maccas, Brandon turned up the radio. Rick Astley's voice boomed and the three of us sang 'Never gonna give you up' with our windows rolled down as we blazed through the main street of Carraway's Point.

'Wanna head out to the beach? Have a dip?' Brandon asked.

'I can't,' Jarrod replied. 'I gotta go to my gran's with Mum. Can you drop me home?'

We dropped Jarrod off and started for the beach. Brandon cranked Jack Harlow loud through the stereo.

'Bruh, this is amazing,' he said. 'It's what freedom feels like.'

'Driving?'

'Yeah, without Mum sitting 'ere.'

We turned down a hill towards the beach. A couple of white boys from school darted across the road ahead of us carrying surfboards.

We parked at the fence, looking out to the waves. Brandon kicked off his shoes and grabbed a pair of slides from the back seat. Then he started along the road in the opposite direction to the beach and the shops.

'Where you going?' I asked.

'I know a spot.'

I struggled to keep up as the hot summer sun burned down on us. I moved further into the shade of the trees and the sea breeze gave me some relief.

After a few minutes, Brandon started down a trail into the bush. He was walking fast, like he was in a hurry and wasn't feeling the heat like I was. After about twenty metres, the dirt on the trail turned to sand and the crashing waves grew louder.

We came out onto the beach. A few people were surfing, and an old woman was walking her dog off the leash, but this spot was quiet. Further away, swimmers and sunbathers crowded the sand near the surf club, where the lifeguards had erected two flags for people to swim between.

'I've never been to this spot before,' I said.

'It's mostly the surfers that use it,' Brandon replied, spreading his towel on the sand. 'They know the waves are bigger round here.'

Brandon ripped off his tank top and jogged to the shore. He didn't hesitate as his feet hit the water. I watched him dive under a wave.

I took off my shirt. My body wasn't anywhere near as solid or fit as Brandon's. My legs and my arms were skinny. My chest wasn't broad like his, and Brandon's chest hair was this black cluster at the centre of his chest, while mine was like seven hairs in different places.

Brandon waved for me to come in, then strode further out. I spread my towel beside his, kicked off my shoes and stuffed my socks inside. I walked to the water and the waves rolled past my ankles, sending shockwaves of cold up my legs.

'You should make one of your movies out 'ere,' Brandon said. 'Make a shark-attack movie.' Brandon was always egging us on to do the things we wanted, to chase dreams. I swear he could see things in us that we hadn't yet, like how I want to be a filmmaker. He was the first person who ever suggested I could actually do it.

———

In Rory's backyard, Jarrod is smoking the bong. When he finishes, he offers it to me, but I shake my head. As the group begins singing along to 'Let me love you' by Mario, I realise I haven't checked my emails today, and today is the day I find out if I got the scholarship. My phone's dead.

'You got a charger?' I ask Rory.

'Yeah, brother, in the kitchen,' he says.

I leave the backyard and it's much warmer in the kitchen. Even though the rain has stopped outside, I'm still all wet from the day.

I find the iPhone charger in the kitchen, connect my phone and take a sip from my beer.

After a few minutes, my phone begins to power on. I take a deep breath. Maybe the email hasn't arrived yet. Even if it has, it's probably a heartfelt apology and words of encouragement, telling me to keep making films and wishing me luck.

I navigate to my emails and the inbox refreshes. Two spam emails appear, along with an email from the film school.

It's here. It's waiting for me to read it. I hover my thumb over the email, count down from three, then tap.

'*Dear Dylan*,' I whisper, reading the email to myself. '*Thank you for your application for the high-school graduate scholarship. We are very pleased to advise that you have been chosen to receive the scholarship for next year.*'

I set my phone down.

I got it. I got the scholarship.

I skim the rest of the email. Orientation day is 28 January. First class is 4 February.

Your film showcased your potential for visual storytelling. We can't wait to join you on your filmmaking journey.

I can't believe it. I actually got the scholarship. I'm moving to Sydney next year. I'm going to study film and become a filmmaker. It's really going to happen.

Suddenly, I don't feel part of the world I am in right now – the world of Rory's house, beers and bongs and backyards.

I hear Jarrod's laughter outside, unplug my phone and shove it in my pocket. I rest my unfinished beer on Rory's kitchen bench and leave the house through the front door.

As I step onto the road, into the cold, a tear rolls from my eye. It's weird to feel so angry and sad and confused, and, at the same time, so happy and excited. It's overwhelming. I need to get home, get out of these wet clothes and climb under my blanket.

When I leave Carraway's Point, I don't ever wanna come back. I'm thinking of all the ways life will be different. No Chopin Drive. No Terry and the rednecks. No Miles Higgins. Sydney seems like another planet to me. It'll be like a dream.

I can't wait to tell Mum. I know she wasn't super pumped when I told her I'd applied, but she'll be proud of me. I'm sure of it. And somehow, I feel like Brandon had something to do with it. The film was about him and me after all.

Headlights turn the corner and shine over my body. In the dark night, I can see a kind of mist, even though it's not that cold. As the car comes closer, I hear the brakes gently squeak as it pulls to the side of the road. The first image flashing in my mind is Terry's face, his evil smile, the hole he said he'd bury me in. I taste the dirt in my mouth like I'm right back there.

When I cross the road and out of the beam of the headlights, I realise it's not a ute – it's a car with things on top, like roof-racks. But they aren't roof-racks – they're unlit siren lights. It's a cop car, pulled over in front of me, and there's a copper watching me cross the road.

I stop, look at the cop car like I'm staring down a bull about to charge.

They've come to find me, to brag to me about their mate who got away with murder. They've come to push me down onto the road, cut my face on the tar, yell at me to stop resisting, when all I was doing was trying to go home.

They want to get me like they got Brandon.

'What are you waiting for?' I shout to the cop car. 'Come fucking get me. That's what you want, isn't it? Walking at night is a crime now, hey? Walking while black is a crime?'

I'm holding my arms out to my sides, like I'm ready for their shots, waiting for the lights to ignite and blast blue and red into the street.

Instead, the door opens and the headlights dim. The copper's body is dark as they start towards me with slow strides, like they're sizing me up, taking my measure.

'Dylan,' a woman's voice says. She takes another step closer, and I realise this copper is Kallum's mother, Constable Smith. She's the Aboriginal cop. 'How are you?' she asks.

Her partner is sitting in the car watching, but Smith is standing in front of me. Her brown face looks purple in the dark. I don't really know what to say to her. I used to know her when I was little. She was Kallum's mum, she was nice. I don't know her now. To me, she's one of *them*. Miles Higgins is *her* friend too.

'I saw you walking here,' she says. 'I wanted to check in on you. I know today must've been hard for you, Dyl. You're so young. This kind of thing is too much for an adult to bear, let alone an eighteen-year-old kid. If there's anything I can do...'

'What could *you* do?' I ask. Her mouth opens, like I've shouted at her. I want to ask her if she could bring Brandon back, if she could turn back time, if she could take her gun and correct this on her own.

Smith shakes her head and there's a tear escaping the corner of her eye.

'I don't know, Dyl,' she says. 'I don't know what the answer is right now, but I'll figure it out. I swear to you.'

I want to call her a traitor, like Mum and Dad have before. I want to tell her it was *her* friends who killed Brandon. I want to tell her I'm ashamed to even be near her, even if she's Kallum's mum and we live on the same street. Instead, I just look to my right, the direction I need to go.

'Do you want a lift home?' she asks.

'Not from you,' I say.

'Come on, Dyl,' she says. 'Let me take you home.'

I sigh. She's a cop, yes, but she's also Kallum's mum. And besides, I'm fucking exhausted. The only place I want to be right now is in my bed. I follow Smith to the car and climb in the back. Her white partner is driving. Smith clears her throat and wipes her tear away. The heater is on in the car and the lights of the cop computer threaten to blind me while I pull on my seatbelt.

On the way to Chopin Drive, I look out the window.

'I'm so sorry, Dyl,' Smith says. I'm surprised she's saying anything to me with her white cop mate in the car. 'I want you to know that I'm gonna do my best to make some changes here. Even if it kills me, the policing is gonna change in this town. This is the reason I joined the force: to make it better for our mob. I've never felt the importance of that more than I do right now.'

The car turns onto our street and comes to a stop in front of my house. Mum's gonna be shook when she looks out the window and sees me getting out the back of a cop car. I better make a quick getaway. I climb out and Smith rolls down her window.

'Dylan,' she says. 'I'm serious about what I said. I'll do everything I can to change things here. I promise.'

I could make a comment about how nothing really matters, how I don't think the kind of change she's looking to make is possible here, with these people. But instead of saying any of that, I smile. I don't know if there's any point hoping for anything good to happen in this town, but I suppose I believe she'll try.

'Good,' I say. I nod to her and she nods back.

THIRTY-THREE

It's 22 January – the day me and Jordy move to Sydney.

It's a sunny, warm summer morning on Chopin Drive. Jordy's new little Hyundai Getz is parked in front of his house. The boot is open and ready for luggage.

'You got everything?' Mum asks as I drag my duffel bag to our front gate.

'Yes, Mum.'

Bree's trailing behind us as we walk out of our front yard and start for Jordy's car up the street.

'You got your toothbrush? Deodorant?'

'Yes, Mum. I'm all set.'

'What about your pillow?'

She's got me – I have forgotten my pillow. I drop my bags in the gutter and powerwalk back inside. In my room, I take my pillow from my bed. My bedroom is the cleanest I've ever seen it. I'm leaving most of my stuff here for now, but the plan is to come and get more once I've got somewhere to live after Jordy's aunt's house.

I always dreamed of moving out, but now that the day has come, I'm a little sad. I'm leaving my home, where I've been my whole life, and a part of me feels like I might not be coming back. That night two months ago, when I found out I won the scholarship for film school, I told myself I would get out and stay out of here for good.

I'm gonna miss this bed, though. I'm gonna miss my room.

I spot a shadow at my window. It's Simba trotting along the windowsill. I slide the window screen open and run my fingers gently over his head. He rubs back into my hand.

'I'll be seeing you, Simba,' I say. 'Look after the neighbourhood for me.'

Simba stares up at me for a moment. Maybe he really is Brandon, and he's come to say goodbye. When I leave this place, I need to leave Brandon behind too. My life is beginning again and I need to move on.

I don't know that he'll ever really leave me, though.

I close the window on Simba and he scampers away.

Mum and Bree are waiting for me out the front, joined by Kathy now.

'So, you're off, son?' Kathy asks.

'Yeah,' I say.

'You be a good boy up there, yeah?'

'Yeah, of course.'

'And don't forget us.'

She gives me a hug and squeezes me tight. After the verdict, I didn't see Kathy for two weeks, then when

I did, her face looked like it had a hundred new wrinkles. She looked run-down, exhausted, but today she's smiling when she lets me go and heads back to her house.

'I told your father to be here at nine o'clock,' Mum says as we start for Jordy's car. I carry my bags and my pillow and Bree pulls out her phone to ring Dad. He doesn't answer.

Jordy's stuff is already taking up half the space in the boot and the back seat. I put in my duffel bag, pillow and backpack.

A few minutes later, Jordy comes out of his house, carrying his own pillow and a blanket. His dad and little sister are right behind him, along with his friend Amber.

'Morning,' I hear, and it's Kallum coming down the road from his house at the end of the cul-de-sac. He's got his backpack.

'Are you coming?' I ask when he arrives at the car.

'Yeah,' he says. 'I decided to take the day off work and come along for the drive. I'll get the bus back on Sunday.'

'Okay, cool.'

Jordy forces the boot down, struggles a bit until it locks.

'We're all set,' he says.

'My dad's not here yet,' I say.

'We can wait,' Jordy says, smiling at me.

'Why don't we all go inside for a cuppa?' Jordy's dad asks. Mum says she's dying for a coffee.

'I better get going,' Amber says to Jordy. 'Don't forget us when you're famous.' He hugs her tight like an environmentalist hugging a tree.

'How could I?' Jordy says.

'I'll miss ya.'

'Me too.'

She breaks from the hug and wipes away her tears. After she leaves, we all walk into Jordy's house. I haven't been in here for years, and it still looks exactly the same.

Mum and Jordy's dad make coffees in the kitchen and the rest of us sit on the couch. Jordy's dad asks Mum how she's feeling about me moving away, and she says she's happy for me that I got the scholarship. She's never really been one for emotions, but I know she's gonna miss me. She's been giving me attitude for the past week, always on my back about cleaning and doing my dishes and leaving the toilet seat up. It was pissing me off until Bree suggested she might be more demon-mother lately because she knows I'm leaving.

Mum and Jordy's dad sit at the kitchen table, talking about times they visited Sydney when they were younger. Mum tells Jordy's dad how she lived in Paddington for a year in the nineties with a friend. She tells him about how they used to hit the nightclubs in Kings Cross every weekend and Jordy's dad tells her he went to a nightclub there a few times when he was freshly eighteen. They talk about how they heard Kings Cross has lost its life now and how we'd never know how good the old days were.

My phone vibrates with a text from Jarrod: *Kill it up there, love ya, remember to call me when ur a bigshot moviemaker*

I text back: *Haha I will*

I hear a car come to a stop outside. I worry for a moment it's Terry and his dark-green ute. I haven't seen him in a while. He must be pretty happy with himself, but also disappointed that he doesn't get to bury me in a shallow grave.

'Hello, hello,' Dad says, peering in through the screen door.

'Looks like it's time to go,' Jordy says. We all move back outside and it's almost ten o'clock now.

'What took you so long?' I ask as I walk with Dad to Jordy's car.

'Sorry, son,' Dad says. 'I had to get Nan. I knew she wouldn't want ya to leave without sayin' goodbye.'

That's when I see Nan, standing with her walker by Dad's car. She lifts one hand and holds her arm out, like she's inviting me to hug her, so I do.

'Hey, Nan,' I say. She hugs me tight and her body feels so small in my arms. She plants a kiss on my cheek and presses her cheek into mine.

'Don't you worry about any of us here,' Nan says. 'Look after yourself.'

'I will,' I say.

'You're gonna have a great life, son,' she says. 'Remember to call me once in a while, okay? Let me know how it's goin' up there.'

'I will.'

Now we're all at Jordy's car: me, Dad, Mum, Nan, Bree, Jordy, Kallum, Jordy's dad, Lewis and Jordy's sister, Josie. The goodbye hugs continue with Jordy and his dad. He and Lewis shake hands, which turns into a half-hug, then Jordy crouches down and hugs Josie tight. They hold each other for the longest time and Jordy has tears in his eyes when he lets her go. He tells her to look after their dad.

We haven't done it since I was little, but I hug my own father. He pats me on the back.

'I love you, son,' he says. 'I know you'll make us proud up there.'

'Love ya too, Dad.'

Next is Bree. She gives me a lacklustre half-hug and rests her head against mine – nowhere near as emotional as Jordy and his sister.

'Don't do drugs,' she says.

When Bree breaks away, Mum is the only one left to say goodbye to. Jordy climbs into the car and starts his engine. Kallum's already in the passenger seat.

I turn back to Mum. Her eyes look glossy and she's sucking in her lips. I hug her. Neither of us say anything, but we squeeze each other tight. There's a lump in my throat and tears begin to burn my eyes. I feel them leak down my cheek, onto Mum's shoulder. I try to ease away, but she squeezes me tighter, keeps me in her arms for a moment longer. When she lets me go, her eyes are wet and red, but she's not crying.

'Call us when you get there,' Mum says. She smiles and nods for me to get in the car.

'I will,' I say. 'I love you.'

'I love you, too.' Mum's about to burst into tears, though she's trying her hardest not to show it, as she brings her hand to her mouth.

I wipe my eyes and climb into the back of Jordy's car. Jordy shifts into drive and we move away from the kerb. I watch Mum, Dad and Bree waving to us, and I wave back. I can see them growing smaller over the tops of our luggage. And – oh my god – Mum and Dad are hugging. Maybe he's just consoling her, but still, it's really nice to see.

Jordy taps his horn three times as we turn out of Chopin Drive. Before long, we're out of town and on the highway. Green fields stretch for ages as we pass the turn-off that leads to an empty hole way out in the bush.

Kallum's in control of the music, and he begins playing some Kylie Minogue song through the stereo.

'Any requests, Dyl?' he asks, showing me the Spotify playlist he's making on his phone.

'Umm, I don't know,' I say. '"Take me home, country roads"?'

'Nice,' he says.

Jordy and Kallum sing along to the song, and I feel like I should join them, but I just listen.

'So,' I say. 'Are you guys gonna try the whole long-distance thing?'

'Yeah,' Kallum says. 'I reckon it'll be all right. I'm gonna try to visit once a month. Bus ticket's seventy bucks. Should be able to make it work.'

'We could even meet halfway on like a Saturday or something,' Jordy says. 'Spend a day somewhere on the coast.'

Kallum reaches across to Jordy's lap and Jordy holds his hand. It's cute to see them in love. Hopefully they can make it work.

The next song comes on – 'Fast car' by Tracy Chapman. No one sings as it plays. We just listen. I gaze out the window, where the green fields have been replaced by bush and mountains.

Suddenly, it feels like we've left something behind. It feels wrong for the three of us to be leaving town, zooming down the highway bound for Sydney.

It was always the four of us – the boys of Chopin Drive. Dylan, Jordy, Kallum and Brandon. He should be here with us, on his way to a new start too.

'He should be here,' I say. Kallum turns down the music, quiet but still loud enough to hear it.

'What?' Kallum asks.

'Brandon should be in the car with us. It wasn't meant to be this way.'

It's a strange quiet that fills the car. Maybe it's because we're all feeling the same thing. It's like I'm mourning Brandon again, realising he is dead for the first time. I think Kallum and Jordy feel that too. We're all feeling it, sitting with the rumble of the road and Tracy Chapman's singing to comfort us. Doesn't help that it's a sad song.

'Remember when we snuck down the river that one time?' Kallum says. 'We followed it for hours out in the bush. Jordy wanted to turn back but Brandon wanted to keep going. We found that deep spot.'

'Oh yeah,' Jordy says. 'The water was black. That was fuckin' scary.'

'I remember you chuckin' a tantrum that we were all gonna die,' Kallum says to Jordy, giggling. '*No, no, what if there's like a giant eel down there.*'

'Shut up,' Jordy replies. 'And Brandon dared us all to swim out to the centre of the black, but you couldn't feel the bottom after a couple of metres.'

I remember this now. It was hot that day, and I was tired from all the walking, but it was exciting. We'd found this big deep spot, an offshoot of the river's flow, where the water was still.

'Kallum went out first,' I say.

'Yeah but he felt something touch his foot a few metres out and turned back,' Jordy says, chuckling. 'And youse called *me* the scaredy cat.'

'You didn't even try,' Kallum jests, nudging Jordy in the shoulder.

'I made it further than Kallum,' I say.

'Yeah,' Jordy says. 'But maybe that was the day we realised Brandon was the bravest. He swam all the way out.'

'Even did a war cry,' I say. 'And he didn't stop.'

'Idiot kept going, roaring like a warrior,' Kallum laughs.

Something I think about all the time: was Brandon scared when he was dying? I think he might've been terrified as he lay there, but once he realised it was over, he might've been okay. He was brave, always. He would've accepted it, then thought about something nice. Maybe about his mum, maybe Simba, maybe that time he swam out to the middle of the black water and hollered his way to the other side.

'I miss him,' I say.

'Me too,' Jordy says.

'Me too,' Kallum adds.

We talk through memories of Brandon. The time we went to the movies to watch the new Fast & Furious movie and two old ladies kept shooshing us and giving us death stares from in front. The time Jordy got bitten by a spider and begged Brandon to steal his mum's car and take him to hospital. The time we all put on wigs and costumes that were meant for the school play and pretended we were rich white people sipping tea with our pinkies outstretched.

I look at the space beside me on the back seat, and instead of the folded blankets and pillows, I picture Brandon sitting there by the window, nodding along to the beat, telling Kallum to turn the music back up and singing 'Fast car' at the top of his lungs. We'd all belt the chorus together and it'd be like Kallum and Jordy never drifted away, and we were always friends who had each other's backs – just like we did then, like the three of us do now.

Feels like he really is here for a minute.

The music plays and I gaze out the window. For the first time in a long time, I can finally imagine a future – a good one.

Me, Jordy and Kallum will go do some touristy stuff before Kallum goes home. I wonder what it'll be like to see the Harbour Bridge and the Opera House in real life. I wonder what my first time on a train will be like; how I'll figure out where everything is and how to get around on my own. I'll see the planes landing and taking off, and millions more people than I'd ever see in Carraway's Point. It's scary, but a good kind of scary.

Right now, Sydney seems so far away, but soon, so will Carraway's Point.

ACKNOWLEDGEMENTS

I'll start by saying a massive thank you to my publisher, Jodie Webster, at Allen & Unwin. Thank you for believing in this story. Fourth book done, and hopefully many more together!

Thank you also to the world's best editor, Kate Whitfield. Thank you to Hana Kinoshita Thomson and Dylan Finney for making my favourite book cover ever! Thank you to everyone at Allen & Unwin who had a hand in bringing this book to life.

I conceived and began the original version of Jordy's story back in 2022 while on a residency at the Varuna Writer's House. I would like to acknowledge the magic that comes from that place, as it has had a lasting impact on me and my writing. Thank you also to Black Rainbow, who funded this residency when I was lucky enough to be one of the awardees of their Black Rainbow Futures Fund.

Thank you to my friends, Gabbie Stroud and Kate Liston-Mills, for always supporting me in the MSH group.

Thank you to my sister Hayleigh, for always being my first reader and my biggest fan. Thank you to my cat Simba for allowing me to insert him into this story.

This book is dedicated to my partner, Matthew. Thank you for always believing in me, answering random questions I had for the book and for always being by my side. Life was chaotic and challenging at times while I was working on this book, but you inspire me every day to never give up on what I believe in.

ABOUT THE AUTHOR

Gary Lonesborough is a Yuin writer, who grew up on the Far South Coast of NSW as part of a large and proud Aboriginal family. Gary was always writing as a child, and continued his creative journey when he moved to Sydney to study at film school. Gary has experience in youth work, Aboriginal health, child protection, the disability sector (including experience working in the youth justice system) and the film industry, including working on the feature film adaptation of Jasper Jones. His young adult novels, *The Boy from the Mish*, *We Didn't Think It Through*, and *I'm Not Really Here* have won and been shortlisted for numerous awards.